THE SONG

EVEN THE WISEST OF MEN WAS A FOOL FOR LOVE

CHRIS FABRY

Based on the motion picture screenplay by Richard L. Ramsey

TYNDALE HOUSE PUBLISHERS, INC.
CAROL STREAM, ILLINOIS

Visit Tyndale online at www.tyndale.com.

Visit Chris Fabry's website at www.chrisfabry.com.

Find out more about *The Song* at www.thesongmovie.com and www.cityonahillproductions.com.

Designed by Beth Sparkman

Edited by Sarah Mason

Library of Congress Cataloging-in-Publication Data

Fabry, Chris, date.
The song / Chris Fabry.
pages cm
"Based on the motion picture screenplay by Richard L. Ramsey"
ISBN 978-1-4964-0333-9 (sc)
1. Country musicians—Fiction. 2. Christian fiction. 3. Love stories. I. Title.
PS3556.A26S66 2014
813'.54—dc23 2014040110

Printed in the United States of America

20 19 18 17 16 15 14
7 6 5 4 3 2 1

Other Novels by Chris Fabry

Dogwood

June Bug

Almost Heaven

Not in the Heart

Borders of the Heart

Every Waking Moment

A Marriage Carol
(with Dr. Gary Chapman)

There is a time for everything,
and a season for every activity under the heavens.

ECCLESIASTES 3:1

FOREWORD

As a pastor, I have the opportunity to talk with people in various stages of romantic relationships. All too often I see them when they are confused and hurting. Much of this discord results from the flood of false messages we receive in today's culture about how to deal with issues of dating, sex, and marriage. So what is the truth? What does God have to say about these things? After all, he's the creator—the architect—of romantic love.

A few years ago I did a series based on the Song of Songs, or Song of Solomon, and I realized how relevant it is in today's world of discarded relationships. Song of Songs is written as poetry, and while that poetic nature makes it beautiful, it can be difficult for people to understand and to connect to their current issues—even for pastors. Some church leaders avoid this book because they are uncomfortable with its up-close-and-personal love story.

That's why our team developed *The Song*, a modern adaptation of Solomon's life through his writings in Song of Songs and the book of Ecclesiastes. We wanted to make Solomon's story accessible to a wide audience—to an audience that might never have read Scripture at all. *The Song* began as a movie and church resources, but to make it available to as many people in as many different ways as we could imagine, we developed it into a novel as well. My prayer is that God will use the story of *The Song* contained in this novel to provide wisdom on issues of committed love, true beauty, and finding satisfaction in relationships. I pray it will awaken love in thousands of marriages. This story offers both hope and this promise to readers: *"Don't quit. Don't give up. God can take the broken pieces and make them beautiful again. It's what he does best."*

I'm grateful for the partnership with Chris Fabry on this project. Chris understands the heart of *The Song*, and his treatment of Jed and Rose's story will hit home with readers in an authentic way. You will have the chance to spend time with them in a longer, fuller way than we were able to show you on the screen. And you'll meet some characters you didn't see in the movie. You might just see yourself or your spouse in their struggles and victories.

I'm proud to have this novel as part of all of our efforts for this project. I hope you enjoy this story and that it refreshes your belief in God's gift of love and romance in your relationship.

Kyle Idleman

Bestselling author of *Not a Fan* and
teaching pastor at Southeast Christian Church

PROLOGUE

JED KING'S EYES ROLLED BACK, his head strangely numb like someone had sapped all feeling from his body. He clawed at his wrist, trying to get the thing there off, and there was blood but very little pain. He leaned back, feeling his will to live ebb.

If this were a song, he thought, *it wouldn't be worth singing.*

His life was a song played in three-four time by someone who came before him. He was writing new verses to another man's tune. The chorus was familiar but led to a place he didn't want to go. And that place was here, slumped back, vision blurred, unable to move.

Someone shrieked and fell next to him. He heard a wail, a keening. What rhymed with *cry*? *Die. Fly. Good-bye?*

It was Shelby, her long brown hair matted and her face without makeup. She didn't look a thing like the pictures taken for the magazines. Now she was frantic and undone instead of exuding that quiet confidence that had attracted him. This self-assured sensation on the violin was freaking out, but he couldn't respond. Couldn't do anything but listen to her scream.

"No, no, no!" she yelled, her voice bouncing off the walls in the bathroom. Where was this place? A hotel? He couldn't remember.

His life had been a constant search for the right word, the right line. A snippet of dialogue between two friends that became part of a chorus. Something his son had said in a moment of giddy clarity, a headline in the newspaper, a question asked by a fan standing in line. And words that would capture the forbidden desire he felt for *her*, for the woman who wasn't his wife.

But now there were no words. They wouldn't come because the feeling was gone. His breath became shallow and his lungs ached and he could only hear his own heartbeat and feel that big fist squeezing inside his chest. The pumping grew slower, tighter, as if his heart were seizing like an engine about to grind to a halt.

"What did you do?" Shelby screamed.

What had he done? A good question. What had he done with all the chances, all the choices he meant to make, with the life he meant to live and the love he promised? He had to write that down. *The love I promised.* But there was no reason to write anything down. It was over. He was over.

"Jed! Listen to me! Jed? You have to stay awake!"

Sure, stay awake, he thought. *Simple. Easy. For everyone but me.*

Shelby slapped him hard but he didn't feel it, just saw her hand hit him and pull back as the tears flowed. "Jed? Talk to me!"

He wanted to. He really did. But there are some things you can't do even if you desire them. There are some choices you can't take back. Words said that can't be unsaid. Rhymes left hanging at the end of sentences. The gap between a good lyric and just a thought that was never completed.

Shelby tried to sop up the river of blood with a white towel, but it was a losing battle. Jed's hands drew into themselves and gnarled like an animal's claws in the throes of death. He could see the posts online in his mind, people sharing the sad news with each other. *"RIP, Jed. What a shame. What a waste."*

News cameras would capture the covered body being wheeled to the back of an ambulance with its lights off, a sign that hope was gone, life was over. The reel would play again and again until the news cycle was over and something else replaced it.

Meaningless. Meaningless. Everything is meaningless. I have seen everything done under the sun. All of it is meaningless.

"Jed! Jed! Say something!"

His eyelids fluttered like a butterfly unleashed from a cocoon, and something bubbled from his soul. A word took root and grew until it stretched to his parched lips and he spoke it in a whisper.

"Rose."

Shelby turned on the shower and the water cascaded, the faucet fully open. Jets pounded, washing his face and matting his hair against his head, and he didn't care if he lived or died or drowned or floated. He didn't care at all.

And then he was somewhere else, at a place in his memory as vivid as his reflection in the steel faucet. Standing in the pouring rain. Then came a flash of lightning and words washed over him.

Pity anyone who falls and has no one to help them up.

He had spent his life trying to gather people who would validate his music. Agents and fans and followers who clung to him. Now he was alone because Shelby had retreated into another room.

He heard pounding and voices.

Two men appeared and lifted him by his arms from the shower as more screaming reverberated in the room. Two other men in uniform restrained Shelby and asked what she was on. Jed blacked out, then found himself rolling on a gurney toward the ambulance. But the lights were on. What did that mean? Was there still hope?

He blinked and he was inside with someone over him, working on him, looking into his eyes as if begging him to hang on. Funny. This must be what fans saw as they watched him perform. Looking into the face of someone performing his craft, doing the very thing he was born to do. Now Jed was the one looking up.

He blinked again and saw the fluorescent lights of the

hospital, the gurney racing through the ER. People in scrubs rushing toward him, sticking him, putting wires and tubes inside him. He wanted to speak, wanted to tell them how sorry he was to put them through this. He wanted to tell *her* how sorry he was. He wondered if he would ever have a chance to speak again, to say the words trapped inside.

Then, like a wave, it hit him. Reality washed over him like that time when, as a kid, he'd been standing in the ocean, not looking, and the tide pulled his feet out from under him. A wave hit him from behind and sent him sprawling, head over heels, into the surf. Out of control.

And then darkness.

The flat line of the heart monitor.

No dark tunnel. No piercing light or brilliant flowers or any of that. No music, no sound. No angels or demons. Nothing but darkness from which the words surfaced, white on black. His life in words. Everything he knew to be true.

I looked and saw all the evil that was taking place under the sun. I declared that the dead are happier than the living. But better than both is the one who has never been born, who has not seen the evil that is done under the sun.

Jed King's life rolled back like a scroll and on it was the good and the bad, the mistakes, the triumphs, the gains and losses and all he tried to keep hidden. Darkness and light. The song he had been singing with every heartbeat.

Part One

CHAPTER 1

HE WAS BORN JEDIDIAH KING and he tried to live up to the name. His father was David King, a vagabond country artist known for his hard drinking and living, at least for most of his career. Jed's father put everything into his music and sang as hard in the small honky-tonks he started out playing as the arenas that hosted him toward the end of his life onstage. He sang and tumbled his way into the hearts of fans worldwide. Men on tractors in the heartland sang along. Women in trailers and mansions echoed the words to "Can't Hold On." He was just a poor man frightened of his shadow, but he learned how to turn his fear into tunes with a message that cut a path and made a connection.

David King gave his son two things other than his name—a love to build things with his hands and a desire to write songs with his heart. Jed had picked up the hammer and saw like his father long before he picked up the guitar. But once he found those six strings, there was no letting go.

He'd watched his father play the guitar since he was young. Watched the placement of his fingers on the strings and the way he strummed or picked. It was as if the instrument were an extension of the man, and every time his father grabbed that instrument, he came alive. He could be dead tired, nodding off on the couch, and then he'd see the guitar in the corner and make his way over and pick it up. His eyes danced as he worked on some new tune or reworked an old one.

Watching his dad's band work together as a team was a holy experience. Something about the process of creating music made Jed want the same.

A man at the music store in their town who didn't know Jed or his musical lineage had let him go into the back room and play the cherry-red Guild Starfire that hung on the wall. Not play it, actually, just hold it. The man told him everything about the guitar—the wood, the craftsmanship, what made it the best. And then he picked up the guitar and began a riff Jed could hardly believe. The guy played with his ear down on the side of the instrument, listening to its inner workings, and he played from memory a song that took Jed's breath away.

"How do you learn to play it like that?"

"Take lessons. Learn the chords and runs." He held up the

guitar. "But music doesn't come from here. You can't learn that from anybody on the planet. Music comes from here." He tapped his chest. "It's something you either have or you don't. Not having it is bad. But having it and not using it is worse."

He showed Jed G, C, and D, then gave him a chord chart from behind the counter and told him to come back in a week. Jed went straight home and found his father's guitar, the one someone special had given him with the crown emblem carved on it. He had written some of his biggest songs on it and said it brought him luck.

Jed picked it up and spread his fingers into the G position, though he found it easier to put the ring finger on the first string instead of the pinkie. He played and it sounded close, but he wasn't pressing hard enough. Then he moved to C and it took him several seconds just to get his fingers down on the right strings and the right frets. How could players possibly change as fast as they did?

He moved to D, just three fingers and strumming four strings, but that was the hardest. He'd seen players move all the way up the neck of the guitar and put their fingers over the strings in a bar chord. Or they played the lead way up the neck one or two strings at a time. But how?

"I wondered if you'd ever pick it up," his father said behind him.

He walked in with those big cowboy boots clacking across the hardwood. Jed swallowed hard and held the guitar out in an apology.

"I saw you the other day when we were working outside. Putting your thumb across the strings. You interested?"

Jed nodded.

"Where'd you learn the chords?" his father said.

"Guy down at the music store showed me."

His father's beard had grown a little longer and his hair was wavy as he sat on the bed. He wore a T-shirt with a pocket, not the normal stage getup people associated with him, and this felt good, natural, to Jed.

"Did he tell you to use that ring finger for the G?"

"No, he said to use the pinkie."

"Good man. He's right."

"But it's easier to use the ring finger for me."

His father smiled. "That's how I play it too. Sometimes I work the pinkie in and use the ring to play the second string right there. Try that."

When Jed couldn't get it, his father took the guitar and showed him—not impatiently, but like a man who tinkers with cars might twist the radiator cap and say, "Lefty loosey, righty tighty."

"Can you show me some more?" Jed said.

"Sure."

The next morning Jed woke up to find a Guild guitar at the foot of his bed. He was playing it when his dad came downstairs to the breakfast table. "Fellow at the music store said you took a real shine to the hollow body he had down there. This one doesn't need an amp. You like it?"

Jed could hardly contain the grin. "I love it."

His father wiped the sleep out of his eyes and coughed, then poured milk on some cereal. "No pressure with that. I'm not giving you the guitar to make you follow in your old man's footsteps. There's a lot of places these feet have gone I hope you never go."

"Like where?"

"We'll have that conversation. What I mean is, I'm not expecting you to make a career out of this. Unless you want to. You understand?"

"Yes, sir."

"You'd be good, you know."

"Sir?"

"You'd be good at singing. I've heard you."

"Yes, sir."

That was all it took and Jed was off and running. Funny how a few words over a bowl of cereal could change a boy's life. Funny how a well-tuned guitar could too.

CHAPTER 2

THERE ARE THINGS in a man's life that can only be learned from a father. These things encompass chord progressions and song structure and how to mow a straight line on a lawn and change a flat. Not that a mother can't teach these—she can—but coming from a father, there is more imparted than how to do the task.

As soon as his father understood how serious Jed was about not just learning the guitar but connecting words to life, he had been involved, listening to Jed's songs, really hearing what was inside. Jed remembered a day at the dock, sitting by the water with his father and picking out a tune on the banjo, his dad keeping perfect time with the strum of his guitar, tapping his foot and sending ripples over the water. Even the fish seemed to enjoy the music of father and teenage son—a largemouth bass surfaced nearby and splashed, nipping at a fly that danced on the surface.

His father coughed into the back of his hand and came away with blood. He wiped it on his shirt, thinking Jed hadn't seen it, but there are some things you can't hide. Some things that can't be wiped away.

The diagnosis came quickly, though it took some coaxing by Jed and a Herculean effort by his mother to get his dad to visit a doctor's office. And then came the slow, long descent that took everyone by surprise.

"I always thought I would die in some plane crash," his father said one night, hooked up to tubes and monitors in his hospital bed. "You die like that and people will never forget you."

"I'll never forget you," Jed said.

His father smiled weakly. "There's a lot about my life I hope you do forget."

After another coughing fit, one Jed was glad his mother hadn't heard, his father wiped his mouth and leaned closer. He still wore the bandanna, though his hair had been cut and his face shaved.

"I was proud you gave up the cigarettes," Jed said.

"I wish I'd never picked them up. But what you think as a kid won't hurt you will come back to bite you. A lot of things will bite you unless you stay away."

Jed waited for more words but there was only coughing

and silence from his dad. When a song came on the country channel, his father reached up and held the remote out with a trembling hand to turn off the power. It was as if he had bench-pressed a thousand pounds.

His hand fell to the covers and he took another shallow breath. "Jed, I made mistakes, but I've made my peace with God. I'm going home."

"Don't give up, Dad."

"I'm not giving up; I'm just ready. If God wants to do some kind of miracle, he can. He doesn't need my permission. But if he wants me to come home, I'm good with that. More than good."

Jed stared at the silent television.

"You can think about it like a long concert tour. I'll just be at a permanent engagement."

"Like Las Vegas."

His dad laughed and then coughed harder, and Jed wished he hadn't tried to be funny. When his dad regained his breath, what little was left, he grabbed Jed's hand. His own hands were calloused from the hard work he liked to do, the carpentry and manual labor. He was a man of music, but also a man who knew the meaning of sweat equity.

"Heaven's gonna be a lot better than Vegas, Son."

Jed just nodded, feeling his chin quaver. He could write a song to that, the comparison of heaven and Vegas.

"I want to see you there someday," his father said. "Will you promise to see me there?"

Jed nodded again but he couldn't speak.

"Follow God, Jed. Do what he says. And it will go well with you. You'll be the man I could never be."

Jed's father had asked them to put Psalm 23, the whole thing, on his tombstone. "So people can read something that will last," he had said. Jed's mother bent down and ran a hand across the crown emblem beside the dates: December 17, 1942–August 10, 2003.

"He would have been real proud of what you said today," she told Jed, her voice cracking. "He would have been real proud of you."

"I wish I could have put all of that in a song for him, before he was gone. So he could have heard it. So he could have helped me . . ." His voice trailed off and she rose, unsteadily, then clung to him and wept. He held her there by that peaceful place until she pulled back and looked at him.

"He wanted to tell you so many things. He just didn't have the words."

"He used them all up in his music, didn't he?"

She smiled through the tears. "Some men never get them out."

"What happened, Mom? Between you two? I'd like to hear your version. I know this isn't the right time, the right place . . ."

"It's the perfect place. Truth works in a graveyard. He would have wanted me to tell you anywhere you asked."

And then came the hard story he'd known was there, his mother choking through half of it. Tears falling like rain.

"You've seen the old videos. You know I used to sing with David. My husband, Bill, played mandolin in the band. I've never heard anybody before or since who could play that instrument like he could."

"He died, right? I read some old news reports online. It was a suicide?"

"The family kept it quiet but it came out finally. We were all devastated. I found him."

"Let's not talk about this now, Mom."

"No, hear me out. Saying all this is hard for me, but to think of you not knowing, or finding out from somebody else, would kill me."

"I've heard the scuttlebutt at the family reunions. Whispers and shaking heads."

"Your father hated those reunions. The story is this. Your father and I had an affair. We broke our vows. It was foolish. I wound up pregnant. I couldn't deal with knowing the baby wasn't Bill's, and David took me to a clinic. It's one of the biggest regrets of my life. His too."

Jed stared at the tombstone and tried to take in the words.

"Bill found out. I think he knew something was going on but didn't want to believe it. And he was so hurt, so angry at what we'd done, that he took his own life. I found him hanging at our house, with a note that said he hoped I was happy with the choice I'd made. First person I called was David."

"I'm sorry, Mom." He waited a moment, letting her wipe

her eyes, before asking, "And that's why Dad's family broke up?"

She nodded. "His wife gathered the kids and left. I've never seen a more broken man. I thought he would drink himself to death, but somehow he got through it."

"You got him through it."

"We helped each other. He tried to work things out with her, but she divorced him and took almost everything he'd earned. I don't blame her. I blame myself for most of it. You think the choices you make just affect you and the other person, but you don't realize how one choice ripples toward everybody. You included."

"Me?"

"When we were married, it was joyful but sad. Your birth signaled a new page in the story. When you were born, it was the best day of my life and your father's. But there was also this bittersweet knowledge of all that we had done. We tried to move forward in spite of the past, our mistakes. But guilt will follow you. Just hang over you like a dark cloud."

"You were a big part of the reason he sang," Jed said. "The reason he kept going."

"The reason he kept going was that God got hold of his heart. And he did the same for me. I'm so ashamed of what happened back there. How we let our passions run. We hurt a lot of people. And we've lived with that. But your father wanted to give you what he couldn't give his first family."

She pulled a weathered journal from her purse and placed it in Jed's hands. "It's all here. He always said that a man has to live with his mistakes. But he hoped he could keep you from making the same ones."

Later that night Jed opened the book and read the scrawled writing, like a gentle touch from his father. Words that breathed life. Words that made sense of the backstory he had discovered.

Meaningless. Meaningless.
Everything is meaningless.
I have seen everything done under the sun.
All of it is meaningless.
Correction and instruction are the way to life,
keeping you away from your neighbor's wife.
Do not go near her door.
Keep to a path far from her.
Do not lust in your heart after her beauty or be captivated by her eyes.

Can a man scoop fire into his lap without his clothes being burned?
Can a man stand on hot coals without his feet being scorched?

Another man's wife preys on your very life.
No one who touches her will go unpunished.

I looked and saw all the evil that was taking place under the sun.
I declared that the dead are happier than the living.

But better than both is the one who has never been born,
who has not seen the evil that is done under the sun.

Jealousy arouses a husband's fury.
He will not accept any compensation, however great it is.
A man who commits adultery has no sense. He destroys himself.
His shame will never be wiped away.
But the one who confesses and renounces sin finds mercy.

As you do not know the path of the wind or how the body is formed in a mother's womb,
you cannot understand the work of God, the Maker of all things.
Who knows what is good for a person—
during the few meaningless days they pass through like a shadow?
Who can tell them what will happen under the sun after they are gone?
No one knows when their hour will come.
Generations come. Generations go.
But the earth remains forever.

Jed stared at his father's handwriting and thought of his own life.

The door opened and his mother slipped into the room.

"He wanted you to have this, too," she said, holding out his father's guitar with the crown on the front, the signature emblem of his career.

"You'll want to keep that," Jed said.

She shook her head. "No. It belongs to you. He wanted you to make some more great music with it. Nothing would please me more than to have you do that."

"I'll never be half the singer he was. Half the writer. Half the man."

"You can be more. Learn from his mistakes. Let his life teach you and give you all you need to be a good man."

Jed took the guitar and something close to electricity shot through him. This was the instrument his father had used onstage and behind the scenes to craft tunes people heard on the radio. How many playlists had this guitar's sound on it?

As he held the instrument in his hand, he knew he was holding more than the legacy of a singer-songwriter. He knew there was more here than the sum of the parts of an old guitar. He was holding the catalyst, the next step, the heartbeat of a father who couldn't speak the things he wanted into the life of his son.

His mother left and he listened to her footfalls down the hardwood hallway. He placed his fingers to play a G chord, then tuned the A string down to G and played the last five strings with the pinkie on the third fret, just like his father had taught him.

All the ache in my heart and the wound in my soul
All the tearing apart at saying good-bye
All the pain deep inside, like a dam giving way . . .

It was just a passing thought, a phrase he wrote in his journal. He sat there all night with his father's guitar, strumming, writing, crying, and laughing. The well of his heart was filling even through the brokenness, and Jed knew what he wanted to do with his life.

CHAPTER 3

As long as Rose Jordan could remember, she had lived the good life that came from a farm, working the vineyard. The smell of grapes in their season, ripening and hanging in clumps, straining the vines with their weight, filled with juice that represented life itself—all of this invigorated her. This was the perfume of her early years, the thing that greeted her every morning when she awakened.

The Jordan family traced their roots back to early settlers who had traveled west and been enamored with the good ground they found in Kentucky. The land had been passed from one generation to the next until the town of Sharon was settled in the 1820s. Family squabbles split the land into two different parcels and mirrored the ripping apart at the seams of the country.

The new century brought with it incorporation, but the vineyard stayed the same, and Rose liked to think that when she looked out on the rows of grapes, she was seeing the same thing that her grandmother had seen and her mother before her, all the way back to the 1700s, when her people first set foot here.

Growing up on a working vineyard was something that chased her brothers away but held Rose in a grip so tight she knew it would never let go. The boys had only seen the constant work it took to bring forth the wine, but she had seen it as life-giving. Like her mother, she drew comfort from the work instead of fatigue, and her sleep was that much sweeter after a full day of labor.

A crusty man of the earth who said no more than he needed, her father, Shepherd Jordan, was a pillar in the community, one of the cornerstones of Sharon, but he led a quiet life. Anyone who needed anything could come to him with their broken tractor or ailing horse or financial problem. Several families who had lived on the edges of his land had found a kind benefactor in Shep as their property grew from a third of an acre or less to three or four acres. What was life about if you couldn't give it away?

Still, the vineyard was not without controversy. There were some in town who said the Jordan family's hands were stained with the blood of grapes and broken lives.

"'Wine is a mocker and beer a brawler,'" Eunice Edwards had said to Shep's face one day on their front porch. She was shaking a finger at him and had the other hand on her ample hip. Rose had been captivated by the floral print dress that clung to the woman like a grape skin. She watched from the safety of the living room couch, the voices wafting through the screened window.

"'Whoever is led astray by them is not wise,'" Eunice continued. "That's what the Good Book says. Proverbs 20, verse one."

Rose glanced at the car and spotted Eddie, the youngest of the Edwards boys, sitting in the backseat, drumming his fingers on the open window. He was about her age and always had a look on his face like he knew more than he did.

"Eunice, I don't disagree with you," her father said. "There's an awful lot in the Scriptures about not being drunk with wine. But wine is God's gift to us. It represents life."

"Shepherd, you've seen lives destroyed because of alcohol. I don't know why you would spend your life on something that tears people apart."

"Anything good can be used for evil. A car can take you and your son out there to church, or you can use it to take you to some bar. The car isn't the problem, it's the heart of—"

"A body needs to get from one place to another. We don't *need* a drink of wine in order to live."

"You're right about that. We don't need wine. But God gave it to us. It's a gift that should be used wisely."

Eunice shot him a look through her thick-rimmed glasses. She punched the bridge of her nose to push them higher. "I'm going to pray for you, Shep. I'm going to pray God will forgive you and convict you of the sin you're committing, and the sins of the fathers down to your generation."

She glanced through the window screen and saw Rose. "You've got a little girl in there without a mother. What would you think if she took to the wine bottle? What'll you do when your boys turn out to be drunks?"

He didn't answer her, though Rose wanted to. She wanted to shout some of the verses that talked about wine in a positive way. It was good for the stomach, Paul had said. And the Bible said not to get drunk—if it meant you couldn't drink it, why didn't it just say, "Don't drink wine"? But Mrs. Edwards would say that the wine Paul drank and what was around today were different.

Rose had walked out onto the porch and stood by her father as the car lifted dust from the driveway. "Why does she have to be so mean?"

Her father gathered her in and she watched the car disappear behind the rows of grapevines. "I suspect it has something to do with her daddy. And her husband. You have to give people who have been smacked around by life a little extra rope, Rose."

"Is that why she's mean?"

"She's not mean. She's just hurt. An animal that's gentle and friendly growls when it's injured. Remember that when people act ugly toward you. They're usually in some kind of pain."

Now, a decade later, Rose remembered that scene as she tried to lift the old dollhouse from its storage area in the barn. It was too heavy and bulky and she needed help, but she didn't want to ask her father. It would pain him to see her get rid of it. After all the work he and her brothers had put into it all those years ago, the cutting and gluing and painting, and the way they unveiled it on her birthday—just days after the run-in with Eunice Edwards—it seemed a shame to part with it.

They had given it to her when she turned nine, less than a year after her mother had died, and she had played with that dollhouse every day that year. There were three stories to it. The kitchen and dining and living rooms on the first floor, along with a nice laundry and craft area (an homage to her mother), then the bedrooms on the second floor, and on the third was a little room that looked kind of like a cupola, where the husband and wife could look out at the land and enjoy sunsets. The level of detail had fascinated her and made her grateful for a dad and brothers who cared enough to try to do something special, something memorable, even if their hearts were breaking.

"Let me help you with that," Denise Lawton said. She was taller than Rose by several inches, with long brown hair and eyes that twinkled when she smiled, and she always seemed to find a way to get her eyes to twinkle. Denise was a drama queen, literally, because she had been in every play and musical at school, seemingly from infancy.

"Wait, you're not getting rid of this, are you?" Denise said. "Rose, you can't!"

"It's been sitting in the barn for years."

"But we played with this when we were kids. You should keep this for your daughter."

Denise tried to move back toward the barn, but Rose pulled harder. "Keep moving—we're going to the truck."

"This is a mistake. You loved this dollhouse."

The thing was getting heavy and marking up her arms, so Rose set it down in the grass and ran a hand over the rooftop and the cupola. "I did love it, but I've outgrown it. And some little girl is going to be so happy."

"It's an heirloom. You don't outgrow an heirloom, you pass it down."

"I don't want my life to be about collecting stuff. If I ever have kids, I can tell them stories about this, about what my dad and brothers did for me. But I don't have to keep it in order to remember. I want to let go of it."

"I'm all for letting go of things you don't need. Uncluttering is fine. But you have to choose wisely. This is a mistake. Trust me. You're going to want this in a few years."

"Okay, stay right here," Rose said, running off. Denise called after her like she was threatening to leave but she was still with the dollhouse when Rose returned with her camera.

"Here, take a picture so I can show all these children you think I'm going to have."

"You are going to have a houseful. You'll make a great mom. People who have great moms become them."

"That's sweet. I think you just gave me a compliment."

"I was complimenting your mom."

Rose knelt by the house and smiled, holding up the

kitchen table and one of the chairs to show the intricacy of the construction. Denise snapped a few photos.

"There. Now let's get this over to the truck."

"You're going to hurt your dad by getting rid of this."

"My dad will be proud that we're helping the family raising funds."

"Always the great philanthropist. Who is this family, anyway?"

"They're from the Nazarene church. Their son needs an operation. They're having a rummage sale this weekend at the church picnic. Who knows what this might sell for."

They lifted it onto the back and slid it close to the exercise bicycle that had been tied down. There were several bags of clothes and books nearby and other things people from their church had already donated. Seeing the dollhouse there with the other stuff made her catch her breath. It was one thing to decide something like this and another to decide not to feel anything.

Rose pulled herself up on the truck's gate and sat. She looked out at the land, the vineyard that stretched out toward the rolling hills. She closed the bedroom door on the dollhouse and heard it click. Such detail.

She smiled. "I remember the musicals we'd do with guys straddling the top of the dollhouse and singing, 'Oooookla-homa!'"

"And the Barbies would always sit in the kitchen and listen, dreamily. Waiting for Ken to walk through after a hard day's work."

Rose closed her eyes and the memories came back sweetly. "You helped me laugh again."

"What are you talking about?"

"After Mom died, after all that happened in our house, the way my brothers coped or didn't . . . They kept living as if they'd lost a Little League game. And how stoic Dad became. I was the only one who cried and I felt bad about it. You let me. You encouraged me to cry. And you were the one who helped me laugh again."

"I just wanted to see the old you come through."

"It was your mom who suggested having my birthday party the next year, wasn't it?"

Denise nodded. "We talked about how sad you were. When you came over, when your dad would let you, you just wanted to stay outside. Sit on the swing and stare at the yard."

"You were good at listening."

"My mom said your dad cried when she suggested the party."

"He did?"

"She said he knew deep down she was right, that you needed things like that, but it was so hard for him to do. Your mom was the one who planned the parties and bought the presents."

"And baked the cake and decorated the house and put the balloons on the mailbox the day of the party." Rose sighed heavily and swung her legs beneath her like a child. "I don't think it was buying stuff or decorating that he didn't want to do. I think it was really hard for him to let a little joy come back into the house. It felt like we were betraying her by laughing again. By celebrating life."

"But she would have wanted you to laugh. That's the crazy thing. And she would have wanted you to keep this dollhouse for her grandchildren."

Rose rolled her eyes. "I'm not ready to think about grandchildren, Denise."

"You're going to have fifteen kids. All of them boys."

Rose laughed. "So what do I need a dollhouse for? And can you imagine fifteen boys in one house?"

"And you'll drive around a school bus to the grocery store."

"I think for that to happen, I'd have to find them a dad first."

"Eddie Edwards has always had a thing for you. And he's cute."

"Puppies are cute."

Denise rolled her eyes and shook her head. "You are hopeless. Guys are falling all over themselves to get to know you."

"I don't see any."

"You won't believe the number of guys who talk about you at church."

"Talking about me and talking to me are two wildly different things. Why don't they do a little of that?"

"You know why. They're all scared of your dad. Don't look at me that way. He's intimidating, you have to admit."

"Maybe a little."

"Saying your dad is a little intimidating is like saying Mount Everest is a bit of a hike." Denise sighed. "He does love you, in that crazy, delusional, special-ops-wine-country-farmer-protective kind of way. But I think your guy is out there. Right now he's waiting. Planning. It's a covert operation."

"What does he look like?"

"Let's see. He's six feet tall with a strong back that will be able to carry this dollhouse alone, anywhere you want. And he'll have blue eyes or maybe green. And a kind face. He'll wear crisp white T-shirts everywhere and jeans that look like they just came off the rack. A little beard down here like Tim McGraw."

"Tim who?"

"The country singer. Come on, Rose, you really need to update your music. You can't stay with the oldies forever."

"I like the oldies. My mom liked the oldies."

"Fine. Then this guy will like the oldies. He'll have all the great hits and listen to the AM station that still plays them."

"You talk like you've seen him. Like you have his phone number."

"I wish. If I knew a guy like that, I'd go for him myself."

"You can have him. I'm done with guys."

"You can't be done when you haven't started. Unless you count Stanley from fifth grade."

"Stanley Hinckley?"

They both broke out in spasms and Rose covered her mouth.

"He brought you flowers, didn't he?"

"Oh, he was so sweet. He used to sharpen my pencil every morning before school started and bring it to me like he'd slayed a dragon. First boy I ever danced with. Only boy I ever danced with."

"Too bad he left you for another woman."

"Who was that?"

"Little Debbie."

"I heard he lost weight, though," Rose said when she could talk through her laughter. "Got on the wrestling team after he moved to Lexington. I saw his picture the other day. Still has that smile."

"See, you're not done with guys if you're thinking about Stanley. Maybe he could move back and work on your dad's farm?" Denise's voice had a mix of concern in it. When Rose didn't answer, she said, "What are you going to do? I mean, you can't stay here forever, right?"

"Somebody has to help my dad, and it's not going to be my brothers."

"Your dad doesn't want you to stay here and sacrifice your future."

"It's no sacrifice to love someone who's loved you all your life."

"What about what God wants?"

"Honoring my dad is a good thing, isn't it?"

"Sure. I'm just saying . . ."

"Just because I don't go off to school like you and have this big vision for life doesn't mean I'm not doing what God wants. You can still find passion in small places. Your hometown. Don't try to make me fit in with your own dream, okay? I think it's great you have big plans. Go for it. But don't try to make me be like you."

Denise winced. "Looks like I touched a nerve."

"No, you put the toe of your boot on the nerve and smashed it."

"You're right. You don't have to leave the farm in order to do what God wants. And maybe someday the guy of your dreams will just waltz up here and plop himself down at your feet."

"If God has somebody for me, he's going to make it happen."

"That's where you're wrong. You have to get out there, Rose. You have to be proactive. You can't just sit and let life come to you. You have to explore. You have to live."

"And you're the person who's saying I shouldn't get rid of my dollhouse?"

"Rose—"

"Denise, I love this place. This is where my dreams are. Where I want my future to be. I'm not settling or hiding; I *am* living."

Denise stared at her for a long moment. "Okay." She sighed. "So the dollhouse goes?"

Rose smiled. "The dollhouse goes."

CHAPTER 4

As soon as *American Idol* hit the airwaves, people told Jed he should audition. They said it was a way to get noticed and get his name out there. But everything in him felt like that wasn't the way to go, that it was somehow cheating his art. He wanted to do this the way his father had, just play his songs and let things shake out. Sing the songs with every ounce of energy inside and see what happened. And that's what he did. He had the advantage of being in the lineage of a famous country artist, so there was interest and intrigue when he first began to play.

One night in a little venue on the south side of Louisville, a man approached.

Stan Russel was fighting hard not to look fifty, but he was losing the battle. His hair was thinning and his paunch broadening. If he wasn't careful, he would wind up with a bowling ball to carry around his middle. He wore a nice suit and looked like the kind of man who could get things done.

"I saw you last week at that little place on Frankfort Avenue. Heard you were playing here tonight."

"Well, thank you for taking the time to come hear me, Mr. Russel. I'm honored."

Stan smiled at Jed's politeness. "You've got a unique talent. Solid technique. Your voice cuts through. Your lyrics seem to come from somewhere deep inside. That's a winning combination, son."

"Thank you."

"Of course, you need some refining, but everybody your age needs that. Somebody to help them take the next step."

"Yes, sir."

"I'm not just saying this as observation. I have a reason to be here."

Jed stayed silent, asking only with his eyes.

"I'd like to represent you, Jed. I think with your talent and the drive you have to succeed and your heritage—" he gave what Jed would affectionately come to call the *Stan stare*—"I could help take you places."

"And what places would those be?"

"What places you want to go? Chicago? LA? I'm not in this to keep you a regional artist; I want to help you go big-time. Radio stations around the country will be playing your songs. You can count on that."

"What do I have to do?"

"I've convinced a fairly big label to give you a shot. What I need is a signature tune. One that connects you and your daddy. You give me that and I'll take care of the rest."

"Every agent who has approached me has told me to knock off the God stuff. Are you going to say the same thing?"

"Quite the contrary. I don't want you to take anything out of your songs that comes from here." He pointed to Jed's chest. "I don't want to hear anything fake. I want to hear the real thing. I don't care if you're an atheist, a Christian, or you believe space aliens are watching us. I want you to sing what you've been made to sing, just like your dad did."

They shook hands that night. Didn't sign anything or make any promises, but Stan handed him his card and Jed slipped it into the hole in his guitar. Then Jed stayed up all night working on something that had been rolling around in his head ever since his father died. It was the truth. And sometimes the truth had a bittersweet way of comforting those who had the ability to look it in the eye.

So when he started writing, the little lick at the start, the muted guitar string jag, gave the perfect feel. He could hear the mandolin coming in behind him, but only that, and maybe a bass line that ran through it. He was writing about his father, but he felt he was writing about himself too. Or what he might be capable of doing if he didn't follow the narrow path.

You can say it was love,
I don't know what I think of that.
Yeah, but somewhere the lines got crossed,
somewhere the vows were tossed away.
But the consequences stayed.
The consequences stayed.

Families torn apart all for the sake of your arrogance.
And somewhere the lines got crossed.
You took what wasn't yours to take.
But the consequences stayed.
Still the consequences stayed.

Yeah, I was born the son of a king
but you don't know what that means, do ya?
You might say it's living a dream
but somehow dreams have a way of coming true
like you don't want them to.

Some would probably see it as an angry song. Some would say Jed was accusing his father and dragging his name through the mud. Others would analyze it and say he had let his mother off the hook, that she'd been a willing participant in the breakup, the breakdown. Jed didn't see it as anything but painting the truth with words. All the family struggles, the alimony, the financial ups and downs, the screaming fans and the ugly side of fame. And how, when you stripped all of that away, a man's life boils down to just a handful of things.

In the last turn he brought it all together, his earthly father and his heavenly one, until it made sense to him.

And to the God in heaven,
give me the wisdom to see this through.
I didn't choose the place I was born
but I have to believe that it was you.
So to the God in heaven,
give me the wisdom to see this through.
Love is a choice worth making,
but even if it's not what we choose,
I'm still the son of a king.

Some songs take a lifetime to live and an hour to write. That's what "Son of a King" was like, and when he finished, he wept because he knew he had something special.

Jed tipped his guitar over and the card fell out. He called Stan at four in the morning and played the song the whole way through on the man's answering machine. Then he fell into a deep sleep that lasted until the phone woke him.

"Can you make it to Nashville today? How long will it take? Bring your guitar and that song."

CHAPTER 5

THE HARVEST FESTIVAL had been her mother's idea. It had started as a family thing, getting people together for games and food and music. When Rose was a little girl, she remembered the extended family coming and camping out on the lawn, sleeping anywhere they could find an empty spot. Late-night games of dominoes and Rook and the sound of her mother playing the piano while voices sang from an old red hymnal in four-part harmony.

Through the years, the festival became more of a celebration and an extension of the vineyard—a way to share the bounty of the harvest with friends. People came for those three crisp days in October to unwind and eat good food and taste something new. There was storytelling and face-painting and they sold pumpkins for half of what you could buy them for at the store. Women from the church brought baked goods and there were hayrides and pony rides and the juiciest candy apples south of the Mason-Dixon, or north for that matter.

The pinnacle of the event was the concert Saturday night. Each year Rose and her dad tried to make the concert bigger and better. Early on they had groups from church, quartets and bands that sang at no cost. One year they had a talent competition, everything from singing kids to a ventriloquist to a guy who spun pie plates, but they finally agreed to hire professionals. That led to several years of bad decisions by her father, who brought in some of the most eclectic performers Rose had ever seen. A man who played the harp and sang falsetto versions of Slim Whitman's greatest hits. Three men who were billed as a quartet—and they'd never had a fourth member even to play piano. They wore impeccable clothing; it was just that the style had gone out in the seventies with shag carpet.

"This year, it's all yours," her dad said this summer. "You pick the singer, the talent, whatever you want. I wash my hands of the whole thing."

"Really?" Rose was wide-eyed and smiling.

"I want to see what you come up with."

"What's the budget?"

When he told her, her face fell. "Dad, that's going to get us more of the same. We have to spend a little more."

"What's a little more?"

She told him and *his* face fell. "We barely make enough to break even as it is, Rose."

"But think of it this way. You get a better artist, someone people know, and more people will come. That means more pumpkins and apple turnovers are sold. More people will want to sample your wines and maybe buy a bottle or two. If we attract more people with the musical artist, they'll be here and hungry and want to take something home with them."

"Who are you thinking about?" he said.

"Leave that to me."

And leave it he did. Which caused Rose more concern because she knew almost nothing about music. Oh, she liked to sing and play the radio, had CDs compiled of her favorite oldies, but music was more background noise to her.

Rose immediately called Denise, who had followed her dream of acting during college and gotten a few good roles in summer stock and dinner theaters. Rose had gone to nearly every production. There had been talk of Denise moving to New York after graduation, but money became an issue and instead a friend had set her up with a studio in Nashville, where she worked as an assistant to a producer.

Nashville was two or three hours away, depending on where in the city you needed to go, so Denise made it home a weekend a month. When Rose called looking for ideas for the harvest festival, Denise went to work and soon after showed up on Rose's porch with a list of ten names.

"They all look good to me," Rose said. "Why don't you pick one?"

"That's not how it's supposed to work. We have to think of the best fit for the vineyard. You don't want somebody singing drinking and women-chasing songs."

"Anything would beat the guy spinning plates."

"Do you want a group that sings gospel?" Denise held up a brochure with a picture on the front. "This family has been around a long time and they have kids who play every instrument you can imagine. They can come off a little like a dog and pony show, though. You know, 'Look at our two-year-old play "Dueling Banjos" on the piccolo.'"

"She'd be a crowd favorite."

"Only after you've had a glass or two of chardonnay. Let's put them aside."

Rose studied the list of singers and entertainers and the pictures that accompanied their names.

"How are things with Eddie?" Denise said. "Still on again, off again?"

"We're seeing each other," Rose said. "Dad still doesn't trust him."

"Do you?"

"You said a long time ago that he was cute," Rose said.

"Don't change the subject."

"I thought finding an artist was the subject."

"It is, but you have to tell me about your love life. I'm interested."

"There's nothing to tell. I mean, we go out a few times a week. I see him in church."

"Church, huh? It's that serious?"

"It's not that serious."

"What about his mom? What does she think of the two of you?"

"She's . . . a little leery of me, I think. Cautious. She thinks we'll turn Eddie into a winebibber."

"Mm-hmm."

"Can we get back to the list? Who's this girl?"

"Valerie? She sang the national anthem at a Braves game and got a recording contract about ten seconds later. She's sweet, but she's got this big voice that might not fit as well with you guys. I see your stage as a smaller, more intimate thing. Which makes me think of Eddie."

"Would you stop with the Eddie questions?"

"I just care about you, Rose. I had a friend who knew Eddie, dated him a couple of times, and she said he didn't just look like a puppy."

"What do you mean?"

"She said he was all paws and lips. She had to smack him to keep him down."

Rose laughed. "I hear what you're saying about the venue—a big-voiced singer probably wouldn't be good. We want kind of the 'vineyard unplugged' feel."

"You're hopeless. Okay, vineyard unplugged." Denise scanned the page and pictures.

"I guess I just want somebody who won't make the young people roll their eyes and won't make the old people plug their ears."

"Then you have to go with this guy. He's a little rockabilly, lots of patriotic stuff—you know, soldiers coming back from war and remember 9/11. And he can throw in some gospel as well."

Rose looked at the name. "Chad Houston? I've never heard of him."

"That's your price category—what you can afford. *I've never heard of him.* Now, if you're willing to pay about $500 more, you move up to *Is he the guy who sings . . . ?* A thousand more will get you *I love that song.* Most of the people you know are out of range. These are regional artists with some following, a record or two, but they haven't made it big. But just think what it'll be like when you have this Houston guy at the harvest festival and then he becomes a huge star."

Rose nodded. "Sounds great. Let's do it."

Denise contacted the right people and Rose had a contract in her hands by late August. The pages were filled with legalese explaining how much to pay Chad, how long he would play, what he needed to drink and eat before the concert, specifics on the sound system required. It all seemed overwhelming until Rose called Denise to ask follow-up questions.

"I'm surprised all that stuff is in the contract."

"Don't sweat it. He'll be happy with a check and a Pop-Tart. Trust me."

Rose signed the agreement and sent the pages back with the payment to secure Chad. Then she started advertising, sending out flyers and posting things online. The local stores allowed her to put a flyer in their windows and the buzz started going around that the harvest festival was going to be the best ever.

That was, until mid-September, two weeks before the festival, when Rose got a call from an agency in Nashville. The good news was that Rose was getting back the money she had put up for the concert. The bad news was that Chad Houston had gone water-skiing in between shows while in California, broken his leg in three places, and was canceling all his concerts for the next month.

"Let me see what I can do," Denise said when Rose frantically called her.

Two hours later Denise was back with a strain in her voice. "It's too late to book any of those other folks on the sheet I gave you, so we have to go with plan B. Or maybe it's plan Z now."

"Who do you suggest?"

"You can't be picky with less than two weeks. I know a manager of a couple people. His name is Stan Russel. I saw him this afternoon and gave him one of your cards. He said he has this guy, Jed King, who might be available."

"He doesn't spin plates, does he?"

Denise laughed. "I'm shooting you an e-mail with his bio and stuff. He's with a label but evidently not with a label—Stan talked about him being let go. It was kind of confusing. But he said he's really good, and he sings about God in his songs."

"I guess at this point we can't be that picky. Is he available?"

"Stan is supposed to talk with him tonight. Promised me he would give Jed your information and have him call you."

"I hope it's soon."

CHAPTER 6

After some initial airplay and buzz for "Son of a King," and a couple of county fairs, it was back to Louisville—the same bars and honky-tonks. Jed once played on a small stage at a truck stop and it was one of the best crowds he'd ever performed for. Still, he longed to see standing-room-only venues with people clapping along and singing rather than eating pancakes with watered-down Aunt Jemima.

One night at a little bar the music was flowing and he felt at the top of his game. He sang with all the passion inside him but that was drowned out by the sound of a pinball machine in one corner and loud conversation through the sparse crowd. When he finished his most upbeat song, there was just no response. Only two women were paying attention, and Jed knew they weren't really that interested in the music. When the set concluded to a smattering of applause, he made his way to the bar for a drink and the women followed. They were both attractive but on the road to trashy.

"Great show, Jed."

"Thanks."

"I'm Laura."

"Katie."

He shook hands with them and smiled.

"Love your stuff," Katie said, winking.

Jed glanced at the bartender, who seemed to be hovering.

"So what are you doing after this?" Laura said.

"Yeah, you want to party with us?"

"Party?" Jed said.

"Yeah, you know." Laura ran her tongue across her lips and touched his arm lightly. "Party."

She said it like she could convey the sexual tension with just two syllables. Like she could explain all she wanted to do with the one word and the way her eyes lit when she smiled.

Jed cocked his head and took a step toward her. "Laura, do you love me?"

She looked at her friend, then back at Jed. "Are you serious?"

He continued, "The mingling of two souls, that's a serious thing. So I need to know that you love me. That, through better or worse, you'll be there for me. For our children."

Laura got the look Jed loved to see. A mix of disbelief and incomprehension. "What?"

"Children need to be loved too, Laura. Not just me. The children." He turned to her friend now, who looked at him like he had a horn growing out of his forehead. "Laura doesn't seem to get it, Katie. Do you love me?"

"You're a freak, you know that?" she said.

"Let's get out of here," Laura said as they left, looking over her shoulder with a glare for Jed that conveyed contempt and disdain.

Jed couldn't contain the smile and turned to see the bartender staring at him, slack-jawed.

"You're crazy," the man said.

"I know. I know. Sorry. Clearly I'm the one with the problem."

"Those girls wanted you."

"Yeah, they thought they did."

The bartender sighed, shook his head, and went back to work.

Jed turned and scanned the crowd, finally finding the person he was looking for in the back. He took his drink and sat in the booth across from Stan Russel.

"How are you doing, Jed?"

Jed stretched and weighed his words. "A little tired. Of playing these places. Tired of singing to people who don't want to hear what I have to say. People who want to drink more than they want to listen."

"I've told you, it's a process. Overnight hits tend to flame out. The best course is slow and steady, building a base of fans. You know that."

"Stan, what happened to our winning combination?"

"I'm sorry things haven't turned out like you wanted. Like we wanted. My hope was that by now things would have taken off, but they haven't."

"And they're not going to take off unless you start booking me into bigger places with more people. Come on, Stan, we will sell more albums if you get me playing bigger venues. This place sells out at like eighteen people."

"I have you in the venues you can fill, okay? There's a bottom line, my friend, and you have plateaued."

"We just need a new approach. On the next album—"

"There's not going to be a next album."

Jed stared at the man, not able to comprehend what he was hearing.

"They're dropping you."

It was a knife Jed hadn't expected. He'd come to the table with all the swagger he could muster, thinking he needed to tell Stan how things were going to be, take the situation under control. But with a few words and a sad look, Stan had pulled the rug out from under him.

"I'll find another label," Jed said, trying to regroup.

Stan gave him a shake of the head. "Okay, man, I'm going to break it down for you. People come to see you for one reason. They loved your dad. Until you find heart or inspiration or something real to sing about, you're just going to be David King's kid."

A manager was supposed to build confidence, show a little faith. Build up the artist when he got down. Tell him things would work out, that they were only one break away from hitting the big time. But Jed could tell that the man who was in charge of his music had given up.

A big sigh. Stan pushed his plastic cup of Coors Light back to the middle of the table. "Your dad was all heart; his songs were inspired. People come to see you because they loved him, and they don't want to listen to you air out his dirty laundry. I'm sorry, Jed."

Funny how something so true could be thrown under the bus so easily. Stan had been excited for the label to hear "Son of a King." Now he was blaming Jed's lack of success on the song he'd thought was pure and honest. To Stan and the label, Jed was just another angry son raging against his parents, rebelling. But they had signed him because of the song and were dumping him because of the same song, which only made Jed more angry.

Stan pulled a business card out of his pocket and handed it to Jed. "A little parting gift from old Stanager, okay? There's a vineyard over in Sharon that does a big harvest festival every fall. They need a musician. They pay well. And it's only thirty minutes away. You don't even have to pay me."

"Are you serious?"

"Yeah, I'm serious."

Jed took the card and tore it in half, then tore it again and tossed the pieces onto the metal table.

"I'm a bridge. I'm on fire." Stan leaned closer, his breath stale with beer. "You are brilliant. Appreciate that."

"Just go," Jed said.

Two hands in the air and Stan rolled out of the booth. "I'm happy to leave."

Jed wanted to run the man down and punch him. He wanted to take his guitar and smash it over Stan's head or toss it through the front window of the bar. Stan just walked away like Jed was nothing. Like that handshake meant nothing, like he was moving on to some other girlfriend and Jed was left standing at the altar.

Jed stood and followed Stan toward the door, trying to think of something he could say, some knife he could plunge with his words. Then he stopped. He turned and went back to the table and picked up the four pieces of the business card. On the front it said, *Jordan Vineyard*.

He retrieved his guitar and let the pieces fall into the hole.

Jed drove away from the city, away from the light pollution, out into the country where he could see the stars. He turned off the music and just listened to the crickets and frogs, the Kentucky night sounds, watching the lightning bugs rise and the stars become brighter and brighter against the dark sky.

In his heart a man plans his course, but the Lord directs his steps.

"God, if that's true," Jed prayed, "I have to believe you're directing my steps now. I think I have a gift. I think you want me to use that gift. And maybe I'm not going in the right direction. I don't want fame like my dad. I've seen what that can do. It just leads to heartache. I know I need something more than fame or money or success."

Jed found a picnic table by the road and lay down on it, hands behind his head, staring straight up. "I choose to believe that you have a better plan for me than one I can cook up myself. You've given me a gift, and if you want me to use that to praise you, I'll do it. If you want me to dig a ditch, I'll do that with everything in me. Or build a garage. Or do anything. I'm yours, Lord. I refuse to let a label or a manager dictate how I live my life. Success is not how many records I sell. Success is how close I follow you. Would you show me how to do that?"

CHAPTER 7

THE NEXT DAY, Rose collected a stack of ads from store windows and deleted the information about Chad Houston online. The last thing she wanted was people showing up expecting to hear one person and getting another. That wasn't fair to anybody. She wished Denise had given her the number for Jed King so she could call him. The only contact information online was a number for his manager, Stan Russel.

She would just have to wait and hope Stan followed through on his promise. She didn't want to tell her father about the change in singers because she knew how he would react, just scowl and say, "Doggone the luck." He would pat her on the shoulder but inside, he'd think he should have done it himself, and she hated that. Hated waiting for her father to see that she really could run the vineyard, that she was up to the task.

Rose pulled up the bio Denise had sent and stared at Jed King's picture. He was holding a guitar with a crown on the front of it and staring into the distance. He had a boyish face that seemed innocent, thin and angular with a chiseled quality. Dark features. Piercing eyes. But there was a sadness to him, a melancholy that made her feel sorry for him. He wore a faded T-shirt and jeans and the picture exuded a "This is how I am, take me or leave me" quality. There was somebody he looked like, a movie star who'd played a country singer once. What was his name? The guy with the hair and the easy smile?

Her cell phone rang and she didn't wait to check the number. How appropriate if she was looking at Jed's bio when he actually called.

"Hey, Rosie," Eddie said when she answered. His voice sent a shiver through her and she wasn't sure if that was good or bad.

"Hey, Eddie."

"Whatcha doin'? Thinking about me?"

"Sure. I'm always thinking about you." *But thinking what is the question.*

"That's what I like to hear."

"And I'm working on the harvest festival."

"Baking funnel cakes?" He didn't mean anything by it or by his laugh, she was sure. Some guys still thought of girls as domestic help—*get back in the kitchen and tend to the vittles.* But Eddie wasn't that way. He couldn't be.

"No, our singer fell through. Literally—he broke his leg and can't appear."

"What are you going to do?"

He said it with a yawn, but he was probably just tired. She closed her eyes and saw his brown hair, those eyes that could stare a hole right through you. Eddie could be so intense yet so fun-loving.

"I'm working on another guy."

"Story of my life."

"What?"

"You working on another guy, that's the story of my life."

"Eddie."

"Seriously, Rosie, if you're interested in somebody else, just tell me."

"What are you talking about? There's nobody else. You know how I feel about you."

"No, I don't. Every time I get close to you, you push me away. Every time I try to show you how I feel about you, you pull back. I don't understand why you don't want me to love you."

"I do want you to love me. Just not in that way. Not yet."

Rose heard his exasperated sigh just as her father walked into the house and called her name.

"On the phone, Dad," she called back.

"All right. I brought dinner when you're ready."

She closed the door and sat in front of the computer again, looking out the window. The evening was her favorite time to look over the vineyard, the sweep of the land bathed in the fading sunlight. The pond that lay like a golden pool at the bottom of the rolling hill.

"My dad's home," she said.

"There's a few of us getting together over at Lake Barkley tomorrow. My uncle has a little cabin and there's a park nearby with picnic tables and a volleyball net and some sand. It's really nice. Peaceful. It'll be fun. No pressure."

"Who's going to be there?"

He rattled off a few names she didn't recognize, except one guy from church. "We could spend the day at the lake and then watch the moon come up from my uncle's cabin. We could watch movies. Or just talk. I want to be with you, Rose."

"That sounds really good," she said, and she meant it. Being with Eddie was always fun.

"We could bring a bottle of your dad's wine. Go out on the lake in the boat."

She closed her eyes and could see the lake, imagine the cabin. It would be nice to get away from the stress, even for a night. Just leave the cares and worries behind.

"What do you say, Rose?"

Her cell beeped and she looked at the screen. A number that began with 502.

"Eddie, can you hold on a minute? I think the singer guy's calling."

He gave another loud sigh. "Sure, I'll be here."

She hit the button and answered with a nervous "Hello, this is Rose."

"Hi there, Rose. This is Jed King. Do you work with the . . . ?" A slight pause like he was having trouble reading something. "Jordan Vineyard?"

"Yes sir, Mr. King. I was hoping you would call."

"I understand you need someone to sing at your fall festival."

"Harvest festival. Yes."

"Can I ask why you waited so long to find somebody?"

"Well, we did have someone, but he was injured in a water-skiing accident."

"You had Chad booked?"

"You know him?"

"I played with him a couple of times here in Louisville. He's a good guy. Not a good water-skier, though."

"Evidently not. So that's why we have this open spot and we were hoping you'd come."

"Well, I'll have to check my schedule and talk with my people and see if my secretary has anything else planned for me."

Her heart fell. "Oh. Well, do you know when you might be able to let me know if you—?"

"I'm teasing you. I don't have any people. No secretary. I barely have a calendar. I'll do it."

"You will?" She was smiling from ear to ear. "That's great! Now, I know there's probably a contract you have with the food and equipment and things you need. Can you send that to me?"

"I don't need a contract. My word, your word, is as good as a contract."

"Thank you."

"I'll show up an hour before the event to set up. I assume it's in the evening, around seven?"

"Right. Come a little earlier and we can get you some dinner."

"Sounds great. I only have a guitar, a banjo, and a table to sell my CDs, if that's okay."

"Sure. I can get someone to help you, if you'd like."

"That would be awesome. As long as you have a microphone and speakers that work, that's all I need. I'll bring the songs."

"All right. Great. We'll see you on Saturday the seventh, then."

"Wait, Saturday the seventh? I thought it was this Saturday."

"Is that a problem?"

"Only that I'll have to wait another week to play for you guys. See you on the seventh."

Rose couldn't stifle the grin on her face. This Jed King was a stranger, but he sounded so confident and, well, nice. Down-to-earth. Not like some of the entertainers she had heard about through the grapevine.

She hung up and immediately remembered Eddie. She

hit the button again but the call had dropped. She quickly redialed, but her phone rang before it went through.

"I can't believe you hung up on me!" Eddie said.

"I didn't. I was talking with the singer about the festival."

"What's his name?"

"It's not important, Eddie."

Another sigh. "Rosie, say yes to tomorrow. The lake. The cabin. That's all I want to hear."

"It does sound like fun."

"It'll be great. We'll leave early in the morning and be back late, so tell your dad."

"I need to get the ads up in the stores."

"You can do that Saturday. Come on, Rosie. Just one day."

"All right. Pick me up tomorrow morning."

"Yes! Oh, we're going to have so much fun. You won't regret this."

When she told her father over cold chicken and mashed potatoes that she was spending the day with Eddie, he groaned. There was a wrinkle above one eye that creased his forehead when something went wrong with a tractor or some joyriding kid took out his mailbox, and it showed up now. She was beginning to see the age in his eyes. He had seemed so strong and youthful when she was little, but the loss of her mother and the boys moving out and the weight of the years had weathered him like an old barn.

"I know it's hard to see me grown-up and making my own choices, Dad."

He tore off a piece of buttermilk biscuit and held it there

like a communion wafer, rolling it and studying the thing before he put it in his mouth. Her father had always savored a good meal. Rose remembered the spread her mother used to put on the table on Sundays and holidays. This rubbery chicken and the prefab mashed potatoes were so far from what they had known, but exactly what they had gotten used to—what they settled for.

"You don't think Eddie's a good choice," Rose said.

He put down the plastic fork and wiped the grease from his hands. "What do you think, Rose?"

"I think he's sweet. He's handsome, he has a good heart, and he really likes spending time with me."

"Is that what he likes? Spending time with you?"

She let the question hang there, wondering if her dad knew more about Eddie than she thought. "He's a good guy, Dad. He's not like some of the others."

"You sure?"

He looked at her with those pale-blue eyes and she realized she was saying this more for herself than for him, more to convince her own heart than to comfort his.

"I got a singer booked today."

"Doesn't ski, does he?"

She smiled. "You heard about that?"

He ignored her question. "What's he sing?"

"I'm not sure. Country, maybe. He's supposed to be good. Denise suggested him."

"You hired a guy and you don't know what he sings?"

"I trust Denise. Plus, it's really short notice."

"He's not some honky-tonk singer, is he? You know, 'Let's get drunk tonight' kind of guy?"

"Denise said he sings about God and a lot of things . . ." Her voice trailed and she suddenly felt like a little girl again, her dad giving her a wary eye about makeup or how much her haircut cost. "I know you don't trust me with this, but—"

"You sign a contract?"

"He said he didn't need one. His word was as good as a contract."

Her dad pushed his plate away and wadded his napkin and placed it on top. "I don't mean to hurt you, Rose. Don't take it that way. I do trust you. You know how I get when the festival rolls around."

"We don't have to do it this year. We could take a year off."

"I couldn't do that to your mother."

"To Mom?"

"I made some promises. You know that."

She had heard the story a thousand times. "Tell me again."

"One of them was that we would do something every year to celebrate life. That's what the wine represents—you know this."

Rose did.

"Your mother always hated the fact that I took my time making decisions. Weighing this against that and the cost versus the risk and what people would think and worries about money. Living that way is not living at all, it's prison. Paralysis."

She had never heard him talk so philosophically about his life.

"Point is, I finally saw it when she was gone. I finally realized that not making a decision, not moving ahead with life because it was hard or uncomfortable, was not really living. So I told her I would change. And keeping the festival going each year represents a little of that change for me."

Rose patted his hand with mist in her eyes. "This is going to be the best festival ever."

He smiled. "You just watch Eddie, you hear?"

On the way to the cabin, Eddie turned on the radio and listened to his favorite morning team. The banter was raunchy and the humor felt cruel at times with the hosts making fun of celebrities or callers, but Eddie hit the steering wheel laughing, having a great time. When they reached the picnic area, there were several cars already there and people throwing Frisbees and playing volleyball. Another group was under a shelter starting the barbecue.

He pulled into the parking lot and switched off the radio. "How come you're so quiet?"

"Just thinking."

"About what?"

"The festival. My dad."

"He doesn't like me much."

"He doesn't like anybody who shows an interest in me."

"He's got nothing to worry about with me. I'm the perfect gentleman." He reached over and squeezed her knee, then rubbed her leg gently. "Let's go have some fun."

Rose didn't know many people at the picnic and she stayed mostly by herself. Eddie dragged her onto the volleyball court though she didn't want to go. She stood up front at the net, right across from Kristen, a girl she knew was interested in Eddie. She was laughing loud and bouncing around in tight shorts and a shirt that looked a couple of sizes too small.

When Kristen spotted Rose, her face lit up. "Hey, Rose, you made it!"

Like she knew she'd been invited? What did Kristen know?

"Hey, Kristen," Rose said. Someone served from Kristen's side and the ball bounced in the sand right behind Rose.

"You gotta get that!" Eddie yelled.

The next serve hit the net and fell at Kristen's feet. She picked up the ball and wobbled a little, then handed it to Rose. "Your turn."

She tried to serve, she really did, but the ball angled out of bounds.

"Give her another try!" Eddie called.

"Yeah, let's see her do that again!" Kristen said.

Rose tried to concentrate on the ball, dropped it and swung underhanded, but again it went sideways and she couldn't look up. She also couldn't get Kristen's laughter out of her head. She spent the rest of the game trying to avoid the ball.

"Hey, you tried hard," Eddie said after the game was over. "No harm in that. Let's get something to eat."

They ate burgers and hot dogs and sat on picnic tables. There was soda, but there was also plenty of beer. The longer the day wore on, the louder the party got, with music booming from an open Jeep and laughter rising along with the smoke from the barbecue.

"I don't think I want to stay," Rose said to Eddie.

"That's fine. We can shoot over to my uncle's place."

He told everyone they were taking off, and once they were in the car, she felt better. As they drove away, Rose caught Kristen's glare from the picnic shelter.

The farther they drove into the countryside, the more remote the area became, and more beautiful. Leaves had turned but hadn't fallen, with every color of the palette on display.

The cabin was right on the lake, built on a slight knoll with a long, wooded driveway and trees that shrouded the dirt lane. It was an A-frame with a heavy wooden door that opened like Eddie was unlocking a freezer. There was a loft upstairs, granite counters in the kitchen, a gourmet stove and a huge refrigerator stocked with food, and hardwood floors that looked like mirrors in the fading sunlight.

"This is gorgeous," Rose said. She stood at the front windows and looked out on the rippling lake water. "Your uncle must be rich."

"He's a builder. He remodeled this with stuff left over from a big job in Nashville. Some software developer had a house built in Brentwood. Waterfalls in the backyard." Eddie walked in front of Rose, blocking her view. "The most beautiful thing here isn't the house or the lake though."

Rose blushed. "He has a boat?"

Eddie laughed. "I'm not talking about a boat. The most beautiful thing here is right in front of me." He put his hands on her shoulders and looked into her eyes. "You're the most beautiful thing I've ever seen. And I know I don't always express it the best way. I'm clumsy. It's because I'm scared, I think. That you won't like me."

"I do like you, Eddie."

He leaned in for a kiss. After a few seconds, Rose broke away and hugged him, then pulled back. "Let's go for a walk around the lake."

"I don't know. There's a lot of bugs out this time of day. But there's a hot tub on the patio. Let's go there."

He took her hand and led her outside, pulling the cover off the hot tub. While he worked on it, Rose wandered off, down to the little boat launch, her mind spinning in different directions. Part of her was glad she was being pursued but another part didn't like the pressure from Eddie.

"Now what are you doing down here?" Eddie said, walking onto the launch.

"I think we should go home."

"We just got here!" Eddie said. "I want to make you dinner. Watch the stars come out."

"We'll be really late driving back."

"Then maybe we should spend the night here."

"Eddie, come on—"

He moved toward her and she backed away, still facing him. Her feet were at the edge of the launch, precariously close, and she put her hands on his chest to steady herself.

"The beautiful Rose," he whispered. "And not a thorn in sight."

"We need to talk about this . . ."

He leaned closer and she could smell the mints he had eaten on the drive. "Just a little kiss. That won't hurt anything, will it?"

Maybe it wouldn't. In fact, she knew it wouldn't hurt. It would feel good. So when she could back away no farther, she planted her feet and lifted her face and let him kiss her. It was slow and passionate and inviting, and she felt something shift in that moment, felt something inside give way, like a surrender. She put her arms around him and he pulled her close. But somehow the shift of weight didn't work and he leaned a little too far and her balance tipped. Rose screamed and grabbed him around the neck as they fell into the water.

"You did that on purpose!" she said when she came up for air, algae in her hair and shooting daggers with her eyes.

Eddie laughed. "You were the one who pulled me!"

She swam to the dock and pulled herself up. A stiff breeze blew, giving her goose bumps, and she scampered back to the house dripping wet. Eddie suggested they launder their clothes.

"No way," she said.

"It's okay. There are robes in the bedroom. Get out of those and I'll wash them."

He gave her a thick cotton robe like she had seen in ads from high-end spas. It felt like she was wrapping herself in a sheep. When she came out, the robe tied tightly, Eddie was bare-chested with just a towel wrapped around himself.

"I need a shower after that dirty lake water. Want to join me?"

"No."

"Kiss me one more time, then," he said.

But this time there was something else in his eyes. A fire. Determination.

Rose moved past him into the laundry room and shut the door, rinsed her clothes and wrung them out by hand, then tossed them in the dryer.

"You sure you don't want me to help?" Eddie said.

"No, I've got it," she called back, her stomach churning like the clothes flopping in the dryer behind her. She had shoved down the feelings about Eddie for a long time and she was beginning to see it wasn't really about Eddie. It was her. These feelings kept bubbling up and she kept pushing them down.

When she heard the shower running, she pulled her clothes out and put them on, even though they were only half-dry. She went out the back door and walked to the road, following the way they had come. A half hour later, after she had reached the blacktop, Eddie pulled up alongside her.

"Rose, get in the car."

"Don't order me around."

"This is crazy. You going to walk all the way back to Sharon? What did I do?"

"I don't think it's going to work with us, Eddie. We're just different."

"I was just trying to have a little fun. I can't help it. You're beautiful."

"Yes, you can help it. You're not a teenager who can't control his hormones. You're a grown man who should listen when I say—"

"Rose, come on," Eddie said, interrupting. "Just let me give you a ride. You can get in the back if you want. I'll be your chauffeur."

She stopped and turned. He leaned over and opened the back door for her. "I'm not leaving here without you. If for no other reason than your dad would kill me. Look at the sun—it's already down. It'll be dark in twenty minutes."

Her purse was in the car, her cell phone inside it. She probably couldn't get service out here, it was so remote. No one was on the road and it *was* getting dark.

She got in the car, sitting in the back. For ten minutes they rode in silence. Then Eddie flipped on the radio and listened while she stared out the window, a tear running its way down her cheek.

Neither spoke for the rest of the ride.

Finally, when he pulled up to her house, Eddie said, "You're not serious about this?"

"Yeah, I am. If you can't respect what I want . . ."

Eddie snorted. "You say I'm acting like a teenager, but you're the one who needs to grow up, Rose."

Rose jumped out of the car and slammed the door.

Eddie rolled down the window and shouted, "How about I find a real woman who knows how to show me she loves me? 'Cause we're done."

Rose stumbled into the house as Eddie's car roared away.

"Rose, what's wrong?" her father said behind her.

She was crying too hard to speak.

CHAPTER 8

JED SPOKE TO HIS MOTHER periodically and she asked him to visit—if he had time. They were growing apart, as a natural process, but he could hear the pain in her voice, the pain of losing her husband and a son who was living independently. He surprised her one day before the concert at the Jordan Vineyard and they ate lunch together and talked about safe things. He told her about the venue but tried to paint it for what it was: a nice gig in the country without a lot of expectations. Then she grew quiet.

"What is it?" Jed said.

"I don't want you to feel like you have to take care of me."

"I don't feel that way. I want you in my life."

"And I want to be part of helping you become who you were meant to be, but I don't want to get in your way."

"You've heard about Stan, right? That he let me go?"

She nodded. "Because of the label's decision."

"You know about that, too?"

She wiped her mouth and took a drink of sweet tea. "He called after he talked with you. He was concerned."

"If he was so concerned, why didn't he stick with me? That's what friends do."

"It's business, Jed. You know that. It's not personal."

"It feels personal."

She thought a moment and it seemed to him like she was pulling up a bucket from some deep well of her life. Finally she said, "That this happened to you is not the most important thing. Life sneaks up and smacks you when you least expect it. It happens to us all. The most important thing is how you handle it. Your response to the struggle."

Like his dad's song, Jed thought. A line from a song on his father's first album Jed had sung when he was learning to play.

Life will take its swings
and life will not hold back
So you gotta dodge and weave and keep your feet
and try to stay on track.

"I've been thinking I might give carpentry a try," Jed said. "Maybe take some time off from music. Still write and play, but let things come to me. There's a contractor I know who—"

"Jed, you'd be a great carpenter—you learned a lot from your dad. But that's not what you were made to do. You know that, don't you?"

"You're my mother. You have to say stuff like that."

"I also was onstage. Sang with some of the best and watched the rest. I've seen those who have it and those who just want to have it but don't. The hungry ones. You've got the natural talent that can't be taught. The intangible quality of a star. And you have the drive, I think. But you also have the heart. A genuine goodness. You can do this without having it change who you are inside."

"You sure about that?"

"I know it."

"Funny, that's exactly what Stan told me I didn't have. Heart. Passion. Inspiration. He says my songs . . . How did he put it? They just sit there without moving people, I guess is the way to say it."

"He's right."

Jed looked at her with a furrowed brow. "Some encouragement you are."

She smiled. "You've gone as far as you have on your talent and legacy."

"Meaning people listen to me because they liked Dad's music. He said that, too."

"I didn't mean that. I meant you've reached a point where you need to make a decision."

"About what?"

"Will you settle for the success you've had and call it good, or will you reach for something more? Something deeper? And how will you define success? Number one hits? Another contract? Lots of money in the bank?"

"Dad had all of that and was miserable for much of his life."

"Exactly. Will you learn from him? Use the manure of life?"

He cocked his head at her.

"It's something your father used to say. Most of life is manure. The challenge is learning to manage the stink and get the benefit from what grows out of it."

"The barnyard philosopher."

They both laughed and it was a welcome relief to the conversation. Then his mother opened another can of relational questions.

"Anything going on romantically?"

"I could ask you the same thing," Jed said.

Another smile, but this one was sad. "After the life your father and I had, I don't think anyone could replace him. I'm open to it, if God would have that for me, but I'm not asking him to fill that void with anyone but himself."

"Fair enough."

"What about you?"

"I've given up on women."

"So soon? Totally? Irrevocably?"

"Janis and I were serious for a long time in high school. You know that. But we were so different. And when she went to school . . ."

"What about Tracey?"

"Sweetest girl I've ever met. She wasn't ready to sign up for what my life is becoming."

"Not interested in being a carpenter's wife, huh?"

He laughed. "Maybe if I became a carpenter, she would be interested."

"So what are you looking for?"

"It's not like I've made a list. I don't have eighty things a girl must have—"

"But if Janis and Tracey weren't the ones, you have an idea."

Jed sighed and put down his fork. "First I want to be the right guy. But I also want to meet a girl who will take me deeper with God than I can go on my own."

"That's a pretty tall order for somebody with no list."

"I think I'll know her if I ever see her."

"And how's that going to happen?"

He thought a minute. A picture flashed in his mind—some girl he had never seen with a knockout figure and a smile that could light a dim barroom. Long hair—or short; he could go either way on the hair.

"I think I'll know her because she'll make me want to sing a new song."

"Be careful about holding this woman to an impossible standard."

"You asked."

"I'm just saying—if you're looking for a woman to inspire you, just be careful not to put too much pressure. Inspiration doesn't come from outside, it comes from inside as you look at the world."

"Is that another one from the barnyard philosopher?"

"That was his and mine." She leaned forward and put a hand on his arm. "In other words, don't wait for a girl to make your heart come alive. That's not her job."

"Sounds like a song, doesn't it?"

"Maybe it is," his mother said. "And it sounds like you're not giving up on women."

"Sure I am," Jed said, smiling.

CHAPTER 9

The tombstone of Lily Jordan sat on a knoll overlooking the pond on their property. Family graveyards were more intimate and meaningful than a big plot of land with stones everywhere, and Rose had been glad when her dad had decided to let her mother rest by the vineyard. It was the spot where her father wanted to be buried as well.

Rose looked at the dash between when her mother was born and when she died, grieving how little of it she'd gotten to experience with her. Her mom had left her letters to open at each birthday until she was twenty-one, but those had ended now. More than ever, it felt like Rose was on her own.

The breast cancer had spread to the lymph nodes before they discovered she was sick. She had hung on until after

Rose's birthday, and then some. But in the end, though they tried to shield Rose from the pain her mother was going through, the disease had taken over and her mother bore little resemblance to the cheery woman who looked out from the pictures in Rose's baby book.

There was so much she wanted to ask now, so much to say, and these trips to her grave helped Rose process life. She knew she wasn't actually talking with her mother and she never heard answers from the grave. There was just a strange comfort in speaking aloud here and saying things she couldn't tell her father.

"I don't know why this Eddie thing has me tied in knots," Rose said to the tombstone, arranging the dandelions and daffodils she had picked that morning to bring here. "He's not a good guy. You probably knew that seeing him in elementary school. It just took so long for me to see it and I don't know why. Even now that I've seen it, part of me wants to run right back, and I know that's stupid."

Rose stood and went around to the other side of the stone on the freshly cut grass and sat in the shade of the oak tree. The breeze lifted the branches overhead.

"I know what you'd say. I've read it enough times in your letters. 'Be the person God wants you to be and run toward him. If anybody is keeping up, ask his name.' I thought Eddie might be like that—he's been in church with us since he was little. Dad says being in church doesn't make you any more of a Christian than . . ." She stopped. "You know what he says. I don't have to repeat it."

Rose stared at the back of the gray stone. Her father's grave would be right next to her mother's one day, and that gave her a chill. The possibility of losing her father had been an overpowering fear after her mother died. She had to be with him at all times, which meant being in school brought anxiety. What if something happened to him? Like Scout Finch in *To Kill a Mockingbird*, Rose had conceded the necessity of school and he promised not to die.

A couple years after that, Rose had a Sunday school teacher who had taught the story of Lazarus. Rose had excused herself and gone to the bathroom to cry. Later, the woman took Rose for tea and asked questions about her mom. That was the crazy thing—after she died, nobody would bring her up, but Rose wanted to talk, wanted to remember. Half of the fear was that she might forget too.

"I don't have good answers about your mom. I think death stinks, if you want to know the truth."

"One of the ladies at church said everything works for good, even the death of someone you love."

"Who said that?"

"Mrs. Bailey." A prim, proper woman with an encyclopedic knowledge of Scripture.

"The worst thing that's happened in that woman's life is a hangnail. She tosses verses like that as if she's throwing the first pitch at a church softball game. These truths aren't slogans or bumper stickers to lob at people who are hurting. And you've had a deep hurt, kiddo. You ever get mad at God?"

"No."

"You know where you go for lying, don't you?"

Rose smiled.

"You don't have to pretend with God. Read the Psalms. Pretending means you cheat both you and God of real life, and that's what he wants to give. Get all the feelings out and ask him to help you heal."

"Did my mom die because I did something bad?"

Her eyes were crinkled and sad-looking. "Is that what you think?"

"It's run through my mind."

"Rose, this is not your fault. None of it. God's not punishing you—this is a wound he's allowed and I don't think you'll ever have an answer this side of heaven. But hang on to this: the same God who allowed Lily to leave is the one who said he would never leave you."

"I'd rather have my mother back," Rose said.

"That's good," the woman said. "That's honest and real and would probably get you kicked out of any class Mrs. Bailey might teach."

"How do you know all this?"

"I lost my own mother when I was about your age. I struggled for years. Ran away from God. Stuffed my feelings, the whole bit. But in God's kindness, he welcomed me back. And I think he let me go through that so I could comfort somebody else—like you."

Now, here at her mother's grave, Rose thanked God for people who hadn't so much taken her mother's place but had held her up while she walked through the pain.

"You always said that good things come to those who wait, Mom," she said. "I guess I'll keep waiting for the right guy, and if he never comes along, at least I'll be close to God."

She rearranged the flowers one more time before she left.

CHAPTER 10

JED DROVE THROUGH the rolling countryside on that crisp fall day. The farmland looked like it was being tucked in for winter, and the trees had turned rusty, but there were hints of life, patches of green here and there. Jed didn't know why God set things up this way, that they had to die in order to live, but it was true.

He studied the MapQuest printout against the steering wheel as the road narrowed. Stan's card that had been ripped up was now taped together and paper-clipped to the top of the page.

He was beginning to think he had missed a turn somewhere when he passed a sign that said, *Sharon, Population*

2,221. What had his life and music come to? He wanted to play big venues but here he was entering a town that was tucked away in some forgotten corner of the world.

The vineyard was bustling with activity when he pulled past the barn to park and his brakes whined, the pads getting a little too close. He was early for the gig, so he walked around to get a feel for the place and the people. Lots of kids and younger parents; that was good. And lots of food.

There were pumpkins and cornstalks and hay bales everywhere. He saw a booth for grape stomping, which made him smile. Lights were strung overhead and he couldn't wait to see the place after dark with the moon above and a crowd of people. It wasn't the Grand Ole Opry, but it paid. Then some doubt crept in. Would he be playing tiny fairs and festivals and church youth groups the rest of his life?

He passed an apple cider stand and the smell of the hot cider brought back a cinnamon-toasty memory, a good one of his mom and dad together at a pumpkin farm when he was little. Just the three of them, and nobody knew who his dad was with his hat pulled down low and a fresh shave. They had run through the corn maze and Jed had turned to see the two of them kissing. He laughed and made fun of them, but somewhere inside, he felt warmth at the sight of them together and touching and kissing.

His father had given him a Styrofoam cup of cider and put a splash of cold water in to make it palatable. Jed could still taste that cider after all these years.

He spotted gourd bowling and other games spread

through the farm like a carnival. Wagons filled with people for hayrides. Parents struggled with strollers on the uneven ground and toddlers walked stiff-legged, looking back and falling.

The smell of caramel apples and cotton candy made his mouth water, and the wine-tasting table drew him like a fly to honey. There was something for every age.

"Jed?" someone said behind him. A sweet voice. He turned and saw her walking through a maze of tables and chairs. She didn't glide, wasn't a specter, but the way she appeared with the sun glinting off her blonde hair made her look like a vision. She wore a white scarf and sweater and her face took his breath away. Was it too much to call her angelic?

"Are you Jed King?" He'd never imagined an angel with a slight drawl.

"Yes," he answered stiffly, like he was reading from a script but couldn't get out any of his lines because his heart was pounding so hard. When he'd heard her voice on the other end of the phone line, he'd cast a mental picture of her, but she did not look like his mental picture of a farm girl.

"I'm Rose Jordan," she said, a hand on her heart. And she smiled. The whole world seemed a little brighter as he looked at her through sunglasses. "We spoke on the phone?"

"Right, right," Jed said, smiling and taking off the sunglasses.

"It's nice to meet you," she said, reaching out a hand. Her little drawl showed up in the word *nice* that came out close to *nass*. Just enough to let him know she was a country girl and didn't need to hide it. She was what she was. Firm grip to the handshake too.

He searched for something to say. "This is your place, then?"

"My dad's." The way she said it was so gentle, a mix of respect and honor. Like she was proud of both the land and her father because they were a package deal.

"It's beautiful," he said. He was talking about the farm but he couldn't take his eyes off her. The hazel eyes. The dimples when she smiled. How old was she? Was she wearing a ring? He couldn't believe he was thinking these things so quickly, but there it was.

"Well, he'll want to know you're here, so . . ."

He watched her, in awe of everything about her, the way she walked, the confidence in her step. He'd seen a lot of beautiful women, but there was something different about Rose. A quietness and peace and gentleness. No, *angelic* was just right.

She didn't turn as she walked. "My father's name is Shepherd, but everybody calls him Shep."

The man looked to be in his sixties, with a weathered face and receding hairline. He was quarreling with some contraption that was set up near the start of the hay maze.

"What's that he's working on?" Jed said as they walked.

"That's a horizontal winepress," she said. "Dad likes to show people how he does things, and when they don't work, he gets frustrated."

"Come on, old piece of junk," Shep muttered as metal clanged against metal.

"Daddy?"

"Yeah?"

"Jed King is here."

The man didn't look up. "Who?"

"The singer?" she said.

Shep put down the tool and stood, squinting into the sunlight, and shook Jed's hand firmly. He had calloused hands, rough and farm-weary. Jed's were not as rough, but the construction he had loved and done since he was a boy had taken some of the softness away.

"I'm sorry to interrupt. I'm Jed."

"Shepherd Jordan," the man said. He was a few inches shorter than Jed. Rose looked at her father with pride, like she was glad she could show him off.

"It's great to meet you. I was just telling Rose this is a beautiful place you have."

"You're David King's kid," Shep said. It felt more like an accusation than a question or observation. But he got that a lot.

"Yes, sir."

Shep looked at Rose, then back at Jed, formulating something, doing some kind of equation in his head. Then, just as quickly, their meeting was over.

"Go ahead, hon, show him to the stage. I got a lot of work to do. Son, nice to meet you."

"All right," Rose said.

"Good to meet you," Jed said.

And the man was back to work without another word. Just a grunt and a groan and more clanging of metal.

"Dad's really sweet, he's just a little stressed."

"No, it's fine," Jed said.

"Who did he say your father was?"

"David King."

She looked slightly bewildered. "So he's a singer too?"

Jed stopped, bewildered himself. He wanted to ask what rock she had grown up under, but he simply said, "You don't know who he is?"

She smiled again, embarrassed now. "Oh, I'm sorry. I don't know anything about music."

Most of the time that was all anyone wanted to talk about. They knew him because of his father. They wanted some tidbit of information, some story about dear old Dad's last days. But here was a person who had no idea about his father's fame.

"No, please don't apologize. It's a good thing. Believe me."

They headed to the stage area, past the snow cone booth, and Jed wondered if there could ever be a more perfect Saturday afternoon in October than this one.

Someone spoke over the loudspeaker, or maybe it was the radio they were piping through the grounds. And then, beside him, a man a little younger than Jed nudged a blonde girl and looked at Rose as if to say, *"Watch this."*

"Hey, Rosie," the guy said.

Her voice changed. "Eddie." There was something painful in the name as it left her lips. "What are you doing here?"

"Tasting wine. It's free wine tasting, right? That's what the paper said."

Eddie wore an open-collared shirt and seemed a little warmer than everyone else at the party. His hair was combed back, and the blonde girl seemed as enamored with him as she did with the wineglass she was holding.

Rose was clearly uncomfortable and Jed wished he could do something to smooth the road here.

"This is Kristen," Eddie said.

"Yeah, I remember," Rose said. Then her voice turned sad. "How are you?"

Kristen's eyes widened as if she'd just seen oncoming headlights. "The wine is really good." She smiled unnaturally like the grapes had gone to her head.

"Thank you. I'm glad you like it."

"Who'd have thunk?" Kristen said. "I mean, Kentucky, right?"

An awkward silence followed and Kristen kept smiling. Her sweater seemed a little tight and her hair was an unnatural blonde. Not that she wasn't pretty—she was. But there was a clear difference in the two women in front of Jed in both style and substance.

"So are you two . . . ?" Eddie said, pointing his wineglass at them.

"No, we . . . just met," Rose said. She seemed nervous.

Jed seized the opportunity and spoke over her. "Yes." He glanced at Rose. "Don't be shy." Then he looked at Eddie, reaching out a hand to shake. "Jed King."

Eddie had a limp-wristed handshake and hands that felt

doughy-soft. Jed guessed he worked some job where he wore a phone headset all day.

"Jed King. As in David King?"

Jed gave Rose a look. "See?" Then he turned back to Eddie. "Yes."

"You're hotter than your dad," Kristen said breathlessly, giving him a once-over. Eddie gave her a shocked look and uncomfortable silence fell over them again.

"Thank you," Jed said, glancing at Rose, who was also smiling.

"Well, there you go," Eddie said, clearly peeved. "You're better than your dad at something."

Jed wanted to hit him with a snappy comeback, but nothing came to mind.

"How's *your* dad?" Eddie said to Rose. Something more passed between them, a daggerlike stare from Rose.

"I don't know," Rose said. "Why don't you go ask him?"

Jed looked back at Shep, who was now kicking at the machine he was working on.

"He looks busy," Eddie said.

"No, no, I'm sure he'd love to talk to you." Her words were fraught with sarcasm and Jed knew, like a walk in a pasture can bring a misstep, that's exactly what had happened on their way to the stage.

"Maybe later," Eddie said. "Excuse me."

"It was nice meeting you again," Kristen said over her shoulder as they walked away. Eddie was nearly dragging her by the arm. Maybe back to the wine tasting.

"Sorry," Rose said, clearly flustered. "It's this way."

"He's a winner," Jed said.

When they reached the stage area behind the barn, she seemed uncomfortable with how simple everything was. "Here you are. Just make yourself at home."

"Thanks."

"And sorry about Eddie. He's a jerk."

"You deserve better."

Her face became tight and she looked away. "I know I deserve better than a guy who'll dump me for not sleeping with him. I just don't know if better exists anymore."

When she looked at him, he was smiling, admiring her spunk and the spark in her.

"Wow, I just said that, didn't I?" she laughed nervously.

"No, it's okay," Jed said. "When I get done playing and you get done with whatever you have to do, you want to hang out?"

Rose took a breath and studied his face. "Look, you seem like a really nice guy."

"Nice . . . ow, that hurts."

"It's only that I just met you."

"Right," he said dismissively, to ease the conversation.

"I don't even like him. But it still kind of kills to see him with her."

She had a far-off look like there was a lot of prelude to the song she was singing. The last thing he wanted to do was chase her away by coming on too strong, too fast, but he wanted to say something comforting, something that would make her like him. So he resorted to what had always worked. The charm and the humor.

"Well, I'd hate to see you die."

She smiled and nodded, then gestured toward the stage. "Good luck, Jed."

He watched her walk away, then replayed the end of the conversation in his head. *"I'd hate to see you die."* How cornball was that? How embarrassing. He had made a good connection with her and that was the end? He'd probably never see her again, he thought.

Then again, maybe she would listen to his music. Maybe she would listen to what was deep inside rather than on the surface. And from that thought a song began to form on his lips—something that sprang to his mind without effort or thought or planning.

Let me cut right to the chase, Rose.
When I see your beautiful face,
I can't help but ask myself, Why?

He couldn't sing a song he'd made up on the spot, after meeting her. He couldn't risk the embarrassment if it fell through. But as he carried his banjo and guitar to the stage, every footstep brought another line, brought another thought, another lyric. This was how he processed events, how he cleaned them up and brought them to life. All the mess and dirt and grit and glorious truth of the human condition could be expressed in a few lines boiled down to a catchy melody that stuck with somebody long after it was sung. It was the magic of music, the magic of words and a tune together.

But would it work with Rose?

Jed sat on the wooden stage, pulled out a notepad he kept in his guitar case and a dull pencil he had brought from a miniature golf place, and wrote down the words as fast as they came to him.

CHAPTER 11

THOUGH HER FATHER was in charge of the three-day festival, Rose bore the brunt of all the small questions of the day. Where to get first aid help for a little girl with a scratch on her leg. How to get the power back on to the cotton candy machine. (It had worked loose from the plug.) Where the restrooms were. She worried that there were some people who were doing more than just tasting the wine this year and that they'd have to be asked to leave. That was Eddie and his friend Kristen. Rose's guess was they had been imbibing long before they came to the festival.

As the sun set, a soft, orange glow enveloped the farm. The only thing left today was the concert by Jed, and all she had to do was introduce him before she could relax and enjoy it. She hated being up front but there was something about Jed . . .

It was his smile, of course. And the stubbly, rugged beard that grew as a shadow on his face. The way he looked at her when they first met made her heart melt, and when he suggested they spend some time together after the concert . . . she hadn't known what to say. After the Eddie debacle, her distrust of men in general made her knee-jerk react to his invitation.

The moon was up now and people moved chairs toward the stage. Parents with smaller children sat at the back or bundled them in strollers and let them sleep. A little rest for the weary on both sides of the stroller. The lights overhead gave a Tuscan feeling, transforming the barn and hay bales into a more exotic venue.

Rose's stomach churned as she walked to the stage. Even standing in front of class and doing math problems at the board had given her anxiety as a child, and she was good at numbers. Other kids didn't seem to mind at all. She guessed some were just made to stand up in front and others were made to watch.

"You ready?" she said to Jed.

He was studying a piece of paper before he shoved it into his back pocket. "Let's go."

She turned and looked at the audience gathered, surprised by how many people had arrived in the past hour. Rose swallowed hard and smiled, just as she caught sight of Eddie and Kristen. The girl was taking another swig of wine.

When she stepped to the microphone, the audience applauded.

"Thank you, everyone. You're in for a real treat tonight. Give a warm round of applause for Louisville's Jed King."

Short and sweet and to the point. Rose hurried off the stage as Jed adjusted the microphone. The applause faded and the speakers squealed a bit.

Over the noise came Eddie's mocking voice. "Nice banjo, Jed."

Kristen said something Rose didn't hear, but she could tell from the girl's laugh that she had crossed over the line of inebriation. Humiliated and feeling sorry for Jed, Rose looked up and found him staring straight at her. His voice filled the speakers.

"'Let me cut right to the chase, Rose,'" Jed sang. "'When I see your beautiful face, I can't help but ask myself . . . Why?'" He extended a hand in Eddie's direction.

Rose stood frozen to the spot. There was silence now, all but the hum of the speakers and some crickets. Then someone giggled.

"And if I didn't need this gig,
I swear I'd flip my lid
And already Eddie would be nursing a black eye."

The audience had expected something else, and Rose sort of wanted to sink into the ground and disappear. But at the same time, she was delighted. Jed was using his music to defend her honor, to stick up for himself, too. And there was power in it—though he was just picking a few strings on his banjo and singing, there was electricity in the vineyard.

"It seems like such a waste
to let him in the way
of what you and I might have one day.
I don't want to quit you, baby.
I ain't gonna split you, baby.
I'd rather give you up than watch you die.
I know loss hurts more than a little,
but he splits you down the middle.
It's time to give good love a try."

People began to stand as the tempo took over, their clapping and hooting and hollering and laughter filling the spaces between. Rose looked at Eddie, who was frozen in his tracks. But Jed wasn't done yet.

"It would be such a pity
just to split you fifty-fifty . . ."

He took a breath and let go with a long, winding, stringing-together-whatever-came-to-mind kind of lyric.

"Especially with some guy who makes fun of my banjo and shows up at a thing with another girl and he knows you're going to be here, he's scared of your dad and

breaks up with the most beautiful girl in the world
for the dumbest reason in the world kind of guy.
Rose, you and I would bloom in no time."

The crowd was on their feet. When Rose finally pulled her eyes away from Jed, she noticed Eddie and Kristen had slunk away. She also saw her father looking at Jed with his hands in his jacket pockets.

And from there, Jed was off and running, and it seemed to Rose that he had power over the crowd. They rose and fell with his ballads. They clapped with the fast songs and cried with the sad ones. There was something free to his voice, the way he played. The songs weren't just things he performed; they were snapshots of his tour of life for everyone to experience.

When it was over, everyone who came up to her said, "How did you ever get him to come to Sharon?"

Rose waited for the line around Jed to disperse, and when it did, she approached and handed him a box of her father's best wine.

He pulled out a bottle and studied it. "Wow. That's really nice, actually." He set the bottle down. "Here, I have something for you."

She took the CD and glanced at it. "Oh, this is great, thanks."

"Really?"

"I think so, but like I said, I don't know anything about music."

"Everybody knows something about music."

"Very little in my case."

"What's your favorite Beatles song? Everybody has a favorite Beatles song. 'Strawberry Fields Forever.' 'Hey Jude.'"

"Well, I've always liked 'Turn! Turn! Turn!'"

He had a blank look on his face, like something she'd just said didn't register. Rose started singing the song and he smiled, his eyes twinkling.

"What? I love that song."

"I love that song too. It's just not the Beatles."

"Yeah, it is."

"No, it's the Byrds. You're thinking of the Byrds."

"Nah. Agree to disagree."

"No, you'd still be wrong."

Rose hesitated, weighing her next question. "The lyrics are in the Bible. Can we agree that God wrote them?"

"Absolutely."

She could see his breath in the chill of the evening, and his nose was a little red from the cold. She should let him go, let him take the box of wine and leave. But she couldn't resist one more thought. She held up the CD. "Too bad my song isn't on here. Never had my own song before." She rocked onto her tiptoes, unsure, then let the words come. "Probably going to ask me out again then, huh?"

Jed demurred. "You know what? I'm sorry about that. I shouldn't have asked you out like that."

"No, that's all right . . ."

"Not without talking to your dad first."

She studied his face. "What?"

"He seems like the kind of guy who would appreciate being asked."

"For my hand in marriage, maybe, but one date?"

"We're going to have more than one date," Jed said.

It wasn't that he said this that took her breath away. It was the confidence with which he said it. "How do you know?"

"I know," he said.

"He's busy with cleanup." She thought a moment. "Monday?"

"Monday," Jed said without a hint of disappointment.

"Good," Rose said and then, with a knowing smile, added, "You're going to need a day to prepare."

Rose couldn't sleep that night. She woke Denise from a dead sleep at 1 a.m. to talk. Her friend groggily asked her about the festival and apologized for not being there, yawning and slurring her words.

"I think I met him," Rose said breathlessly.

"Met who?" A little more clarity in Denise's voice.

"The guy I'm going to marry."

Now wide-awake, Denise said, "You mean Jed?"

They talked for two hours and Denise seemed even more excited than Rose about the future.

"How are you going to tell your dad?" Denise said finally.

"Jed's going to do that. Monday. He's going to ask for a date."

"Are you serious?"

"He suggested it."

"You need to take all your dad's guns away. Start hiding them now."

"He'll be fine," Rose said, though she wasn't sure that was true.

She was still awake when she heard her dad come downstairs the next morning, and she joined him in the kitchen.

"Thought you'd sleep in today," he said. "It's been a long weekend."

"Nope. Not skipping church."

He nodded and poured a cup of coffee. Her dad wouldn't let the festival interfere with church services and she wouldn't either. They talked about the festival—the things that worked or didn't yesterday and what it would be like this afternoon. But he didn't bring up Jed at all and that troubled her.

On the ride home from church she asked what people had said about the concert.

He looked sternly at her. "Did you know Eddie was going to be there?"

She frowned. "I'm not Eddie's keeper anymore. In fact, I never was."

"I was surprised he showed up. And that he had his new girl with him."

"You and me both," she said. "It was pretty painful seeing them."

"His mother cornered me in the fellowship hall this morning."

"Did she complain that you made Eddie drink too much?"

"That was the gist of it. I wanted to tell her a thing or two about self-control and some other fruits of the Spirit. But I held my tongue. I'm working on patience."

Rose smiled and loved her dad for not flying off the handle at everybody who deserved it.

"She was upset about that singer, too. Said he made a fool out of Eddie. That's what she'd heard."

"I can't argue with her. He put Eddie in his place."

"How'd he find out about you and him?"

She told him the story of what happened and he listened as he drove, his fingers tightening on the steering wheel when she described the jab Eddie took at Jed.

"Daddy, after the concert Jed apologized."

"For what?"

"For the song he sang about me. He said he should have talked to you before he ever asked me for a date."

"Is that so?"

"I thought you'd appreciate that."

"Maybe coming from somebody else, I would."

Her heart began to race and she turned toward him, her voice strained. "What do you have against him?" As soon as he looked at her, she knew she'd tipped her hand, that her dad could see all the way to her heart.

"I don't have anything against him personally. In fact, I think he has good taste if he likes you. I just don't like his stock. An apple doesn't fall far from the tree. Nor a grape that grows on the vine."

She stared out the dirty windshield. "I'd like to go out with him."

"Rose."

"What if God brought us together?"

"Horse collar," he said. It was the closest thing to a curse word she would hear him say. "Is that how you think God works? Some singer blows in and takes a shine to you and you're ready to run off with him?"

"I'm not running off with him. But this is something I'd like to do. And I'd like you to meet him again and this time do more than squint at him."

"I was busy."

"Horse collar." She turned toward him again. "Would you talk to him? If you don't think he's a good guy, I'll . . ."

"You'll what?"

"I don't know what I'll do. I'll try to listen to you. I always have."

"But you're not promising anything," he said.

"Would you meet with him tomorrow? Just give him a chance?"

"Tomorrow?" he said with surprise. "He don't waste time, huh?"

Her father didn't speak the rest of the way home and all through the afternoon he remained aloof. Rose wanted to call Jed and give him a time to come, but she waited. She knew her father was ruminating, thinking about things, stewing.

And it had been her experience that once he owned something, once he got comfortable with it in his mind, she had a better chance with him.

They ate a late dinner of leftovers that night, after all the festivities were over and the barn was cleaned. When he'd finished, her dad rose from the table and threw some scraps out the back door for the critters. He washed his plate and headed toward the stairs, the wood floor creaking underneath his weight. Then he stopped and put his hand on the wall. It was stained dark from all the times he'd stood this way after reading the morning paper and getting the ink on his hands.

"Tell him to be here at three o'clock."

CHAPTER 12

JED DIDN'T TELL ANYONE about meeting Rose—didn't call anybody, didn't e-mail a friend or tell his mother—but she was all he could think about when he woke up the day after they met. In some ways he wondered if it was all a dream, if he had made up the whole thing, found this gorgeous woman in the country who turned out to be a figment of his imagination.

But Rose was real. The connection they'd made the night before was real too. And he could tell so much about her from that chance meeting, if it was chance at all. She had morals, scruples. She didn't sleep around to gain the affection of some jerk who didn't care about her. She was hardworking, loved her father and the farm. She took joy in what she did. There was so much he observed about her in that short amount of time. The way she interacted with people, the way she talked with little children—everything about her captivated him.

She didn't need the limelight, either. In fact, she seemed so humble in the way she presented herself, the way she was almost embarrassed to get up in front of the crowd to introduce him. She was giving, had a good sense of humor, a great smile, and she was a knockout.

The only things between them and lifelong happiness were her father, her lack of understanding about music, and the fact that the Beatles didn't sing "Turn! Turn! Turn!"

Sunday evening, Jed held up the taped-together business card and studied the number. If this all worked out, he needed to call Stan and thank him not only for the gig but for the love lead.

He dialed the number and Rose picked up on the first ring.

"I was getting ready to call you!" she said.

"Really?"

"My dad said you should be here at three tomorrow. To talk."

"Sounds ominous."

"You have no idea."

"Is that all he wants to do, talk? He doesn't want to chop me up in little pieces, does he?"

She laughed. "No, medium-size pieces are more his style."

Hearing her voice again made him warm inside. He'd known a lot of girls, but there was something different about Rose. And not just because she didn't have a clue about his father. She liked him for who he was, not whose son he was.

"How did this afternoon go?" he said. "At the festival?"

"It was good. Not as many people as last night, but then we didn't have Jed King here this afternoon."

"I really enjoyed playing last night. In a strange way, I needed that."

"What do you mean?"

He gave a heavy sigh. "My career, my music—it feels like it's at a standstill. Or that it's headed for the landfill."

"Nice rhyme."

"Thank you. And not just my music, my life. The whole package. So coming out there and playing and meeting you did something. I wish I could bottle that feeling and sell it."

"Even if Eddie tried to ruin it."

"Eddie actually made things better. I mean, I probably wouldn't have sung your song if Eddie hadn't tried to throw a wrench into things."

"Eddie's good at throwing wrenches."

"What I'm saying is, it felt good to just be myself and do what I do, from the heart. It felt natural, you know?"

"I do," she said. "And from the response we got, you need to keep doing what you're doing, no matter what anybody says."

"I appreciate that," he said. "And I can't wait to see you and talk more about you and your dad and . . . everything."

"See you at three, then?" she said.

"Three it is."

He didn't have to look at his MapQuest printout once. The drive to Sharon was like going home. Rose was sitting on the front porch when he got there, and it made him think of a Bruce Hornsby tune about coming back to an old love.

He walked to the house, unable to take his eyes off her. She reached out a hand and led him inside. "He's waiting for you in his study. Right through there."

Jed peeked in and saw the man's boots on the floor next to a bearskin rug. "Think I'll survive?" he whispered.

Rose just smiled and watched as he walked through the door.

Shepherd Jordan rose and shook his hand and told him to sit. There were two leather chairs in the room and Jed sat facing the man. The first thing he noticed was the stuffed wolf staring at him. There was a turkey in the corner in full plumage. A bear stood upright behind him. Skins were draped across the backs of both chairs. On the mantel over the fireplace was a . . . Well, he had no idea, but it looked fierce.

"Wow, this is pretty impressive," Jed said. "Did you kill all these?"

"Mm-hmm." Shep sat with a grunt and crossed his legs. A hot cup of coffee steamed on the end table next to the man.

Jed sat forward with his elbows on his knees. On his drive, he'd rehearsed what he would say. He would take the lead and put things on the table. He had looked in the mirror and said, "Mr. Jordan, I only met your daughter Saturday night, and I can tell there's something really special about her. I'd like to get to know her better. But I'd like to ask your permission to do that. To see each other."

He would be strong. He would look him in the eye and shoot straight because that was the kind of man Shep Jordan was. But until he walked into this room, Jed had no idea how many straight shots Shep had taken.

Before Jed could say anything, Shepherd began. "Mr. King, I don't know you." Then he stopped. Just sat there and stared at Jed like he was taking aim, looking through the crosshairs.

"That's true, sir," Jed stammered. So much for strength and confidence. "And you can call me Jed if you like."

Shep Jordan didn't want to call him Jed evidently because he immediately said, "So what makes you think I should let you date my daughter?"

Deep breath. "At the very least, Mr. Jordan, you know that I'm the kind of guy that's willing to ask a very intimidating man if I could date his daughter."

Shep shook his head and responded quickly. "No, that says more about me than it does about you."

This was going to be harder than he thought. Jed softened his voice. "I just want you to know that I respect you and that I respect Rose."

The man bit the inside of his cheek and stared at Jed. "You sing about God in your songs, don't you?"

"I sing about things that I'm passionate about."

"Like Rose?"

"You heard that, I guess."

Shep sat forward and an edge came into his voice. "I love Rose. A lot. And I have always tried to protect her from certain kinds of men out there. Just to be honest, men like your daddy."

There it was. The shot over the bow. The knife in the gut. The sins of the father being visited on his son, the ghost of David King haunting him again, this time a specter that would keep him from something good.

"He sang about God too, didn't he?" Shep said, and Jed could feel him looking through him to his lineage.

It pained Jed to defend his father because there was the public side of him that made a huge mistake. Several of them. But Shep didn't know the man like Jed knew him. Didn't know the turn he had taken.

"I know he made mistakes, Mr. Jordan. But he learned from them. So did I. I won't repeat them."

A crash outside the door nearly sent Jed through the roof. Something dropped on the floor and clattered. A creak by the door and a shadow underneath told Jed it was Rose. She was listening.

Shep turned back to him and stared. Jed stared back, trying not to blink.

"Trust is earned. You get it an inch at a time. You got here by three and I appreciate that. You passed that test. So you can take my daughter out this evening." He leaned forward and put his hand on the back of the wolf. "But you have her back here by ten tonight."

"Thank you, sir." Jed stood and held out his hand. "I won't let you down."

Shep looked at his hand, then shook it hard like he was working a pump handle. "I'm not giving you the chance to let me down, son."

Jed nodded and smiled.

Shep lowered his voice to a whisper. "Don't waste her time. If you know it ain't clickin', end it. And no matter what, don't break her heart."

"Yes, sir."

"And keep your hands to yourself, you hear?"

CHAPTER 13

ROSE DECIDED not to suggest a restaurant and let Jed choose. He drove them an hour away and they talked in the car, Jed asking questions about the vineyard and her life on the farm. She started out nervous—about what she wore (she had changed clothes four times before finding the right combination), about how the fatigue of sleepless nights would affect her ability to hold a coherent conversation, even about being nervous. But as soon as they started talking, it felt natural and easy like she'd hoped it might be.

The restaurant was fancier than she expected but she loved the crisp white linen tablecloth and the candlelight. Everything was so romantic, down to the wine Jed chose—which was from her father's vineyard. Apparently he had made a deal with the head waiter to serve it.

After dinner, Jed took her on a river walk, where they talked more. Rose asked about his father and about growing up in the home of someone famous. He seemed a little guarded, a little reserved about his childhood, and she didn't pry. If things worked out between them, there would be time to talk about all of it.

Was she already thinking that way? Already thinking about a long-term relationship? She couldn't believe this went through her mind, especially with the promises she had made to herself after Eddie. She wasn't interested in men. Didn't want anything to do with them. And now here was Jed with that voice and those soft-blue eyes and the easy laugh. When he put his arm around her in a gentle hug, it was like fireworks going off through her body.

It wasn't until after dark, when Jed took her to a coffee shop called Perkfections Café and Bar, that they talked about her father.

"I'm not going to lie, your dad freaked me out," Jed said. "Just a little bit."

"Well, you're going to have to tell me all about it because I wasn't listening or anything."

Jed laughed. "Okay, since you weren't listening, I'll give you the highlights. He loves you a lot. And he has quite the collection going on in that room."

"Yeah," she said, unable to hold back the laughter because it was true. "My friend Denise says he stuffs more things than the pillow factory."

"That's good. I'll have to remember that one."

"And you're right that he loves me. He's shown me that in a million ways."

"So you really didn't hear anything? I thought I heard something drop on the floor outside the door."

"I was dusting," she said. "My mother's jar fell from the table in the entry."

"It didn't break, did it?"

"No, it's wooden. It means a lot to me. She gave it to me before she died."

"How old were you?"

"Eight."

"That's tough. To lose someone you love that early."

"It was. And that's partly why my dad means so much. He saw me through it. He was there every night I cried myself to sleep. Even though he handled it differently."

"Not as emotional?"

"Right. He takes things in stride and just puts one foot in front of the other and moseys on down the road. But it affected him too. He was telling me the other day about the festival—he does it partly as the fulfillment of a promise to my mom."

"That's really sweet. I'll bet you look like her."

"That's what people say."

"So she was beautiful."

Rose rolled her eyes. "How long have you been working on that line?"

"No, seriously, it just came out. There's no working on something that comes that easy. And it's true."

She laughed and blushed, feeling like there was something right with the world again.

"You want to see something from my past?" she said.

He looked at his watch. "I promised your dad that—"

"Come on, it's on the way home."

They drove toward Sharon and came to a wide place in the road with some old school crossing signs. "Pull over there. By the front walk."

The place was dark and gloomy like a haunted house. The stars shone as brilliant as diamonds, and the frogs and crickets sang like they had microphones and amps.

"This is the elementary school where I went as a kid. I can walk you through every classroom in that building and tell you the things that happened to me each year."

Jed squinted. "There's broken windows. Do they not use it anymore?"

"Structural problems. They closed it a year ago. Built another one on some land that doesn't flood."

Jed picked up a rock and tossed it at the front of the building, hitting a windowpane that cracked. "What happened in that classroom?"

"Mrs. Taylor. Third grade. That was the year my mom died."

He was quiet for a minute, then picked up another rock and hit a pane on the other side of the school. "What happened in there?"

"Fifth grade. Mrs. Adkins. She had a little aquarium we all took care of. She loved fish and animals. One day somebody found a bird by a tree on the playground and brought it to her and we decided to nurse it back to health. She set up an incubator that kept the bird warm and we tried to feed it. The little thing started to make a comeback until this mean kid . . ." She searched for his name. "I think it was Romey. Yeah, Romey McCallister. He was new to the school that year and didn't fit in too well. I think he'd been held back a couple of times because he was a head taller than Mrs. Adkins. Well, I caught Romey picking the bird up. Mrs. Adkins had told us not to touch it at all, but here he was manhandling the poor thing."

"What did you do?"

"I yelled at him to put it down. And he said, 'It's gonna die anyway.' Mrs. Adkins was out of the room and there wasn't a soul sticking up for the bird except for me."

"What happened?"

"Romey dropped him. Dropped him down into the nest with a plop. And it made me so mad I couldn't see straight. Everybody just sat there and watched him. Like sheep. So I gritted my teeth and rushed him and slammed him into the wall with everything in me."

"And he wasn't a little guy."

"No, he probably had fifty pounds on me. That was the only time I ever got sent to the office. I can still remember the principal's face seeing me in there. He was so surprised. I was wearing pigtails and a pink bow in my hair and Romey had this big bump on his head and they gave him an ice pack."

"Sounds humiliating for Romey. But you were feisty."

"I still am. For things I believe in. For things I want to protect."

Talking with Jed was unlike any other conversation she had ever had with a guy. He actually asked questions. He wanted to know things about her instead of her always having to carry the conversation. And Jed never once brought up how big of a fish he caught or the latest trade of this player to that team.

Rose began to see that dating Jed was not going to be like dating a boy. Sure, he had some rough edges and things he needed to work on. He had been consumed by the search for a music career and that artistic side drove him, she could tell. That could easily come between them. But it could also draw them together and forward as they moved through life.

There it was again. Together. For life. What was she thinking? Why was she letting her mind go that far that fast?

Of course, it didn't help that every time she looked into his eyes, she got queasy in the stomach. His dark hair, the shadowy beard, square jaw . . . and those eyes. When he opened the door for her at the coffee shop, he touched her shoulder to guide her inside and she felt the tingle run to her toes. He was definitely eye candy, but he was more. So much more. And she wondered what their children might look like with his dark features and her blonde hair.

Wow. She really had to stop that. Once she started imagining what their children would look like, it was pretty much all over.

When he took her home and said good night on the front

steps at 9:55 on the nose, he didn't kiss her. Didn't hug her. Didn't make any physical advances apart from taking her hands in his, but that was enough. She wanted to kiss him passionately and hold him, but she held back.

"I really enjoyed tonight," he said. "I'd love to see you again. Soon."

"I'd like that too," she said. "Maybe you could come here for dinner with us. Tomorrow night?"

"I've got a meeting at church tomorrow night," her dad said from inside the front window. "How about Wednesday?"

Rose laughed and so did Jed. They agreed on Wednesday. He leaned in and whispered something she didn't hear.

"What was that?"

"I told you it would be more than one date," he said.

She smiled and nodded. And as Jed drove away, she could have sworn she heard a chuckle from the other side of the screen.

CHAPTER 14

JED'S DINNER with Rose and Shep wasn't perfect; there was a certain tension in the air with her dad at the table, a certain sense of protection he provided like a bear waiting to pounce. But Jed loved the conversation and interaction between the two of them. Rose cooked the meal, though Shep insisted on baking his famous corn bread and supplying the wine that went with the chicken and pasta and salad.

"Corn bread is good with everything," Shep said. And he was right.

"I'd love to hear more about your mother," Jed said, taking a sip of wine. He glanced at Shep. "If it's okay to talk about."

The wrinkles on the man's forehead faded for a moment.

Then he gestured with a hand to ask away, though he didn't say anything.

"How did you two meet?"

"Oh, you don't want to hear that."

"Come on, Daddy. I like that story."

Jed wiped his mouth with a napkin and smiled at the man, inviting him further. He was so rough and unapproachable, but there was something about him that reminded Jed of his own father. He couldn't put his finger on it.

"We were both war babies. Born in the early forties. My daddy worked for her daddy on his farm from time to time."

"They were from the wrong side of the tracks," Rose added.

"You want to tell this or you want me to?" Shep said.

"Go ahead. I'm just making sure Jed gets the whole picture."

Shep sat back and put his hands behind his head and stretched, closing his eyes. "I can remember the first time I noticed Rose's mother. She was a year younger than me and there was this field near the elementary school where we played baseball and tag and red rover and such. The sun was coming up and there was dew on the grass and across the field came this pretty little thing with braided hair and her books held close to her chest."

Rose touched Jed's arm and mouthed, *"It was like a picture."*

"It was like a picture," Shep said. "Pretty as a speckled pup. I'd seen her on her farm, at school on the playground. But I'd never really seen her."

"Do you remember your first date?" Jed said.

"That took a long time."

"To convince her to go out with you?"

"To convince her parents that it was okay to go out with me."

"He was from the wrong side of the tracks," Rose repeated, grinning. "Have I mentioned that already?"

"I think I remember something about that," Jed said.

"My family didn't have much. My daddy worked hard, though, and taught us the value of a day's labor. He just didn't see as much of a return as Lily's dad. But I figured out pretty quick that my best shot at getting to know her would be at church. Their family was always at church. Every time the door was open, they'd be there."

"They sat by each other during Sunday school," Rose said.

"I was coming to the party without much. I didn't know Jesus from Jehoshaphat. Couldn't find Genesis in the King James Bible. But they made us memorize the books, in order, and that was about the hardest thing I'd ever done. I could barely spell my own name, let alone say *Deuteronomy*. Lily taught me a song with all the books in it."

"You sing?"

He waved a hand. "It was a kids' song."

"He used to lead singing at the church we went to, didn't you, Daddy?"

"The only thing I did was get everybody started and try to stop them at the same time. But in the middle of all of that, in the middle of having ulterior motives about getting to know Lily, I found somebody else."

Jed raised his eyebrows. "Another girl?"

"No. Somebody bigger. I always thought church and religion were for people who needed some kind of crutch. I believed in God from the time I was a little thing. But I was a take-charge kind of guy. Make your own breaks. Even as a little fellow. But when I started reading the Bible, when I started looking at the stories and the way God moved in the hearts of people, real people, I wanted him to do that same thing with me."

"That's when Mama got interested in him," Rose said.

"Now why don't you just go on and tell the whole thing," Shep said, shaking his head in mock frustration.

"Mama told me that Daddy was rougher than a cob before they met. In school and all, he would be the first one in a fight. The first one jumping into the swimming hole. But after God got hold of his heart, he channeled all that energy and desire in a different direction."

"I'm still rough as a cob," Shep said, putting a pat of butter on his corn bread. "But Lily put some talcum on me. Softened me up a little."

"How did you convince her parents you were good for Lily?" Jed said.

Shep gave him a knowing look. Like the man understood the irony of the question. "I guess I wore them down over time and proved I was worthy of their daughter. Lily's dad was a tough old bird and her mama was sweet as huckleberry jam. But cross her and you had a fight on your hands. I sat right here and asked for her hand in marriage."

Jed sat back and looked at the room. "This was your mother's house?"

"It goes back to the Civil War," Rose said.

"To 1863," Shep said. "The original farm was almost three hundred acres. Dairy. Tobacco. Corn. You name it. They passed the farm down from one generation to another, and when Lily and I married, her parents gave us a wedding present of about ten acres on the little knoll above the pond. We were going to build a house there, but I got a job at the sausage factory and we moved closer to that. Then, when Lily's parents took ill, we came back here to help."

Shep pushed his plate away and stared at Jed. "Time for you to do some talking. Tell me about your mama. Is she doing all right?"

"She is. Every now and then she'll hear one of his songs on the radio and have a bad day. But I think she's living with the loss of him and the weight of some of her own mistakes through the years."

"She was in his band, wasn't she? Married to one of his guitar players."

"Daddy, maybe we shouldn't talk about that," Rose said.

"It's okay," Jed said. "Yeah, they were friends. Sang together. Traveled together."

"Her first husband took his life, as I recall."

"He did. And that's the kind of thing that will haunt you the rest of your life, if you let it. But God forgave them. The past doesn't have to define you."

"True," Shep said.

He threw Jed some more questions about where he'd grown up and what life with his father was like, the fame and the travel.

"He was more than just a singer and songwriter," Jed said. "Most people only saw him as the public guy in the lights. He taught me how to build things. He was a really good carpenter. That's the first thing I noticed when I walked in here, how solid this house is built. The curve of the staircase. The care and craftsmanship."

"We've worked hard to keep it up," Shep said. "But you don't sing much of your daddy's songs, at least judging from Saturday night. I would think people would want to hear those."

"They do. And maybe if I went that direction, I'd be more successful."

"But you don't want to go that direction."

"I'm trying to hear my own songs, Mr. Jordan. I'm trying to not live in his shadow or use his fame. I'll sing them at some point, I'm sure."

"And if you don't make it with the singing?" Now the man fixed him with a stare and the weight of the question hung in the air like woodsmoke from a burned-out campfire.

"The way I look at it, if I put God first, everything else will fall in place."

"That's not a bad answer," Shep said. He stood and took his plate to the sink. "Why don't you two take a walk. Show Jed the knoll I told him about."

"Leave the dishes, Daddy. We'll do them later."

"No, I'm doing the dishes tonight. You cooked this meal. Now go on. Get out of here."

Rose smiled at Jed and grabbed her sweater and they walked toward the barn. When a cool breeze blew the autumn leaves, Rose crossed her arms in front of her.

"Winter's coming."

"Happens every year, doesn't it?"

"What's your favorite season?" she said.

"I like the new growth of spring. And the heat of summer. And the cold of the winter when you can snuggle up in front of a fire. But I think my favorite is fall."

"You like the change of colors in the leaves?"

"Sure. But most of all I like it because it was in the fall that I found a Rose."

She pushed him and ran for the hill, and he chased her, listening to her laugh echo across the hillside and wondering if her father was watching out the window as he did the dishes. Had he run after Rose's mother up this hill?

"This is it," she said, catching her breath. "This is where they were going to build their little house and start a family."

"What a view," Jed said. "A great place to build something. You can see for miles. You can see the future from here, I'll bet."

She took him down to the pond and he skipped a rock across the water.

"How do you do that?" she said. "Every time I try, it's . . . Well, watch." She picked up a rock, angled her body, and threw it in with a kerplunk.

"It wasn't great," he said. "The trick is, you have to pick the right rock."

"Is that so?"

"Yeah. You want it flat so it'll glide on the surface of the water."

"Like this?" she said.

"Perfect. Try again."

She did and again it went kerplunk.

"Yours skip like ten times," she said. "How do you do that?"

"My dad was legendary at slinging these things. Lethal, some would say. Come here."

He stood behind her and put a rock he had chosen in her hand. She fit perfectly against him, like a hand in a glove. Her perfume, her hair—everything about her was intoxicating and he had to focus on the task and not let his mind run.

"So you take it right here with your index finger out like that. Pull back but not over your head. Sidearm it, right? And flick your wrist at the end."

She rested against his body and, over her shoulder, gave him a look like she understood and was feeling the same strong pull that he was. And when she threw it this time, she slung it like his father had shown him, flicking her wrist enough that the rock sailed onto the water and skipped, just like his heart did when he heard her victorious squeal and laughter.

"I did it."

"You did it."

And it was in that moment that Jed could see them together. Could see them skipping rocks when they were older. Maybe a few children around them. He could see them here on the farm or in a house in Louisville or maybe Nashville and making trips on the weekends. Could a man see all of that on the second date? Or was this an illusion, something he wanted to see that couldn't be achieved?

No, it was real. The feeling in his heart was as real as the splash of the water and the ripples on the pond.

You have stolen my heart, he thought. *You have stolen my heart with one glance of your eyes.*

And she had done that. The only question was if he had done that for her.

CHAPTER 15

WITHOUT A MANAGER and with no recording contract, Jed felt untethered from the music world and everything he'd tried to build. There was a comfort in having people who worked out schedules and told you where to go and what to do while you concentrated on making music. But with the untethered feeling came a strange sensation of freedom. He was free from the expectations of people who wanted him to be something he wasn't.

Someone from a Christian college in Campbellsville, Kentucky, had been at the concert at the Jordan Vineyard and gotten his number from Rose. That gig led to a church in Lexington inviting him to play at a Friday evening coffeehouse event. The dates were spread out and there wasn't much money involved, but Jed felt his roots growing deeper in his art, that there was a bigger purpose to his singing than making money and garnering praise. And that bigger purpose kept him coming back to Rose.

She was all he could think about. He kept a mental picture of her smile with him when he fell asleep each night, and their conversations rolled around in his head on the drive home and at odd moments.

"I was basically raised by my father . . . and two brothers," she'd told him during one of their talks.

"Where are they?"

"Louisville. They weren't cut out for wine making, so they bailed."

"Think you'll ever bail?"

"No. I love it. And family's important to me. I guess I could find a career to pay for all the stuff I'll eventually throw away or leave to someone else when I die. But family's forever, right?"

Those words echoed in his mind, and his response as well. She'd agreed to disagree about the Byrds singing "Turn! Turn! Turn!" He agreed to disagree about family being forever.

"Your brothers ever come back?"

"They didn't come to the festival. Too busy, I guess. Too many memories, maybe. They're not mean, just wandering."

She turned it back on him, grilled him about his own family. His relationship with his father, his mom, and the broken family his dad left.

"I have two half brothers and a half sister."

"Are they musicians too?"

"I don't know, really."

"Why not?"

"They refuse to talk to me."

"Why?"

When he hesitated, she apologized and he waved her off. And he spilled the whole thing about the affair between his dad and mom, the baby conceived and aborted, and his birth. Rose listened intently as if she were reading the most interesting book about the most interesting person in the world.

He took her to see a country singer he knew at a place in Nashville. A man he had fronted for once who probably didn't even remember him, but he was sure to remember Jed's father. They sat at a table in the back and talked over the music, and he wasn't sure what he liked better—being alone in the car talking or here talking. Just being with her was all he needed.

"Do you wish you were up there?" she said when the band took a break.

"Part of me does. It's kind of inside me to want to take the stage. It's all I've really done except for the carpentry. But it's the same, you know. Writing a song, building something. Singing and hammering are twin sons of different mothers. As long as you're doing it for God, it doesn't really matter what you do."

"That's how I've always felt. There's this verse in Psalms that keeps coming back to me. From Psalm 37." She sat up straight and closed her eyes. A vein showed in her forehead as she concentrated, and he thought it was the most beautiful vein he'd ever seen. "'Trust in the Lord and do good; dwell in the land and enjoy safe pasture. Take delight in the Lord, and he will give you the desires of your heart.'"

Jed stared at her, taking her in. He felt like he'd found a gold mine in her heart.

They were sitting on the couch, a couple of weeks before Christmas, drinking wine and watching a rerun of *It's a Wonderful Life* on TV. Shep had fallen asleep under an afghan in his favorite recliner. The man had accepted Jed's presence and things had gone from tense to inviting in the Jordan home. Jed had helped with winterizing the vineyard as the farm went into its yearly hibernation. Shep actually seemed to like having Jed around, though he still put on the wary attitude every now and then. Tonight his heavy, rhythmic breathing was the undertone to their evening, the background noise that made things a little less romantic than when they were alone.

Jed smiled. "You don't snore like that, do you?"

"I hope not," she said.

He put his arm around Rose and drew her close, and it felt like everything in the world was melting away.

Jimmy Stewart and Donna Reed were in an impassioned embrace on their wedding night, rain falling through the holes in the roof of the old Granville place. Ernie and Bert were singing "I Love You Truly" just outside the window. Jed thought that might be a good song to remake. Maybe he could do something with the harmonies.

"This is my favorite," Rose whispered. She was holding a coffee table book with pictures of vineyards from around the world. On one page was a white chapel surrounded by rows of vines. She wrote in red on a sticky note, *Love this!!!* and drew an arrow on the note to the picture.

She snuggled close, and Jed smelled her shampoo and felt the softness of her hair against his skin. He rested his stubbly cheek against hers, put his lips to her ear, and said, "I think I love you, Rose Jordan."

Then he took her chin in his hand and kissed her. After a moment she drew back and stared at him, the firelight flickering in her eyes. Jed waited, wondering what she was thinking.

Rose set the book down and without hesitation kissed Jed again, this time putting her hands behind his head and pulling him toward her. He kissed her deeply, tasting the wine on her lips.

Then he heard something in the room. Or better yet, *didn't* hear something—her father's snoring.

Shep cleared his throat. "Hey, you two. How's the movie?"

"It's okay," Rose said as she sat back quickly.

"It's not as good as the wine, Mr. Jordan," Jed said and saw Rose roll her eyes.

"That's good to hear. Maybe I'll stay awake to watch the rest of it."

"I think I need to be going," Jed said.

"Don't leave on account of me," Shep said.

Jed took a last sip of wine and put on his coat. "Need to get home. I think I have a song to write."

Rose stifled a laugh and walked outside with him, standing on the porch.

Jed took her hand. "I love you, Rose."

She smiled. "I love you, too."

Jed played a coffeehouse near Louisville with Rose right there in the middle of the crowd. He had asked his mother if she wanted to come but she wasn't feeling well. Shep didn't like driving at night—something about his eyes not being as good as they used to be.

Jed had almost finished his set and was ready to play his last song when something came over him. Maybe it was the polite applause he was hearing or the look on Rose's face when he sang the words that came from his heart. Maybe he just missed his father and wished he could have a piece of him back again.

"I don't normally do this," he said. "But here's one you might know.

"I cannot hear, I have no sight.
Dark is near and your blinding light.
Can you hear me when I cry,
  catch me when I fall?
'Cause I can't hold on."

It was the chorus to one of his father's famous songs and he circled back around and sang it from verse one all the way through with all the feeling his dad put into it. The guitar picked up the subtle pain and longing, and he glanced at Rose, who seemed a little surprised by the applause at the beginning. By the time he was done, the room was crazy. Not over-the-top standing ovation, but a quiet homage to the words and music that flowed from father through son.

Later that night, sitting on the back of Shep's flatbed Ford and staring into the vast sky, then into Rose's eyes, which seemed to give him the same feeling, things became clear to Jed in a way they never had.

"You were really great tonight," Rose said.

"I'm glad you think so."

"Everyone thought so."

He turned his head. "Well . . ."

"That last song, people really liked that one."

"Yeah," Jed said, hearing a little sadness in his voice.

"What?" she said.

"That was my dad's song."

The look on her face said it all, and he wished he hadn't told her.

"Aww, I'm sorry."

"Don't be. It's fine. It's a good song." He thought for a moment, debating whether or not to tell her what was going on inside. What was really going on. And then he looked at her face, the love that was there, and he couldn't hold back. "You know, sometimes I think about letting it go. Music. I look at you. Tonight. I look at the stars . . . I see God here."

Rose studied him, something turning over in her mind. "If you could ask God for anything and you knew he'd say yes, what would you ask for?"

A thousand things floated through his mind. Turn back the clock. Keep his dad from dying. Keep his family from all the pain. Make him successful. Give him a billion fans. But above all that, one thing rose to the surface.

"I'd want to be wise. That way I could live right. And really live. And if I did sing, it'd only be because I had something to say."

"Then you should just ask for that," Rose said. She shifted on the back of the truck and plugged her ears. Jed thought this must have been what she looked like as a little girl on the playground, stopping her ears from somebody's words, her hair hanging down. Beautiful.

"I won't listen," she said. "Go ahead."

So he did. He spoke the words to the sky as if he were talking directly to the Almighty. "God, I want to be wise." And then he added, "Please."

Rose unstopped her ears and looked into his eyes. "You feel any different?"

He let the question hang there and suddenly, as if God were reaching down and showing him the path, Jed saw the chapel from the book. He saw his father's hands on wood, rows of vines stretching toward the sun, and behind them the white chapel and the steeple rising above.

He stood and looked into the shadows where he knew the knoll rose on the hillside, then turned. "You think your dad would let me build a chapel here? At the vineyard? Like the one in your book. With the sticky note thing."

"Why would you want to?" Rose said, a slow smile creeping over her face.

"So I could marry you," he said.

The look in her eyes said all he needed to know. Said everything about the future. Their future.

"I'll ask your dad. And I'll build the chapel," he said. "Marry me."

She nodded—couldn't seem to stop her head from bobbing up and down—and then she was off the truck and in his arms, laughing and crying at the same time.

When they were still again, looking into each other's eyes, he said, "Let me do this. Let me build you a chapel."

"How long will it take?"

"A year?"

Rose groaned and shook her head. "I can't wait that long."

CHAPTER 16

The next day, Jed showed up unannounced before breakfast and asked if he could speak with Shep in his office. The man stared at him, then glanced at Rose, who was grinning so wide it nearly blinded them.

Jed sat in front of the man he hoped would be his father-in-law, in the same chair with the same animals looking on as when he asked to date Rose. Strangely, the furs and stuffed animals comforted him this time. They were at least some company while he watched the man listen to his halting words.

"Mr. Jordan, I think you know by now that Rose and I are in love."

"Mm-hmm. At least what you might call love."

"Sir?"

"*Love* is an overused word, in my opinion. People love baseball teams and lattes. They love popcorn shrimp and crunchy peanut butter or the smell of a new car. That ain't love."

Jed nodded.

"Love is a commitment. Love is not just saying something, but doing something about what you say. Anybody can say the word, but few actually say it and live it. You understand?"

Dry-mouthed, Jed nodded again. "And that's what I want to do, Mr. Jordan. I want to show your daughter that I love her. I've told her that, but I want to make it official."

"And you think she'll say yes?"

"I know she will," Jed said, leaning forward. "Mr. Jordan, you told me to date her and see if things went well. To cut it off if it didn't go anywhere. To protect her heart. Well, it went somewhere. And I did protect her heart. But she's stolen mine. I've respected her and you. I've tried to prove to you that I'm not like some other guys."

Shep nodded. "And you know what? You passed the test. I was wrong about you. At least I think I was. You've done everything I've asked and more to make my little girl happy."

"Thank you." Jed almost choked on the words. "So you'll give your blessing?"

"For what?"

"For marriage. I want to marry your daughter."

The man squinted like this was a new idea to him. He

dipped his head, then uncrossed his legs and stood, reaching out a hand. "Get you a blood test."

"Excuse me?"

"Get you a blood test to make sure you don't have one of those diseases and I'll give my blessing."

"Sir, that's not going to be a concern because I've—"

"Good. You shouldn't have a problem getting the test."

"No sir, you're right. No problem at all."

Shep shook his hand firmly. "You pass that final test and you're in."

After Jed's blood test came back clear and Rose's did too (she felt like it was the least she could do for him), she read every book about marriage on the planet. She knew the five love languages in Swahili by the time the wedding rolled around.

Pastor Bingham at the church was excited to walk through premarital counseling with them. "Most people prepare more for the wedding ceremony than they do their marriage," he said in their first session. "Best gift I could give you is to see what struggles you're going to have down the road and work on them now rather than later."

And that's what he did. They talked about starting a family and when. They talked about debt and who would do the domestic chores, food shopping, all the way down to which way the toilet paper roll should go. Well, not quite that far, but close.

"You'd be surprised at how much acrimony there is over

the little things," Pastor Bingham said. "Most of the time couples store up the hurt and don't deal with it until they're ready to give up. By then, they've forgotten what the original problem was. I don't want to see that happen to you."

The further they went with the sessions, the clearer it became that Jed and Rose were not only compatible, but seemingly made for each other. There were differences, of course, and Pastor Bingham said those differences could either tear them apart or be used to draw them together. Though Jed was up-front and onstage, he liked his privacy. He loved being alone. He was a thinker. Rose needed friends and loved her family.

"This is the type of thing you have to anticipate," the pastor said. "Rose, what happens if you're invited to a party and Jed doesn't want to go? What happens down the road if Jed's music doesn't take off? Doesn't pay the bills? Will you work?"

"I want to help my dad with the vineyard," she said. "But I don't want to work outside of that."

"What happens if Jed goes to work for a company? And what if that company insists he move to Dallas or Seattle or Green Bay? What do you do then?"

"Jed wouldn't ask me to leave here," Rose said.

"I know being here is important," Jed said. "She said something to me when we first started dating. It was . . ." He thought a moment. "She said family was more important than stuff, things that eventually get thrown away. Family is forever."

"And you agree with that?"

"At the time I didn't. But I see what she's saying now."

Rose's heart swelled when she heard her own words coming back to her through Jed's voice. She wouldn't have expected him to remember that conversation from months ago.

Pastor Bingham nodded and asked the next series of questions, but the one about moving unnerved Rose and kept her up thinking until the wee hours of the morning. What if they had to leave the vineyard? Would she be able to go?

The next evening they were having dinner with Jed's mother. They had spent some time together, and Rose hoped this would be a relationship that would help Bethany move forward, sort of a Ruth-Naomi situation. So far Bethany King had been a little distant, although pleasant and cordial, but Rose hoped she would warm over time.

When Rose showed her the engagement ring, Bethany's mouth dropped.

"Where did you get this?"

"I've been saving for a house," Jed said. "Just decided to invest in something to go inside it a little early."

"It's beautiful," Bethany said.

"I didn't want anything fancy," Rose said. "I'd have taken a twist tie for the garbage bag if that's all he had."

"I'm happy for both of you," Bethany said with a smile. "Have you set a date?"

"We're looking at the first weekend in October," Rose said. "It'll be almost exactly a year from when we met."

"And your pastor is okay with that? With having it go that fast?"

"We've been through the third degree with him, Mom," Jed said, something off with his tone. "A year's enough time if you're sure."

"It's really been eye-opening," Rose said quickly, trying to help calm the conversation. "We have so much in common, but we also have a lot to work on." She took Jed's hand. "And I'm looking forward to the work."

Bethany patted Rose's other hand and smiled, but sadness was etched on her face. Her hair had turned gray and it was something she didn't try to color away. Jed said it was as if she had finally become comfortable with who she was, and who she was encompassed all the loneliness of widowhood.

"I wish you all the best with your work. You're getting a good man. And I'm happy to be getting a daughter."

CHAPTER 17

By the time October was in sight, everything was ready except for the chapel.

"You're getting married in a frame of two-by-fours," Denise said, looking at the knoll above the farm.

"I think it's beautiful," Rose said. "I want to put white sash up all around it, and flowers."

"You should move it to a church. You might still be able to find one."

"Don't you think it's romantic that it's not finished? It signifies we're just starting out. We'll put up the drywall and the roof as we go along. Just like we're building our marriage."

"Cute. Wonderful. But what if it rains on your metaphor? The extended weather forecast calls for showers."

"I don't live my life by the Weather Channel."

"Well, maybe you should consider it."

"Let the winds come and the rain blow. If you build your marriage on a solid foundation—"

"Enough with the metaphors and parables or whatever they are. Let's get practical. October here can be windy or rainy or cold. Or all three."

"If it's bad, we'll move the ceremony inside."

"Where? Into the barn? The house, with all those dead animals wandering around?"

"Denise, it's a small wedding. There's only going to be thirty people or so."

"And the musicians and caterers and photographer."

"Look, if this were your wedding, I would never suggest it, but I'm different. And I appreciate your help and all the planning you're doing."

"I think it's a mistake," Denise said, shaking her head. "And it's a bad omen."

"What is?"

"Getting married in a building that's half-finished. Rose, this shows he's not really committed. He's more interested in his career than he is the relationship. Don't you see?"

"I've encouraged him to focus on his music. I believe in him. Don't you see that? We're in this together and I'm glad he wants to pay the bills. He's very conscientious."

"Good for him. I'm glad he has paying gigs even if he doesn't have a record contract or a manager. But if he can't finish the place where you're getting married, can you trust him to do the other hard stuff? Think about it, Rose."

She did think about it, and at first she dismissed even the thought that Jed wouldn't follow through on a commitment. But every time she looked at the chapel, the wood gleaming in the sun and the leaves bright with color against the hills, a little doubt crept in. Surely he would always choose her over every other thing, though. He wouldn't let her down.

Will and Zack, Rose's brothers, made it to the farm early on the morning of the wedding. Rose could tell it was difficult for her father—the boys coming back. They had, in a sense, rejected his way of life, and it brought tension to the house the minute they walked inside.

"You just focus on you," Denise said. "Let the boys take care of themselves."

Rose did, and before long she heard cars pulling in and voices of people setting up tables and taking chairs to the chapel. To think all this fuss was for her, as a bride, was against her constitution. Part of her just wanted to elope or find a justice of the peace and avoid all the bother. She had lived her life trying not to put people out in any way. But the dream of a real wedding with a real dress and the walk down the aisle with her dad won out.

Bethany King knocked lightly and came inside her room. She shook her head and beamed. "You couldn't be any more beautiful," she said.

"You don't look half-bad yourself," Rose said.

"I just wanted to see you one more time before the ceremony and see this dress on you again."

"It was such a great day when you went with us to pick it out."

"I'm so glad you invited me. And I want you to know how happy I am for you and Jed. You're going to be great together. He's so taken with you, Rose."

"Thank you. For everything."

Rose sat obediently while Mavis Treadwell came to her room to work on her hair. The woman had styled every bride and prom queen in Sharon for the past two decades, and Rose wasn't about to break the string. The woman primped and brushed and styled, and when it was time for the veil, Rose looked in the mirror and couldn't wait to see the look on Jed's face.

"Your mama would be right proud of you today," Mavis said.

It was hard to even think of how her mother would react. It had been so many years and the memory of her had dimmed. Still, as Rose looked at her mother's photograph by the mirror and the carved wooden jar she now kept by her bed, she smelled a sweet aroma that hung in the air like perfume, like some exotic oil that had been poured out and spread around.

Her father came in and she stood and faced him.

"What do you think?" she said, twirling once for his delight.

"I think if you were any prettier, we'd have to cover our eyes as you walk down the aisle. You look gorgeous, punkin."

He'd called her this as a child, and the memory of his voice calling out good night to her brought tears.

"Oh, now don't do that!" he said. "You'll get us both going."

She wiped away a tear with a tissue and some mascara came with it. Without looking at him, she said, "Am I doing the right thing, Daddy?"

His voice was low and gravelly. "You're doing a good thing, Rose. You're doing something pure and holy by joining yourself to someone who wants to lay down his life for you."

"I'd do the same for him."

"I know you would. And that's why you two are gonna be all right."

"You really think so?"

"Yeah, I do. And if he's not everything we thought, he'll answer to me."

"You gonna tell him that before or after the service?"

"He already knows."

"I expect he does," she said.

The door opened and Denise appeared, all smiles. "It's time. I'm headed over to sing your triumphal entry song."

"You ready for the walk of death?" her father said after Denise left.

"It won't be that bad, Daddy."

Before Rose got to the front steps of the chapel, she heard the guitar quietly strumming and Denise's soft voice wafting over the hills like a gentle breeze. As soon as she and Jed began talking about the service, Rose had known she wanted

Denise singing "I Love You Truly." The words and music would be the perfect way to enter the assembly.

Jed's family, other than his mother, was absent, and she was glad someone had suggested they even the two sides by putting her family on his half of the chapel too.

Her throat caught when she saw her brothers smiling and wiping away tears. She wasn't prepared for that. She thought they were devoid of emotion.

"You're doing great," her dad whispered. "Just keep moving, punkin, or we're going to have to wring that dress out like a sponge."

And then Rose smiled and enjoyed the rest of the walk and her father's easy smile and grace as they reached the front of the chapel and he put her hand in Jed's. She teared up when Pastor Bingham asked, "Who gives this woman to this man?"

"Her mother and I do," her father said, patting her hand. And then she and Jed were alone.

Pastor Bingham read from 1 Corinthians 13 and gave both a charge to practice love at every moment, and before Rose knew it, she was looking into Jed's misty eyes and promising to love him forever and they were exchanging rings and to a joyous crowd they kissed.

It all happened so fast, she thought.

They walked out of the chapel and down the hill to the reception, where they enjoyed the fruit of the vine and songs and stories.

It was a day Rose would never forget. A day she didn't know would ever come. A day she had waited for all her life.

CHAPTER 18

SHE WAS POETRY and rhyme and everything he could ever imagine that was good in the world. And Jed couldn't help remembering words of passion uttered thousands of years before.

Like a lily among thorns is my darling among the young women. I am my beloved's and my beloved is mine.

They drove to a secluded cabin in Indiana, right on the Ohio River. It was owned by a man who had produced three of his father's biggest albums. The man heard about the wedding and offered it to them for the week, no charge. "Call it a favor to your old man," the producer said.

Jed accepted with gratitude and as soon as they arrived,

he knew it was perfect. He brought in their things and they looked at the rooms and the wraparound porch outside. And then he took Rose in his arms and kissed her with more urgency and passion than at the wedding or the reception. He was tender but could hardly control his hands and eyes.

The most exciting part of the embrace was that Rose was equally pursuing him—if not more so. Then she pulled away for a moment, a strange look on her face.

"What?" he said.

"Can I be totally honest?"

"Of course."

He thought she was going to say that she was scared, afraid she'd do something wrong or not be pretty enough in some way. Truth was, he was nervous too.

"I'm starving. Do you think there's anything to eat here?"

Jed laughed. "Didn't you eat at the reception?"

"I was busy talking with people and taking pictures. Denise said that would happen, that I'd forget to eat and would be starving by the time we got here."

He smiled. "Wait here."

He ran to the car and opened the back. The caterer was going to toss the uneaten vegetables and dip, along with a fruit tray. Jed had looked at all the leftover food and asked if he could save some in a plastic bag. He'd meant to store it in Shep's refrigerator, but he'd placed the food in the back of his car and forgotten about it until he unloaded their luggage.

"My hero," Rose said when he brought the food inside. "I can't believe you saved this!"

"I'd like to say it was advanced planning, but it wasn't."

They sat at the table and Jed lit two candles and they ate vegetables and dip and fruit until they were full. As they laughed at how hungry they were, Rose brought up the night Jed had bought her ice cream. It had already been chilly outside and he had asked her to dance with him to help her warm up.

"Want to dance again?" Jed said.

Rose bit into a strawberry and the juice ran down her chin. She raised her eyebrows. "We're going to do more than dance. And this time I'm not going to just kiss you good night."

He leaned forward and kissed the juice from her chin and their mouths met, sweet and wet.

She took his hand and led him upstairs to the loft suite, and still clothed, they faced each other without reserve, silhouetted by moonlight through the window. He brushed back wisps of hair from her face.

How beautiful you are, my love! How beautiful! Your eyes are doves. Your lips are like a scarlet ribbon, Jed thought.

He shook his head. "You're beautiful." He gently traced her cheek and chin with a finger.

She blushed.

"I want you to know that. Did you know you're perfect?"

You are altogether beautiful, my darling. There is no flaw in you.

"I love you," he said.

"I love you," she said, and the look in her eyes said more

than the words. He leaned forward and kissed her again and they fell into each other's arms.

Later as they slept, wrapped in each other's arms, naked and unashamed, Jed dreamed. He was on an island, alone, stranded. Every day he would make it to the beach and look out on the ocean for any kind of movement, staring into the distance, and with each day the longing became more intense, more heart-wrenching.

His eyes snapped open at 4:44—that's what the clock beside the bed said in big red numbers. He would never forget it or the empty feeling the dream left. Like a bad wine that lingered on his breath. But seeing Rose in bed next to him, this thing of beauty and grace and innocence, set his mind afire. And the words came along with a melody—something that rarely happened. The words and music were just there, like ripened grapes on the vine, ready to be picked.

He eased out of bed and grabbed some clothes and his guitar and crept downstairs.

CHAPTER 19

ROSE AWAKENED and turned in the morning light to see Jed, but she was alone. She wrapped a sheet around herself and looked out the window at the river meandering past the cabin, unable to believe that they were married or that they were here in this place of beauty.

She went downstairs thinking he might be in the kitchen making breakfast, but he wasn't there. For a split second she thought of those horror stories about honeymoons where one spouse was robbed or fell to their death and her stomach tied in a knot—until she heard the strum of the guitar.

She followed the sound outside and the chilly October morning raised goose bumps on her skin. She was surprised to see him sitting in a rocking chair, his face turned toward the river.

"You're up early," she said.

"I had a dream."

Rose took the guitar away and settled on his lap, snuggling close. "About what?"

"Your new song. You want to hear it?" He was like a kid with a new toy he'd gotten for Christmas.

She gave him a look of longing, just a raised eyebrow. "Maybe later," she whispered, leaning into him again, her hands exploring.

He playfully pushed back. "Did you have something else in mind?"

"Yeah, something." She rubbed noses with him and the desire rose in her. If it wasn't so cold, she would have thrown off the sheet right there in the rocking chair. In fact, maybe it wasn't too cold.

"Me too," he said. Then he thought for a moment and smiled. "Well, I think *something* will be incredible after you hear this song."

How could it be better? she thought. How could anything eclipse the expression of love between a man and wife? How could a song . . . ?

In a split second she made the decision not to hold this against him, not to think the worst. Not to complain about how cold she was or hungry or in the mood to go upstairs and enjoy each other again.

So with her feet cold and her stomach growling and the

desire white-hot inside, she sat in the other rocking chair but put her foot on Jed's leg, where she knew it would be hard for him to concentrate.

He started playing a constant downbeat with his pick—*bum bum bum bum*—and when he sang the first line, Rose knew she was hearing something other women complained they never heard. She was hearing his heart.

"I've been waitin' on you to come along,
seeing notes on a page but not the song."

That was it, she thought. His life, her life, had been about playing something neither one of them could see written out, but together they were making the music.

"Had a hole in my heart, things so strong,
only a woman like you could take me on."

She drank the words in like new wine.

"There's a plan for us, a hand divine.
Though waiting was worth it,
now you're my wife.
We've been taking our time, doing this right.
Tonight I'm not gonna just kiss you good night."

Her words. He had used her words in the song.

Jed stopped playing and opened his eyes to look at her

as if hoping he had bought the right birthday present. Rose could hardly speak, her mouth open in speechless awe. She couldn't see through the blur of tears.

"Play the rest," she managed.

And he did. The more she heard, the more she liked, and the closer her heart was drawn to this good man. And she knew they were going to make beautiful music all day long.

CHAPTER 20

JED HUNG ON ROSE's every word. She was his biggest cheerleader—he knew that—but he had no idea how big until she breathlessly told him what she had done.

"You called Stan?" he said.

"I had to tell him that you're back like never before. And that this song is evidence."

He let that sink in. He was initially upset that she would do this behind his back, but he also loved it that she believed in him this much. "What did he say?"

"He was cool at first. Then I quoted some of the lyrics. He was impressed but still kind of acted distracted."

"That's the classic Stan put-off."

"So I told him if he didn't want to hear the song, I would call the Trammel Agency—they would listen to it."

Jed raised his eyebrows. The Trammel Agency was one of Stan's competitors. "What did he say to that?"

"He said to be there at nine tomorrow morning. In the studio. They have a session planned at ten and he wants to hear you play it."

Jed broke out in a wide grin. "You're kidding."

"I'm not. This is it, Jed. I can feel it."

"I kind of wanted to have more songs ready."

She rubbed his arm and drew closer. "More songs will come. You have to let them simmer. But he needs to hear this one."

"Can you help me with the simmer part?"

She blushed and they laughed and embraced.

Jed stayed up late that night tightening the lyrics—making sure it was exactly what he wanted—and Rose was right there. And when he was sure, she took the guitar from him.

"Let's practice something else before we go to sleep," she said.

Jed jumped out of bed the next morning ready to go. Rose was slower to get moving but the smell of freshly brewed coffee brought her to life. They made it to the studio a half hour early and sat in the parking lot, talking, laughing, and trying to calm Jed's nerves.

"It's funny how I can stand up before any number of

You have stolen my heart with one glance of your eyes.

My son, pay attention to my wisdom,
turn your ear to my words of insight.

I am my beloved's and my beloved is mine.

I said to myself, "Come now, I will test you with pleasure to find out what is good." But this also proved to be meaningless.

What do people gain from all their labors at which they toil under the sun?

A time to mourn . . .

. . . a time to embrace

For the lips of the adulterous woman drip honey, and her speech is smoother than oil. Keep to a path far from her . . .

. . . for your ways are in full view of the Lord, and he examines all your paths.

To everything there is a season

And a time to every purpose under heaven

Love is the power that heals.

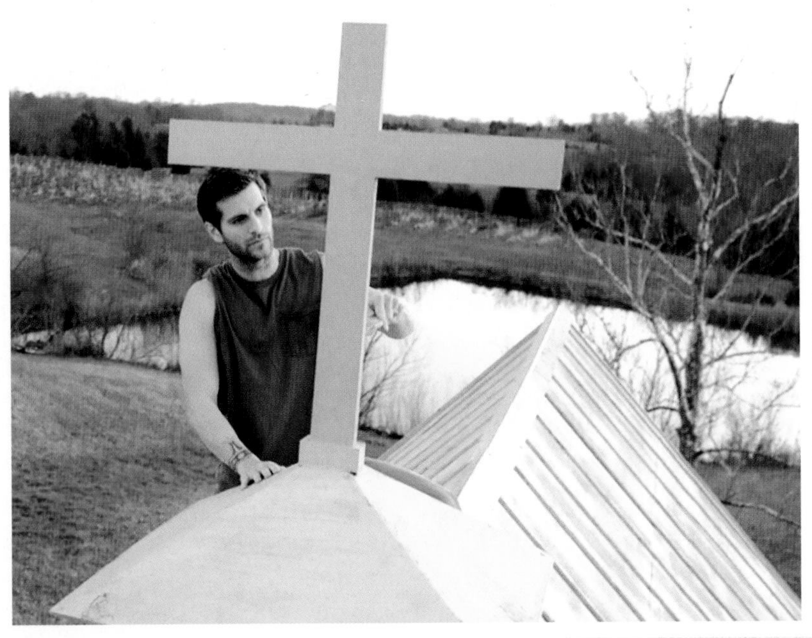

people, but it's the audience of one or two decision makers that makes my knees knock."

"Show them your heart like you've shown me."

"That's a little scary."

"It's what Stan's looking for. Heart. Soul. 'The Song' is amazing. Just look at me when you're singing it."

And that's what he did. After the awkward handshake with Stan and a guy from the record company who had dropped him, Jed picked up the guitar and looked at Rose, then closed his eyes and pictured himself on the front deck of the cabin by the river and the words flowed. He just left everything out there for them and when he was finished, he looked up. Some of the session players had come in while he was playing and stood listening. Stan looked stunned. Rose smiled, her teeth tight together in anticipation. Like he'd done the best job he possibly could.

"Where in the world did that come from?" Stan said. "That was—that is fantastic. It's the heart we've been looking for, man." He looked at Rose. "Did you help him with that?"

She glanced at Jed and gave a grin. "He wrote it on our honeymoon."

"So you did help," Stan said, laughing and nudging Jed with an elbow.

Groans all around and laughter and Rose's face turned a deep crimson.

Stan and the other man spoke in hushed tones in the corner; then Stan went into the control room. Through the open door Jed heard, "Dave, can we push the ten o'clock back an hour? I want to lay down a rough track of this right now so I can take it to the label."

And that's how it worked, though it took a lot longer than an hour. The recording they finished that afternoon went to the label and the raw, spontaneous, energy-filled track was what they used for the single.

Three weeks later, after several days in a row when Rose struggled to get out of bed, Jed suggested she see a doctor. "This is just not like you," he said.

He drove her to the afternoon appointment at a building filled with all kinds of doctors' and dentists' offices. He thought they would give her an antibiotic and she would be fine. Or perhaps they would find something ominously wrong. When she didn't come out of the office, he began to be concerned. Then a nurse peeked out and called his name.

They do these kinds of things when someone gets cancer, he thought.

He walked in and found Rose with a crumpled ball of tissues, her eyes red.

"Hey," he said, sitting by her. "What's wrong?"

The doctor shook Jed's hand. She was in her thirties and seemed all-business. "Mr. King, your wife suggested you be here for the results of the test."

"Test? I thought Rose just had the flu or something. What does she have?"

The doctor glanced at Rose, who waved a hand as if telling her to break the news.

"Rose has an *illness* that won't clear up for a few months. Eight, to be exact."

"You can predict it like that? What kind of illness?"

"It's a baby, Mr. King. Your wife is pregnant."

He looked at Rose, then at the doctor, then back at Rose, who was smiling through her tears. His mouth dropped open and he couldn't shut it. "But I thought . . ."

"I don't know what happened," Rose said.

Jed smiled. "I do. We made a baby. Rose, we're going to have a baby—can you believe it?"

She shook her head.

Jed looked at the doctor, who seemed to be content just to take the scene in. He took Rose's hand. "You are going to be the best mom in the world. I can see you with that little baby in your arms."

"But it's so soon. I thought we'd have time together. Just the two of us."

Jed nodded. It was a loss, of sorts. Having a child this early was not the plan, though they hadn't given pregnancy a specific spot on their calendar. "This is a gift from God. A surprise, yes. But a gift that's going to change us and bring a lot of joy."

Tears brimmed in his own eyes now. They hugged and Jed whooped so loudly that people in the podiatrist's office at the other end of the building could hear.

"The Song" released as a single to limited airplay on a few stations, but something happened about a month later. Call it word of mouth or a groundswell—it was big. Stan said they needed to take advantage of the wave that was growing, so Jed put his band together from a few of the guys he'd played with through the years and they began playing moderate-size venues.

"I don't want this to get in the way of us," Jed said to Rose before going on the road.

Rose shook her head. "No, this is us. This is just an extension of us. Let's go for it. Together."

CHAPTER 21

AFTER THE HONEYMOON, Rose had moved into Jed's apartment in Louisville until they could get a bigger place. Her dad offered to help them with a down payment on a house, but Jed refused. He wanted them to be as independent as possible from both sides of their family. They squirreled away the money that came from his concerts and the advance from the label and put the cash gifts from the wedding into a savings account.

Rose called her dad each day. He'd hired a teenager from a neighboring farm to come in and help him, and it sounded like the boy was good for Shep. There had been some problems in the kid's family and being around someone stable, like Shep, was a gift. And a strong back was what Rose's father needed most.

Rose traveled with the band from town to town while Jed performed and wrote new songs for the next album. Some of the songs came fast and poured out like a bucket tipped over. Others came in drips and drops, sort of like he was pulling at a thread that led to another and another until he grabbed hold of the whole cord. These songs were equally good, sometimes better, and he loved the process of finding the rhyme and tunes and just the right phrase.

In the meantime, "The Song" rose to number seventeen on the country charts. That it was Rose's song had knit them together every time he performed it, every time they heard it on the radio. One night when the crowd swelled and Rose stood in the audience, he caught her eye and pointed at her, giving her the look that melted her heart. The look that said, *We're together in this. I can't do this without you. You're the reason for any success we have.*

The only drawback to their life together, other than the traveling and staying in hotels, was the troubling scene at the front of the stage each night. Girls with low-cut tops and short shorts pranced and danced to try to capture his eyes. And it wasn't just the teenagers. Older women with freshly colored hair dressed like teenagers and acted just as inappropriately. When Rose was quiet later that night at the hotel, Jed asked what she was thinking.

"I see all those girls, all those women looking at you. Some are innocent, but I can tell others are sending messages."

"I only have eyes for you," Jed said, rubbing her belly and feeling the baby kick. He laughed and pushed on the hand or foot moving inside and marveled at what was happening inside her.

Her body was changing and her heart was too. It was no longer just Jed and her—there was another person in the mix and that scared her. Could she love this little one like she loved Jed?

When she got to her seventh month of pregnancy, Rose knew she couldn't travel any longer. The rumbling of the bus and the lack of privacy made her long for home, but Jed's apartment was tiny and the neighbors were loud. He had been looking at houses in Louisville, about a half hour away from Sharon, and the more Rose thought about it, the more she knew this was the best for them—not to say good-bye to what she'd always known but to separate from her dad. Leaving wasn't really a matter of distance; it was a matter of the heart.

Jed struggled with the move too. He didn't want to take Rose away from her father. He felt the same kind of guilt being away from his own mom so much while he was on the road.

His mother had been there for him through all the childhood struggles, all the rejection of the rest of the family, the ridicule and scorn. He told Rose about a night onstage in middle school when he'd tried so hard to play one of his father's songs but things didn't go well. His mother had been there long into the night, helping him see that life wasn't perfect and you could learn something from every performance. She'd been his biggest cheerleader. She wanted him to succeed and fall in love and start a family. But her emotion at the wedding, that melancholy look, hung over both of them. She had lost a husband, then another, and now a son, although it encouraged Jed to think that she'd be gaining a grandson.

Rose's dad made a show of telling her she should leave, that she should begin anew with her husband, but it was a gift that was half-wrapped and didn't have a bow.

They visited the vineyard a few weeks before Rose's due date and before they closed on the house in Louisville. They had scraped enough together to qualify for a balloon mortgage on a place near Cherokee Park. From the start, they'd fallen in love with the house—all that space inside, all those trees in the back, and a yard big enough for a swing set and playground when the baby grew into a toddler.

Shep had been telling them that the family dog, Duke, was getting older, slowing down, whining at odd hours, and his appetite wasn't good. As Jed petted the old dog, he knew it was time. He could see it so clearly but Shep and Rose wanted to hang on.

"If you want, I can take him to the vet," Jed offered. "It might be easier for you if you let me do it."

Shep set his jaw. "No. I don't need a vet. Come on, Duke."

"What are you going to do, Mr. Jordan?"

"We're gonna take a long walk."

The man got his rifle and Jed looked at Rose, who watched Duke through misty eyes. She tried to say something, then looked away.

Jed followed Shep outside, not asking permission. Shep grabbed a shovel as he passed the barn and Jed took it from him and carried it as they walked up the hill.

"You don't need to watch this," Shep said.

"I want to come with you. My dad said there are some things a man should never have to do alone."

Shep stopped. "He said that to you, did he?" He studied Jed for a moment, then moved on.

It took a long time for Duke to make it to the pond, and when he did, he leaned over and sniffed at the water. Then he kept walking, stiff-legged, up the embankment toward the tree line. It was painful to watch, and Jed couldn't help thinking it would make a really sad song. He could call it "The Long Walk." Words and images ran around his head like they did with every song.

He watched the older man, weathered hands wrapped around the gun barrel. His gait and the dog's were the same, stiff-legged and slow. *It's the longest walk he'll take,* Jed thought, *but there's a friend by his side. You can take a long walk if you have someone who loves you nearby.*

Jed saw the reflection of the sky on the surface of the pond. A lonely crow passed overhead. When they got to a spot near an oak tree, not far from the grave of Rose's mother, Jed sank his rounded shovel into the earth and smelled the fresh, loamy soil.

"I guess this is as good a place as any," Shep said.

Jed thought of another walk up a hill. The weight of the world and a cross on a man's shoulders. A man in Roman garb with weathered hands driving nails into flesh. Maybe it wouldn't work to compare that with this, but the image moved him. Jed dug a little deeper as the dog sat in the grass, his eyes tired, his tongue hanging out.

"I've known he was in pain for the longest time and I just couldn't bring myself to do this," Shep said.

"It's hard letting something like that go. Something good that's been here so long."

"I think this old dog kept both Rose and me alive. The boys too. He brought light to a house that turned dark fast."

"You're doing a good thing," Jed said. "You're doing a kind thing."

"Yeah, but it don't feel kind. I'd rather see him crawl off somewhere and let nature take its course. Just have him disappear."

"Maybe he's returning the favor," Jed said.

Shep cocked his head. "What do you mean?"

Jed stopped digging for a minute and leaned on the shovel. "Maybe he knew you needed help all those years ago. He knew he could fill a void. He helped you get through the pain of losing your wife and the pain of your children losing a mother. And now he's giving you the chance to pay him back. To let him go. End his suffering."

Shep put a hand on the dog's head and held it there like he was passing on a blessing. The dog closed his eyes and whimpered and tried to get comfortable on the ground.

"Letting go of something you love is the hardest thing, ain't it?" Shep said.

Jed thought of the irony, the same thing the man was going through letting go of Rose. "But it's because you love him that you can let go," he said.

Shep looked up with red, pleading eyes. Jed kept digging until there was a heap of dark earth and a hole deep enough that critters wouldn't disturb the sleep of Shep's old friend.

"Why don't you let me?" Jed said. "You go on back to the house."

"I'll see it through," Shep said. He got down on his knees next to the dog and put his face close and Jed had to look away. There are just some things too holy to watch. Dying is not a spectator sport and dealing with it is as personal and intimate as any act on earth. There were no words that passed between the man and the animal, just a closeness that spoke all Shep needed to say.

The man stood and picked up the gun and Duke didn't move, not a flinch or a twitch. He was just resting when the shot rang out through the countryside and echoed off the hills. Quail rose from a nearby thicket and flew into the air, almost in formation, Jed thought.

He helped Shep gently pull the dog into the hole and then

spread earth over the body. When the mound was rounded, Shep grabbed some rocks and made a small headstone.

As they walked back to the house, Shep put his arm around Jed and without looking at him said, "Your daddy was right."

CHAPTER 22

ALL THROUGH THE PREGNANCY Rose swore she would never have another baby. It took such a toll on her body, and her hormones were all over the place. Denise talked her down from the ledge several times, coming to her home and sitting with her at the kitchen table. Rose was happy about the baby. She was glad they were starting a family, but all the emotions swirled and made her wonder about her ability as a mother.

"I know I can help my dad with the vineyard," she said to Jed late at night on the phone. "I know I'm competent and capable of doing just about anything, but this mother thing scares me to death."

"You're not doing this on your own," Jed said.

"I know you're going to support me," she said quickly. "But you also have a job to do."

"I'm not talking about me," he said. "I'm talking about God. Rose, he's going to be right there with you, giving you the energy and the patience and the love you need. You're going to be an amazing mom."

"Maybe I'm just scared that in all of this I'm going to lose something."

"Lose what?"

She held back at first, then managed to choke out, "Myself. I look at the moms in church and their kids become their whole life. And that's good. Children are a treasure and they're important, but if your whole life centers around your kids, don't you lose yourself?"

Jed was silent on the other end of the phone. He waited so long she wondered if maybe he had gone to sleep. Then he said, "Maybe in losing yourself you actually find yourself. Maybe instead of making you feel like you're dying inside, this baby will make you come alive in a way you've never been before."

Rose didn't like the words at first. It sounded like she was the only one doing the losing. But as the birth neared, she treasured his thoughts.

Jed canceled a show and caught a plane when the doctor confirmed the baby was coming. Relief flooded Rose when he walked in and took Denise's spot beside her.

Holding his hand, watching his face, gave her comfort, but it didn't take the pain away. When he watched the machine charting the rise and fall of the contractions instead of looking at her, she grabbed his arm and dug her fingernails in. "Look at me, don't look at that stupid machine!"

Her intensity surprised even her, but Jed responded well and was right in her face the rest of the way through, all the way until the last push. It was his eyes, always the eyes—the way they scrunched when he laughed and smiled, and then the tears of joy at the miracle of life they beheld.

All her questions, all the fatigue and nausea and swelling and pain, vanished the moment she held her son. She and Jed had made this child together. He was a miracle God had performed through the love of a husband and wife. There was a song in there; she was sure Jed would find it, something beautiful and mystical and praiseworthy.

Jed stayed home for a week, doting on Rose and holding Ray and singing to him. He finished painting Ray's room and putting up the Noah's ark trim on the wall. Rose rested and recovered, looking in awe at the little hands and feet and listening to his beating heart. Watching someone so tiny and helpless and dependent on her made her well up with feelings for her mom. How Rose wished she could be there to see her grandson. But her father's reaction was priceless. He didn't weep, exactly—her dad wasn't the weeping kind. He just stood in the corner and held Ray, rocking back and forth, staring at him like he was the next king of England.

When Jed went back on the road, Rose felt a loss. She was in a new neighborhood with no friends or relatives close. She spent weekends with her dad in the old house, but that felt like cheating. She knew she was just trying to get through the transition, this space in time when two had become three, but something gnawed at her. She *wanted* Jed to be a success. She *wanted* him to write great songs and become everything he was meant to be. But what price would they have to pay?

She was at her dad's house for a visit when Jed returned a week later and surprised her. He marveled at how much Ray had grown. "I don't want to miss any of this," he said. "Him rolling over for the first time. First steps. First words."

Rose smiled at Jed, knowing he meant it. "You were right, you know," she said.

"About what?"

"About losing myself. I was so scared that I wouldn't measure up as a mom. But once you hold that little man in your arms, there's no going back to the old life. And I do feel alive inside like never before."

Jed smiled at her in the way that said another song was percolating. *"Alive Inside."* That would be a good song for the second album, she thought.

Ray got fussy and Jed placed him at Rose's breast. Jed sat in a chair and watched the two of them. Rose glanced out the window at the chapel in the distance, still half-finished.

CHAPTER 23

EVERY TIME JED CAME HOME, he got the feeling that this was where he needed to be. Not that the road wasn't good or fun; it was. But it was also a lot of work. It was exhausting to travel and stay in cheap hotels and deal with the drama that always came with musicians and life. But he knew this was what he'd been called to do. It was the thing he did that stoked the fire inside and kept him going.

The truth was, he needed both. He needed the anchor of home, Rose and Ray, in order to do the thing he was made to do. Untether him from that and his songs were just flailing in the wind. The passion and pain and heart came through when he wrote and sang about that deep, committed love he was just beginning to understand.

He told Stan not to schedule anything around Ray's first birthday, and the man grudgingly complied. Jed had a whole week to be at home, and even this early, he could tell that having Ray was going to be a blast. He could see himself in the stands at Little League games or maybe even coaching a team, though he didn't know much about baseball fundamentals. He could learn. He would just be there for his son, encouraging him, praising him for any little success, and correcting him when he needed it.

He told Rose to go out with a friend one night, that he would watch Ray, and her eyes lit with excitement. She called Denise and they planned to meet halfway. Denise was now planning her own wedding and they had a lot to talk about.

She kissed Jed, just a peck on the cheek, then turned and gave him another that sent a different message. "Don't fall asleep before I get back."

He smiled and watched her drive away, then sat on the floor and watched Ray toddle from one room to another, testing the boundaries of their baby gates.

Jed fed him dinner, amazed at how much food stuck to Ray's face. Then it was in the bath, into pajamas, and snuggling together on the couch with three of Ray's favorite books. Jed could feel the little guy's energy leaking out with each page turn. Ray relaxed on Jed's chest and his arms fell at his sides and he yawned. When they were done, Jed carried him to his crib and gently laid him down.

"Good night, buddy."

He was on the way to the kitchen to clean the dishes when he heard a voice.

"Drink!"

Ray was standing in his crib, one arm draped over the side. "Drink."

"Okay, I'll get your cup; then you have to go to sleep, okay?"

It was like bargaining with some Middle Eastern terrorist group. Once Ray saw he could get a drink, he asked for another story. And when Jed gave in and said, "Just one more," Ray asked for another.

Rose had said it was best for Ray to stick to a routine at night, and Jed had tried to follow it, but the little guy looked so cute and Jed didn't want him dehydrated when Rose returned. And what was the problem with giving him one more story? Or a snack from the fridge?

When Rose walked in the door, Ray jumped up from the couch and yelled, "Mama!"

Jed quickly turned off the cartoon they were watching. "He wouldn't go to sleep."

Rose smiled at Ray and he held out his arms. She carried him upstairs to his crib, then returned to Jed.

"Jed, I told you the routine. Why didn't you follow it?"

"I tried. I really did."

From upstairs they could hear Ray's crib creak as he pushed and pulled at the railing. "Mama?"

"This is really important. When he gets off schedule, he gets cranky during the day—it makes life a lot harder."

"I know. I'm sorry. He asked for another story and I gave it to him, and once I got him out of there, it was all over. But it's one night."

"Don't tell me it's one night. I know it's one night."

"I'll take my guitar in and sing to him. That always puts him to sleep."

"No! You're not going up there. He needs to know that when it's time to sleep, it's time to sleep."

"Just one song."

"If you sing him one, he'll want two. And when you're gone, he'll want me to come in there and sing something."

"Maaaaaaama?" Ray said, starting to whine.

She shook her head. "He's exhausted."

"Look, I understand. Part of it is I don't get to see him as much and when I do . . . I'll follow your rules. It won't happen again."

"They're not my rules. They're our rules. This is not for me, it's for Ray."

Jed looked at the floor and listened to the crying begin in Ray's room. Everything in him wanted to march up there and pick up his son and hold him until he went to sleep.

"How was dinner with Denise?"

She gave him a look as if saying, *"Don't try to make this better by asking questions."*

He threw his hands up and walked into the kitchen, beginning the dishes he hadn't done. Peanut butter was smeared all over the high chair and it took him longer to wash and dry everything. Ray was in full meltdown when he finished, so he walked outside and sat at the end of the driveway, where he wouldn't hear his son's wails.

A plane passed overhead and he watched, wondering where it was going. Every plane, every bus, reminded him that he wasn't on the road. Every song on the radio he heard was another song he hadn't written or sung. There was something pulling him, something strong that tugged at a deep place.

He looked back at the house and saw the light in their bedroom go out.

Part Two

CHAPTER 24

SHELBY BALE sat in a booth at a bar in Hartsfield-Jackson International Airport in Atlanta. She had flown on her own dime for this meeting and had slept on the plane, with a little help from the pills in the bottle that her friend Vivian supplied. It was 3:15 in the afternoon and she had only been off the plane a half hour, but she really needed a drink. This was an important meeting, a game changer, a life changer. She was twenty-five and as hungry as any starving artist could be.

Stan Russel lumbered through the door, sunglasses, polo shirt, hair slicked back. A paunch in front that would probably keep growing and cause heart disease if he didn't get some exercise. He looked to be about fifty and she couldn't see a wedding ring. Wasn't important information, at least not yet.

She hadn't fired her manager, but if things went well with Stan, she would drop Barry Staver like a rotten banana, which was exactly what Barry reminded her of in looks and odor.

Shelby smiled and waved Stan over. He ordered a drink and joined her.

"I have a proposition," she said when he sat.

"You get right to business, don't you?" Stan said, smiling and glancing down.

Men were always glancing down with Shelby and she liked the divided attention. If she could distract them with her eyes or her smile or a curve here or there, it made getting what she wanted easier. She also liked it when they followed the trail of body art she sported, though the tattoos were a last resort.

"If I want something, I go get it," she said. "And this is a win-win for all three of us. I'm dumping Barry."

"Wait, all three of us?" Stan said.

"I want you to manage me."

"What's wrong with Barry?"

She gave a pout. "You know Barry. Not the brightest spotlight on the stage. Certainly not a spotlight like Stan Russel."

"And you think I can help you."

"We've been playing venues way too small. I know you don't believe me, but it's true. If I were any closer to the audience, I'd have to set up behind them. In most places there's not room to open my violin case."

He laughed and actually snorted. The alcohol and her jokes seemed to loosen him.

"That song of yours, 'Confetti'—that's a kickin' little tune. Really smooth. The airplay you've been getting with that alone should have you fronting somebody."

"Exactly. And we're working on some new stuff that's just as good. Even better. I mean, things are really coming together. And the band is tight. Ricky's guitar, my fiddle."

"Your fiddle is awesome, no question. You have a presence onstage. But why aren't you working this out with Barry? He should be able—"

"Barry is over. I want you. We have a loyal following and things are growing. Have you seen our Facebook page? It's exploding. The places Barry books us sell out fast, but we're ready for the next step."

"What are you saying? And who is the third person who benefits from this?"

"I want you to pick us up. Take over the tour—there are only three dates left and then I'm free. I want to open for Jed King."

Stan stared at her, then threw his head back and laughed more loudly than was comfortable for the room. "You and Jed King? That's a good one, Shelby. That's like booking . . ." He thought for a minute but couldn't seem to come up with a comparison.

Shelby responded before he had a chance to shoot her down. "I know it looks weird up front, but think about it. We bring our fans, he brings his—we fill up a venue neither of us can fill alone."

"And his fans complain about your show and your fans say Jed plays too much God-squad stuff."

"Not gonna happen. Both audiences are exposed to each other. They'll love it."

"Exposed. Pun intended?"

She arched her back and sat up straight and the man's eyes wandered again. "I know we're a little more edgy than what Jed does. He's got the purebred, wholesome-guy, family-man thing going. And I have a reputation for pushing the envelope. But I think we could be good for each other. I'll tone down some of the stuff we do onstage."

"You shouldn't change what's working for you."

"It's not changing, it's adapting. Every species has to adapt in order to survive and become stronger. The truth is, we'll make Jed's shows more exciting. We'll bring an energy that he'll have to match. It'll push him a little. And he'll bring legitimacy to what we do. Everybody wins."

"Do you even know his music?" Stan said, draining his glass.

"My stepmom was into his dad's music, so I grew up with David King. When I was old enough to get out, I'd go to concerts and saw Jed in this little place, back before he got married."

"Before he broke your heart by getting married."

She smiled sweetly. "You hear that a lot, I'll bet."

"Jed has a lot of lady appeal, but he's not a player."

We'll see about that, Shelby thought.

"I knew he'd make it someday; that was clear. The lyrics, his looks, and that voice of his. He's a good musician, too. Even though you weren't always sold on him."

Stan raised his eyebrows. "You do know a few things, don't you?"

"I know enough to be dangerous." She reached out and took Stan's hands, turning them over. "You have an interesting life line." She traced the lines in his hands and could feel the power she had over him.

"And you think my lines and Jed's lines mesh with your lines?"

"I can feel it."

"How does your band feel about this?"

"They're as fed up with Barry as I am. It's time for a change. For you, Jed, us, and the music."

"Well, I'll admit at first blush it feels a little far-fetched." Now he took her hands and turned them over. "But I think we might be able to work something out."

She pulled back from him. "This is strictly a deal about the music. You understand?"

Stan lifted his hands. "It's business. I got it. But I need to talk with Jed. Get his blessing on the whole thing."

"I thought you were the manager."

"I am."

"Then why can't you tell him what's best? I mean, if you feel it as strongly as I do, he'll go along."

"I try not to force things on my artists."

"You don't think Jed will approve?"

"I'm sure he'll be on board if I approach it the right way. If I decide this is a good idea."

"You've decided, Stan. You know it. This is a gut thing,

intuition. This will be huge. So surprise him. Surprise the audience. Where's Jed's next show?"

Stan pulled out his calendar. He was old-school. Probably was being dragged kicking and screaming into the digital age, still at the rest stop on the information superhighway. "He has a few days off right now. His anniversary. Doesn't go back out until a week from tomorrow. It's Boston."

"Perfect. Our last gig is Sunday in Ohio. We'll head toward Boston and get the team to blast social media and fill up the place."

Stan nodded slowly. "Yeah. I can see this working out well for all of us. I'll get a contract together."

They shook and Shelby couldn't believe how easy it was or how quickly fortunes could change. She was going to finally meet Jed King.

CHAPTER 25

Rose felt conflicted as their fifth anniversary approached. Jed had suggested they get away to some deserted island, just the two of them. They didn't have a boatload of money, but concert attendance was growing and with that came more time away. There was always a cost with success.

The conflict in her heart wasn't about celebrating—it was leaving Ray behind. Her dad was overjoyed at the idea and told them to spend a whole week away. Jed saw nothing wrong with the plan. "Ray will have the time of his life at the vineyard!" And that was true. But . . .

There always seemed to be a *but* in her life these days.

Rose worried about her father's health. He had seemed

to slow down in the past year and there were times when he didn't have the stamina for things that were so easy only a year earlier. Seeing her dad every other week or so helped her realize the slow decline that was happening. His breathing was labored at times when they'd visit on the weekend. She'd pull up with Ray while her dad was working in the vineyard and he would hurry to the car, out of breath and putting out his hand for stability.

There was no way she could convince him to go to the doctor. He only went to the doctor when he was in so much pain he couldn't "sit up and string beans," as he would say. She worried that she'd one day walk into the house and find him slumped over in his office among all those stuffed predators. She'd been so committed to her father and the vineyard, and seeing one diminish and the other flourish was difficult.

"Stan manages a guy who has a condo in Cabo. He's offered it to us."

"Where's Cabo?" she said.

Jed told her about the spot on the Mexican coast with the bluest water and clean beaches and the feeling of being a million miles away from everything.

"Why don't we do something closer?" Rose said. "We could take Ray with us and he could play in the sand. He's never seen the ocean. And he'd be tired by dark." She said that last part because she knew Jed would want to "connect" on vacation.

Jed frowned. "You know I love Ray. He's the light of my life. But we need some time alone. Just me and you, like it used to be, you know? Before I go back out on the road. Let's make some memories."

"Jed, when are we going to start making memories as a family? The three of us?"

Rose didn't want to be a nag and certainly didn't have to have everything her own way, but there was something that bugged her in this and she couldn't put a finger on it. She didn't want the separation that success bred, but she also wanted Jed to be who God had created him to be. To sing the songs he'd been given and make beauty from the pain of life. That's what audiences connected with. It was why he was becoming more successful. His songs struck some deep chord in hearts and lives and people were responding. She didn't want to put her foot down about their vacation. That sounded controlling and motherly and anything like the wife she wanted to be. She wanted Jed to be a strong husband who would see the problems they were facing. She wanted him to understand, without being told, how hurtful some of his choices had been to her. Little things were building and compounding like interest on a credit card. And this anniversary celebration was the sliver in the finger that kept sending signals to her brain, a constant throb that wasn't going away. But it seemed so small. It was silly to make a big deal about this.

Rose pored over her old scrapbooks of family vacations when she was younger. Her mom and dad and brothers searching for seashells at Myrtle Beach. Those were some of her best family memories of all. Why couldn't Jed see that? Why couldn't she get him to understand?

She had heard that a man's heart would naturally turn toward his work and providing for his family. That was a good thing, a God-honoring thing—but it could also mean the man got his worth from what he did, and she could see how easily Jed could get lost in his career and abandon the family because of his art.

But she knew the same was true for her. Motherhood had opened her heart in ways she couldn't believe, but there was a subtle pull toward Ray because he had become the most important person in her life. He was helpless, after all. He depended on her for everything. And she would do anything for him. She knew this could push her away from the person who helped her create Ray.

This had been stunning to Rose. She thought the hardest part of marriage would be the wedding preparation. She had no idea it would be so much work and take so much mental and emotional energy and time. The conflict with Jed scared her and she wanted to bury it, just put a good face on things and move on. Bringing stuff up, like the anniversary trip, was not her style. She was the pleaser, the one who simply went along with the program and tried to make people happy. That's why things had become so difficult and pronounced when Ray had been born. She wasn't just speaking for herself any longer; she was speaking for the two of them, and a divide was growing between them and the man they both loved.

The truth was, she and Jed were both busy, and if there was anything that could kill the heart, it was two people who were busy with good things going in different directions.

Separate lives with separate agendas going separate ways did not knit hearts together.

She stewed on the decision, talked with Denise, longed to be able to talk with her mother, and was careful not to bring it up with her dad. Then, two weeks before their anniversary, Jed came to her, a smile on his face and an envelope in his hand. "I split the difference."

"What do you mean?"

"Open it."

She pulled out a brochure with dates written on it in blue marker. Across the top Jed had scrawled, *Rose and Jed's Island Family Anniversary Getaway*.

"It's a little island just off the coast of South Carolina. The rental house is ours for five days. It has a pool in the back—with a gate around it so Ray can't wander in on his own. He can play in the sand all day or swim in the pool, and you and I can walk the beach with him and talk and read and do . . . whatever. I don't know about the ocean temperature this time of year, though."

She hugged him and smiled. "It's perfect," she said. "Especially the 'whatever' part."

Rose wanted to go right then. She felt like a child who couldn't wait to pack her suitcase. Couldn't wait to tell Ray what he was about to experience.

"Oh, and I called Ronny over at the feed store in Sharon," Jed said. "I asked if he'd go by a couple of times while we're gone and check in on your dad. Real quiet-like so he won't know we asked."

Rose beamed. This was what she wanted. Someone thoughtful, decisive, and caring. She would make the vacation a memorable one for Ray and Jed.

Jed built sand castles with Ray and took him into the surf. Rose sat under an umbrella and watched. They stayed at the beach too long on the first day and got burned, then spent the rest of the week with the smell of aloe trailing wherever they went.

Ray was a ball of energy until darkness hit and then he was out, just fall-into-bed tired. Jed tucked him in and found Rose sitting outside under the moon.

"Wish we could take a moonlight walk on the beach," she said.

He sat in the beach chair next to her and she climbed onto his lap.

"This is not a bad compromise," he said.

And it wasn't. The next few days were restful and playful and romantic, as he'd hoped. The spark was back in Rose's eyes and Jed promised himself he would take more time off, spend more time with his growing family. He'd do it not just for them, but for himself.

The day before they left, the phone rang in the house. Jed had turned off his cell and didn't make contact with the outside world, but somehow Stan found the number.

"Just making sure you're ready for Boston," Stan said. "It's going to be a dynamite venue for you."

"I'll be there."

"And I wanted you to know there's going to be a little surprise, too."

"Surprise?"

Stan chuckled. "See you in Boston, Jed."

CHAPTER 26

SHELBY BALE sat with one of her best friends backstage at the venue in Boston. It was their first opportunity to open for Jed and the excitement level was high.

Vivian Lee played the stand-up bass in Shelby's band, and she shared Shelby's zest for life and living on the edge. There wasn't much they hadn't tried together. There were pills Vivian had introduced Shelby to and there were plenty of substances that Shelby had given Vivian. Nothing that debilitated them or kept them from performing, of course. And in some ways, the things they drank and took enhanced their energy onstage.

"I've just figured it out," Vivian said, downing the last drink of Scotch from her glass. "This is not about us breaking free from Barry or playing bigger venues. This is about Jed King."

Shelby laughed. "How do you come up with these conspiracy theories?"

"I saw you looking at the poster outside. Shelby, he's a married man. This is a Christian band. I mean, they play some crossover stuff, but the guy has a reputation."

"So do I," Shelby said.

"You're going to do this, aren't you?"

"I'm following my heart," Shelby said. "I'm letting my passions carry me wherever they will. He doesn't have to respond."

Vivian raised her eyebrows and nodded toward the hallway. "Your passions just walked by in tight jeans and cowboy boots."

"He's here?" Shelby said.

"Whoa, you should see your face right now."

Shelby checked in the mirror, then turned to Vivian and smiled devilishly. "Okay, I'm going to do it." She raised a fist and Vivian winked.

Jed turned as she walked to his dressing room door. He was even more handsome in person than he was in his press photos and videos. He was taller than she thought, not a giant, just a pleasing height, and his beard had grown fuller than the last photo she had seen. He had that chiseled look of a model on romance books, but she knew there was more to him than his looks.

She pulled out a cigarette and caught his eye. He approached the door and put his hand on it as if he were protecting his domain.

"Hi," she said in her little-girl voice. As soon as she heard herself, she regretted saying anything before he did.

"Can I help you?" His tone wasn't gracious. He seemed annoyed more than anything, which took her aback.

She put the cigarette in her mouth and pulled out her lighter. "Well, you actually already have, Jed. I just, um . . . I . . ." She flicked the lighter and saw him staring at the flame. In a gesture of goodwill she handed the cigarette to him and he took it before she held out the lighter for him. But instead of smoking it, he tried to blow out the lighter.

"I don't smoke," he said without smiling. "And I definitely don't sleep with groupies. So—"

She couldn't stifle the laugh, throwing her head back in both shock and amusement at his words. When she composed herself, she said, "I heard you were really religious—"

"I take it you're not."

"I'm spiritual."

"Isn't everybody."

Shelby looked behind her, forming her next phrase, her next introduction. She wanted another chance, another shot at a first impression. "You just have no idea, do you?"

"About what?"

She lowered her voice and took a step closer to him. "You know, normally I would be really, really offended. But you are just so cute. And now I get to have a secret and that's always fun, isn't it?"

She stared into his eyes, into those deep pools that had come up with some amazing songs. And she was sure that there were more inside that heart of his. Better songs. Songs that went deeper than he could ever imagine.

He shook his head and pushed her backward. "Okay. It's good to meet you, whatever your name is—this whole thing is great."

She protested but he closed the door before she could say anything else. And that was Shelby's first meeting with Jed King.

Later, when the applause crescendoed for the band, Vivian yelled, "Did you meet him?"

Shelby nodded and smiled. "It didn't go exactly as planned. He kind of shut the door on me. Thought I was a groupie."

"You are, in a way."

"He had no idea who I was."

Vivian nodded toward the shadows behind the stage as Jed walked up behind his manager. The drums began the next song and the crowd responded to the screaming introduction of "Confetti."

"Show him who you are," Vivian said.

Shelby sang with her usual flair and abandon and her fiddle was on fire—Charlie Daniels had nothing on her tonight. The devil could go on down to Georgia; Shelby had come to Boston and to Jed King.

"Take me, shake me,
And break me into two
Million little pieces
Spread all over you

"I wanna fly up to the roof
And come down when I'm ready
I want my head down to my toes
To feel like confetti."

After their opening set, Shelby looked for Jed to explain and tell him it was okay that he assumed she was a tramp. But Stan headed her off and pulled her behind the stage, speaking over the noise in the hall.

"You give me that kind of energy, that kind of performance every night, and Jed will be opening for you."

She hugged Stan and kissed him on the cheek. "That's sweet of you to say, but I have no designs on showing Jed up. I just want to be the best opening act he's ever had."

CHAPTER 27

ROSE WAS BUSY with Ray, trying to contain his energy, which was a full-time job. She loved the different stages he'd been through, not counting them in years but in things that fascinated him. She had taken pictures of him during his "feet" stage when he'd grab them and hang on. Next came the "mobile" stage and then the toddler months when he focused on standing and wobbling to her before he fell. He transitioned from an obsession with dinosaurs—books, plastic figures, stuffed dinosaurs, dinosaur movies—to the drums. Now he couldn't get enough of playing his father's music on a CD and whaling on the drum set Jed had bought him at one of those warehouse club stores. Jed was rarely home, so it was easy for him—he didn't have to deal with the noise. But Rose was glad for the outlet for Ray, and some of the things he said, some of the ways he mangled the lyrics, were just too cute. She texted Jed some phrases he'd said and recorded them on video to play for him. Finally she had collected so many that she started writing them down in Ray's baby book.

Before the vacation, they had fallen into a pattern of Jed being home for a few days and then being gone for two weeks, and it was honestly becoming harder having Jed home. He didn't respect the routine she had given their son. Jed wanted him to stay up and play, wanted to wake him after he'd gone to sleep—which was great, she loved seeing Jed have fun with Ray, but he didn't seem able to understand the consequences the next day when a sleepy little boy would become cranky because he hadn't gotten enough rest. It was a small price to pay to see the two of them bond over music or games, but Rose began to see Jed's presence as a competition of sorts. Jed would bring Ray candy from the road or the airport where he'd been the night before, while she was trying hard not to reward Ray with food or ruin his diet with a constant barrage of jelly beans and Tootsie Rolls. Once when Jed had taken Ray to a movie, her son had thrown up as soon as he returned and she looked in horror at the red stain on the hardwood.

"He ate a bag of Twizzlers," Jed had said. "I couldn't stop him."

This was exactly the kind of choice a parent had to make for a child, she thought. You didn't buy a big bag of licorice and turn a four-year-old loose. You had to be the one to limit.

But she had to give Jed points for being interested in his son. Some dads didn't change diapers, didn't want to be bothered with the day-to-day stuff of fathering, and Jed seemed to revel in it.

Jed had played Boston the night before and Rose checked her phone in the morning but there was nothing from him. She heard a door slam outside but didn't think much about it until Jed walked in with his overnight bag and a bouquet of flowers. Rose smiled as Ray jumped into his father's arms.

"This is a nice surprise. Did a show get canceled?"

"No, I wish. I fly out tomorrow morning, actually. I'm sorry. I just had to come home, you know?"

Ray looked into Jed's eyes, tried to get him to break his stare with Rose, and finally Jed looked at him.

"Do you wanna be in my band?" Ray said.

Jed gave him that exaggerated face of a doting father. "That's exactly what I want to do. It's why I came home. I'll tell you what, you go upstairs and get that ready, all right?"

Jed put Ray down and he ran up the stairs with abandon as if he'd just won the daddy lottery.

Jed looked tired, but there was something in his eyes as he held out the bouquet to Rose. There was always something in his eyes when he came home.

"These are for you," he said, handing her the pink roses and drawing closer.

"Thank you. Is everything all right?"

Jed kissed her ear and embraced her. "Yeah. I just wanted to be with my wife, you know?"

She did know, but she didn't want to say anything negative about it. She fought the feeling, pushed it down, and playfully looked at him, smiling. "Don't start what you can't finish."

"Nap time?" he said.

That confirmed it for her, that he had come home with one thing on his mind. His need. His desire. And again she pushed the thought down because she was glad he desired her. She was glad he had eyes for her. And she wanted to be there, but what about her needs?

She laughed, covering the thoughts swirling in her head. "No, I'm afraid we've outgrown nap time. I miss it. I'm exhausted." He should have remembered that from the trip to the beach. She looked at him, wanting to tell him everything in her heart with her eyes, wanting him to see through to her soul. "Tonight," she said gently. "I promise."

He smiled and pointed a finger at her. "Tonight. I'm gonna hold you to that."

She rooted around for a vase for the roses and tried to focus on him, his life, his traveling. "You couldn't hold out another couple of weeks, huh?"

When he didn't answer, she looked up and could see it in his eyes. Stan had extended the tour.

"How long this time?"

"Three months." He said it like he regretted the whole thing and was waiting for her to say it was all right, she understood. But Rose couldn't say it. And something deep inside began to swirl, along with the feelings she'd already stuffed.

"Stan added Shelby Bale to the tour." He said it like she ought to know who that was.

"Who?"

He answered, looking at the floor as if it were something he had practiced so he could get it right. So she wouldn't be mad. Like a little boy who had been caught playing the drums too loudly.

"She's just this singer with a cult following. I get her fans, she gets my fans, and we book a lot more shows and make a lot more money."

That stopped her. She looked at him and caught his eyes. "Do you need more money? Or fans?"

"It's not just that, Rose." His voice was soft and comforting, reassuring, but his body language spoke something different. The you-don't-understand-any-of-this posture, which only made her back stiffen.

"Then what?" she said, back to work again, picking up some of Ray's toys and putting them in the toy basket. LEGOs and stuffed animals and figurines that wound up in the oddest places.

"I'm helping people. I know it sounds stupid, but in my own way, I am."

She kept working, kept picking up, kept her hands busy.

"Look, I get e-mails and people coming up to me saying I'm helping their life make sense," he said. "That they were about to give up and they heard one of my songs."

And how about my life? she thought. *How about making my life make sense? How about us being a team together instead of two people growing apart?*

"People are looking for stuff, Rose," he continued, his voice pleading now. "Meaning. Hope. God."

That last one sent her over the edge, though she tried not to show it. He was going to use God to justify his choices? He was going to throw himself into his work and pit her against God?

"If I don't tell them, they're not going to hear it," he said, concluding his sales job. Like she was supposed to buy his vacuum cleaner or supplements or newfangled food processor.

She stopped and looked at him. "Jed, your biggest fan is upstairs, and he needs you a lot more than God does."

It sounded almost blasphemous coming out of her mouth, but it was true. This wasn't about serving God or his family. The two weren't mutually exclusive.

"Bring him," Jed said quickly like he'd been waiting for this response. "And come with me."

"So he can sleep on buses and jets, getting dragged from hotel to hotel? What kind of life is that?"

"It's not a life, Rose. I'm talking about three months." His tone was dismissive, and if she had been pushed off the edge, now she was gaining momentum for the plunge.

"Which will become a year because you won't have a reason to tell Stan no." She was surprised by the speed with which she came up with the argument and threw it at him.

And then she added the coup de grâce. "You'll have me to play groupie."

Now it was Jed's turn to get his back up. "What is that supposed to mean?"

"Feels like you don't come home for me anymore. It's like you come home for . . ."

Sex. She wanted to say *sex*. But she didn't have to. What had been such a beautiful thing between the two of them had slowly become an obligation for her. And for him it was like oxygen. It was why he was back with roses in his hand.

"Let me fix that," he said. He closed the distance between them and his voice grew higher. "Please, I'm trying to fix that. If you come with me, I'd see you every day."

And what does that mean? she thought.

"I'd see Ray every day. We'd spend time together. Please."

So he could play some portable drums with Ray during the day and play with her after the show. No wonder she felt like a toy.

"It's not just Ray, Jed."

As soon as she said it, she saw the recognition on his face.

"What?" He smiled, trying to lighten the mood. "Your dad has a dead bear in his living room, Rose. I'm sure he's gonna be fine. Please."

She couldn't smile, couldn't match his playfulness. What she was saying was serious. "No. He's not doing well, Jed."

He looked at her, his eyes searching for some kind of bridge over the gulf between their hearts.

Ray bounced back into the room clutching two drumsticks

and ready to jam. "Daddy, do you want to be in my band now?"

Jed looked from Ray to Rose. He seemed caught between the two of them. Or maybe caught between something else, she couldn't tell.

"I'm sorry," she said. It was the best she could do.

He touched her shoulder as a gesture of goodwill, as a peace offering. A promise that they would get together in some demilitarized zone later on and hash the problem out and come to a satisfying answer. Jed was the eternal optimist, thinking everything would be all right given enough time and smiles and roses.

"Yeah, buddy," he said to Ray. "Come on. Let's go."

And the two were off, upstairs to their world of guitar and drum solos. After drums there was a board game Ray liked to play. And after that, dinner that Rose prepared. Then Jed let Ray pick out his favorite movie and they watched it from the floor, sitting together with her dozing on the couch. He took Ray upstairs and with the door open, she could hear Jed reading from Ray's children's Bible. He was on the story of Solomon, and Ray kept asking questions about all the mistakes that Solomon made and why he chose against God.

"What did he do?"

"He married a lot of women and they convinced him to do some bad things."

"Like what?"

"Worship golden statues and that kind of thing."

"How many was he supposed to marry?"

"Just one," Jed said. "After that, there's always trouble."

"I want to marry Mom," Ray said.

Rose stifled a laugh and closed her eyes to listen.

"There's rules about that in the Bible too."

"I can't marry Mom?"

"No, she's my wife."

"But you don't live here."

Jed paused for a moment and Rose listened closely.

"Yes, I do. I have to be gone for work for a long time, but then I get to stay home. That's coming soon, okay?"

"Okay."

The conversation continued but Rose drifted off, her sleep sweet on the couch. There was something about falling asleep here that reminded her of her childhood. At the end of her mother's life, Rose would get out of bed and tiptoe downstairs to where she slept, in a bed set up in the living room. Rose would bring a blanket and a pillow and sleep on the couch across from her, sometimes holding her hand.

The next thing she heard was Jed's voice saying, "Rose? Rose?"

She opened her eyes, exhausted, the full weight of the day on her eyelids. It was like lifting fifty-pound dumbbells just getting them open.

"Ray's asleep," he said expectantly, that hungry-tiger look in his eyes.

"I fell asleep," she mumbled.

"Yeah, you did," he laughed.

She couldn't hold her eyes open any longer, so she let

them fall and drifted off, hearing him repeat her name in the distance.

She felt the cover being pulled up around her shoulders and his kiss on her hair. And then she was gone, dreaming of walking along a stream with Jed, skipping rocks and laughing. When she looked up, the stream had turned into a rushing river and Jed was somehow on the other side of the river, standing with his arms crossed, staring at her. That was all she remembered when she awoke, the haunting sight of Jed alone and so far away.

She looked at the window from the couch—it was light outside but still early according to the clock. Thinking she would surprise Jed, Rose crept upstairs to their room only to find the bed empty and his overnight case gone.

Through the window she saw the limo pulling out of the cul-de-sac. He hadn't woken her to say good-bye.

"Mom?" Ray said from his room. "Is Daddy still here?"

"No, Son, he had to leave. I'm sorry."

She heard the drumsticks click together. "Mom, do you want to be in my band?"

CHAPTER 28

THE HUM OF THE PLANE lulled Jed to sleep like it always did. He never had any problems crashing on the plane ride, no matter how short. Over the din of the engines and the game they were playing behind him, he fell asleep. The band members knew better than to wake him.

He felt his chair bump and a voice close to his ear startled him.

"When are you gonna stop being so rude?"

He sat forward and turned to see Shelby Bale hanging over the back of his seat. He'd never seen a nose ring that close before. He'd never heard such a sultry voice.

She reached out a hand. "I'm Shelby."

"I know," Jed said.

"You know now," she said.

Jed put a leg in the aisle and turned farther to face her. She had long brown hair that framed a pretty face. Dimples that showed when she smiled and dark eyelashes. Perfect teeth. Just a hint of perfume. She had tattoos on her arms, and he guessed on other parts of her body, and wore dark fingernail polish. Shelby projected a bad-girl image onstage and in the songs she sang, but there was something equally vulnerable to her style. She didn't seem too "bad" close-up. And certainly not hard on the eyes.

"Why didn't you just tell me who you were?" Jed said.

She shrugged. "Kindness. I was being nice."

"How was that being nice?"

Her smile faded. She was serious now. "For a moment you felt wanted and . . . it's a good feeling, isn't it?"

Jed saw two of his band members glance at him, overhearing Shelby's words. He narrowed his focus on her and tried to think of some comeback. Before he could speak, she pushed away from the seat.

"Unless turning me down was unpleasant. If it was, I'm really sorry. You can let me know how I can make it up to you."

Her voice, her facial expressions, her body language, the way she spoke so close to his ear, all of that let him know she was interested, she was pushing toward him. Or maybe that's just the way Shelby was with everyone. Just her personality.

No matter which was true, Shelby was right. It did feel good to be wanted. It felt good to be pursued.

He watched her walk down the aisle, unable to avert his eyes. She glanced back and smiled when she caught him looking.

The next two nights were a blur, crisscrossing the country in the Gulfstream. He'd have to talk with Stan about a more reasonable tour schedule, but there were rumblings of Europe that would only mean a more grueling travel schedule and more time away from his family. Something had to change.

Jed was onstage in Raleigh, North Carolina, when something did. It happened out of the blue, something he couldn't have predicted or prepared for.

He was singing "All I Wanna Be" in that slow, somber, plaintive voice of his, as if Rose were standing right there in front of him and he were telling her of his desire from the heart.

"What is all this for?
I wonder as I'm walking out our door again.
What is all my talk going to?
When all I want to be is with you.
All I want to be is with you.

"There is nothing that's new under the sun,
I ain't doin' nothing that hasn't been done.
I've let lies be truth to me.
When all I want to be is with you."

When Jed got to the lyric "I want your love, I want your touch," his heart ached as he thought of Rose and how good it felt to hold her. He was lost in those thoughts when the audience responded. The applause felt out of place. He thought perhaps something was happening in the crowd that he hadn't seen, but they were clapping and pointing toward the stage. That's when the violin began a heightened rhythm with a few short strokes of the bow.

We don't have a violin player, Jed thought.

He turned to see Shelby smiling and quickening the pace of the song. Jed was so upset he couldn't see straight. He wanted to scold her for coming onstage during one of his signature ballads, but the band joined her and matched her rhythm, turning the ballad into something different. She was calling the shots with the guys now and he wanted to rein them in, but the music was like a swollen river and he couldn't paddle upstream.

He sang the next verse as she continued to lead the instruments.

"I miss you more with every mile,
I go to bed just to dream of your smile
You're a garden view with a thousand hues
All I want to be is with you.

"And with every good-bye it gets harder to try
When all hope seems lost, the heart just dies.
But there's life if we see this through.
All I want to be is with you."

Shelby played along, underscoring the tune with her violin, and on the next chorus she began singing harmony. It made the sound more full and rich as her voice mingled with his own. In fact, the whole song improved with her presence and Jed knew it now, not just because the crowd was going wild, but also from the feeling he had inside.

When the song was done, Shelby wasn't. She cranked up the tempo with just her violin, coaxing the whole band to follow, and follow they did, the crowd clapping along at a feverish pace.

Jed was in it now, in the rhythm with the guitar and feeling the movement, the life Shelby was bringing to the stage. And what happened was incredible—there was no other way to describe it. Each member grabbed the song and rode it to the end.

When the music stopped, Shelby smiled at him and he hugged her with one arm and said, "Good job." Jed waved as the entire band got up and walked backstage. The crowd was going wild, calling them back for an encore.

"That was awesome," Jed said. "So good."

Shelby couldn't stop smiling. "Thank you."

"I knew you were good, but that was just ridiculous."

Stan came up behind them. "Guys. That was magic. That was absolute wizardry. I need three more months of that, okay? You got it. You can do it."

Jed looked out at the crowd and for a fleeting moment thought of Rose. She was not going to react well to three more months of travel and being away. But the crescendo of the crowd was too great. No way he could stand up to Stan. "All right."

"Perfect!" Stan said, and he was off.

Jed looked at Shelby. "Do you know any more of my songs?"

She gave him a smile, a grin like a Cheshire cat. "I told you, I'm a fan."

"What do you want to play?"

"The one they came to hear," she said.

The crowd jumped up and down as they took the stage and Shelby began the slow melody of "The Song." Jed and the others joined in and Shelby moved toward the microphone.

"Okay, I always thought 'The Song' needed a lady's touch. How 'bout y'all?"

The people at the front pushed toward the stage, hooting and whistling.

Then Jed stepped to the microphone. "That may be true, but I don't see a lady up here right now."

Shelby feigned outrage. "Jed, you just try to sing the song and I'll see what I can do."

The crowd was enjoying their repartee, the back-and-forth of two talented artists at the top of their game.

"I've been waitin' on you to come along,
seeing notes on a page but not the song . . ."

Singing next to Shelby, looking into her eyes, Jed felt something stirring. She was the perfect touch, the oil to the gears of the machine they had going, and he couldn't believe Stan had found her and brought her along.

That night in his hotel room, he thought of Shelby, the way she'd responded to subtle changes in his delivery. The way her violin filled in the missing pieces and took them to another level. And how easy it was to watch her play. There was something about her that drew him and he imagined her coming to his hotel room door and knocking.

He shook the thought away and picked up the phone to call Stan and tell him they should rerecord those two songs with Shelby and put them on a live release. The energy they conveyed was captivating.

"You like her, don't you?" Stan said. "You love what she brings to the stage."

"Absolutely. She's the best thing that's happened to us since . . . since you and I got back together."

Stan laughed. "Can't argue with you there, big boy. You two are creating some buzz. People are taking notice. And I have news. Europe is not just a rumor anymore. I'm booking London, Dublin, Amsterdam, and a whole lot more. We're taking this show to the world. It's gonna be a few months to iron things out, but I can't wait to see you guys set those countries on fire."

With Europe came more travel, of course. And with more travel came the distance between Rose and Ray and him. Jed hung up the phone and stared at the ceiling. There had to be a way to make his marriage work. There had to be a way to keep them growing together.

He pulled up the contact list on his phone and clicked on Home. Then he looked at the clock. It was 2:30 in the morning. No way Rose would be up. And the conversation would just keep her from getting the rest she needed to see Ray through the next day. He put the phone away and made a mental note to call first thing in the morning.

CHAPTER 29

ROSE TUCKED RAY into bed and read him a story from his Bible. He liked David killing Goliath. He liked Noah and the ark and the animals. But most of all he liked Jesus and the stories about him helping people.

"Why did they want to hurt Jesus, Mom?"

"They didn't like what he said. Didn't like it that so many people were following him."

"What did he say that made them so mad?"

"That God was his Father. People back then didn't understand that God could be a daddy to you."

"Like my daddy?"

Rose looked away. It had been a long time since she'd

felt anything but hurt toward Jed. As his career ascended, his heart seemed to be drawn further away from his family, from the things that really mattered. She tried to think of something positive to say.

"Your daddy tries hard to love us," she said. "He's a good provider. And that's what God does, he provides for us."

"But God isn't home very often, is he?"

"That's where things get a little hard to understand. God is always home. He's always waiting for you to come to him. And your daddy wants to be with us, but his job takes him far away."

"Why doesn't he just work at the vineyard like Paw Paw?"

"He could. But God has given him a gift, just like he gave his daddy—your other grandpa you never got to meet. And your daddy wants to use the gifts God gave him."

"His songs, right?"

"That's right."

Ray thought for a minute. "Mom, is it okay if I don't become a drummer?"

She smiled and kissed his forehead. "It's okay with me if you become anything you want to be."

She prayed with him and turned out the light but left the door open a crack so he could see the light from the hall. She must have gotten it right for once because he usually asked for a little bit more light.

Her life had become this day-to-night routine, picking weeds and watering a life. Food and dishes and grocery shopping and staring out the front window. She'd found a ladies'

Bible study just down the street and the women were sweet. When they found out she was Mrs. Jed King, they made a big fuss, but then she became just one of the women. Someone with hurts and struggles like the rest of them. But no matter how good the study, she couldn't bring herself to open up and talk about her real problems. That would somehow betray Jed, she thought.

She headed to the sink as the front door opened and Jed walked in, his beard more full than she had ever seen it. He looked tired and road-weary but she couldn't bring herself to run to him and hug him. There was so much of the past down deep, the best she could do was say, "Welcome home."

"Thank you." He put the suitcase down and came behind her, putting a hand on her waist and leaning in. "Where's Ray?"

"He's asleep."

"Good," he said softly. Gently he brushed the hair from her neck. "Hi."

Rose stiffened. "I'm really tired, Jed." She said it without feeling, without much hope. She tried to communicate something between the lines of her own song, but Jed wasn't listening, wasn't reading the music.

"Me too. I'm exhausted. I've been gone a long time."

She sighed heavily and went back to the dishes. "How long are you home this time?"

He retreated from the kitchen like a hurt puppy. Like a child who'd been told he couldn't have the extra cookie. "The tour was great, Rose. Thanks for asking. I had a great time."

She turned her face to him. "I know how the tour was. I have the Internet. That's how I get to know my husband."

He shot her a glance. "You have the money, too, right?"

"You think that's what I care about?" Her voice was pleading, hurt.

"I think you care about your dad. And I can feel it. Every time I'm lying in bed. By myself."

"Thinking about all *you* care about," she mumbled.

"Rose, if that was all I cared about, I could get it. I wouldn't have to come home."

She stared at him, disbelieving. How could his heart have turned so cold? Who was this man staring at her? "Can we at least talk first? 'Hi, honey. How was your day? How was your year?'"

"Don't exaggerate. Don't act like I haven't seen you all year. Like we don't have this same fight every two or three weeks."

"No, no. Those times, I was trying to get you to do something romantic."

"I was just trying to do something romantic."

"I've had to lower the bar since then . . . you know, ask you to talk or do something else besides just walk in and grab me."

"How awful for you, to feel desired by your spouse. It's a terrible thing."

They were into it now, a full-throttle fight, and Rose could see his body tense. Before he could speak again, she snapped, "Just leave me alone, Jed."

"Forgive my insensitivity, Rose, but I don't have a lot of experience in that recently."

She turned and moved away from him.

His voice rose in intensity and volume. "Maybe you can tell me what that's like."

"Leave me alone, Jed!" she yelled.

And that seemed to bring him to his senses. "I'm sorry," he said. He moved toward her now but she pulled into herself like an injured animal.

"I'm sorry. I shouldn't have said that." He took her hand and looked into her eyes.

Just then Rose heard the sound of small feet padding on the hardwood. She turned to see Ray looking at them from the other end of the kitchen. His face was contorted as if he were trying to understand a story that didn't have a moral to it. A story with a sadly-ever-after ending.

"Baby, come here," she said.

"Hey," Jed said. "Hey, buddy!"

Ray ran to Rose and she picked him up and held him in her arms.

"What's wrong, Mom?" Ray said.

"Nothing, baby. Everything's fine. It's okay. I just miss your daddy." She looked at Jed and for the first time felt like they connected. "That's all. Let's go to bed."

Rose was on her side of the bed, turned away from him, when Jed slipped beneath the covers. There was a Grand

Canyon between them and no words or actions could span the gulf. At least that's what she thought.

"I know I've hurt you. I know you don't want to hear that I'm sorry for the things I've said. I get that. But I have an idea. Let's go to your dad's place. We can leave in the morning, early, and go over there and stay all day. Stay a few days if he'll have us."

"You think that's going to solve everything between me and you?"

"No, I don't think it will solve anything. What it'll do is give us some time together. I think that's what we need. And you need to see that I want more from you than just, you know. Just me grabbing you."

Rose was crying now, wet tears rolling onto her pillow. She didn't want to give him the satisfaction of knowing he'd made her cry like that, so she let them fall without brushing them away.

"I think I'm at a crossroads here," he said. "We've hit this level where everything has come together and we either go to the next plateau or we fall."

"You talking about us or the band?" she said.

"Us. But it applies to the band too." He propped himself up against the headboard and sighed. "Remember that night when I asked for wisdom? When you encouraged me to do that?"

"I remember."

"I feel like God honored that. Like he gave me what I asked for. He gave me you. And he gave me the music that's touching people's hearts. I love what I do. I hate the travel. I hate being away from you. But I love singing my songs and making music that feels like it's changing the world a little."

He rolled over, not touching her, but getting closer. "I'd give it up in a minute if I had to. If it meant I was losing you, I'd give it up totally. But I don't think it has to be either-or. I think we can make this work. I also feel like I've failed at the most important hearts I've been given to reach. Yours and Ray's."

"What are you saying?"

"Come with me to your father's place. Let's pack up Ray and head to the vineyard. I can work on the chapel. Man, it's been so long since I even thought of that place."

Rose rolled over and looked at him. "You mean it?"

"It'll be good for Ray. And Shep too."

"He's been wanting to take Ray to that malt shop in town. The one with the pony ride in the corner."

"It'll be good for us. No agenda. No grabbing."

"I'll believe that when I don't feel it," she said, a little smile on her face. And that coaxed a smile from his.

"Let's do it, Rose. Let's get away. Together."

She rolled back over and stared at the wall. "You think you can get up that early?"

"I'll set my alarm."

They were on the road by six and Rose felt a strange sense of newness with Jed, a sense of hope she hadn't felt in a long time. His words had haunted her all night, though. If she asked him to give up the music and choose their family, would he really do it? Could he? And did she want him to give it up? He came alive when he played his songs. It was as if God were reaching down and giving him something each time he wrote a new song. Did she want to stop that? Could she ask him to give it up?

One of the Bible studies her group had gone through contained a whole section on forgiveness and how important it was. It asked, if we truly possess forgiveness from God, can we give that forgiveness to others? And if you're not ready to forgive another person, can you really say you're ready to be forgiven by God?

These things rolled around her head as they drove to the vineyard. Her father was outside to welcome them—except he only had eyes for Ray. The sullen man who walked through life with a blank expression or a scowl lit up like a Christmas tree when he saw that little boy. He hugged Rose and welcomed Jed, but there was something about that child that opened him up like nothing she had ever seen, and Rose wondered what this had done to his heart, them coming to the vineyard to spend time with him.

"You don't mind if I take him?" her dad said after they were in and settled.

"Maybe you should wait for lunch. He's got his squirt gun out and ready for you."

"We'll let him work up an appetite then," he said. Then he coughed and leaned against the wall for the tenth time that day. Yes, she was counting.

"Daddy, are you sure you're okay?"

"I'm no problem," he said. "Old dogs slow down, you know."

"Old dogs should go to the doctor."

He looked at her with sad eyes. "I'm fine, Rose. Really. Just get me to the malt shop on time."

She smiled and touched his arm. "Make sure that . . ." She was going to ask him to lay off the sugar with Ray. Have him order a fruit smoothie instead of a chocolate malt. All she could think about was the Twizzler episode with Jed. But she bit her tongue. "Make sure you have a good time with him, okay?"

"Just being with you three is a good time for me," he said. Then he coughed again and waved her away when she started to speak.

They worked through the morning clearing some brush from the vineyard, all of them wearing gloves except for Ray, who was in attack mode with his squirt gun. He attacked Shep and Jed and it was fun seeing the men in her life in a playful mood. The way Jed treated Ray, the kindness he showed, the tenderness and caring and easy conversations he had, drew her heart toward them both. It was turning out to be a glorious day.

Ray downed Jed with a perfectly placed shot to the shoulder; then he turned the water gun on a clump of grapes. "I'm making them grow faster," he said.

Rose pulled the gun down and drew Ray close, talking as much to her husband as to her son. "That's not how it works.

If you try to force them, you'll get bad grapes. You gotta be really patient and gentle."

She looked at the fruit of the vine. "Treat 'em right. Give 'em time. And when they're ready, they'll let you know."

"Okay," Ray said.

She turned and glanced at Jed, his bandanna corralling his hair. He smiled and nodded. "Okay," he whispered.

Later, when her dad had gotten his truck started—and that seemed no small feat the way the engine ground and chugged—Rose watched him pull away with her son down the driveway and to the road and out of sight. Something stirred at the sight of them leaving, an emotional tug like she was losing them. Like they might have an accident. Or her dad could have a spell while he was driving and run off the road or into the path of some other car . . . But that was just the fear taking hold. And if she lived her whole life that way, she'd be paralyzed. Love told fear to hit the highway. Perfect love believed the best and acted on the truth and not what might happen.

She looked at the knoll above the pond, where Jed was at work on the chapel. The wood had aged in the years since he first started the framing, but it stood tall and the memories of their wedding came flooding back. The sounds of the wood saw and the hand drill putting screws in the drywall rolled over the vineyard. He was putting the windows in and making progress with the work when she walked up in her dress and her cowboy boots, and the sunlight framed her face with a golden look that she hoped would distract any man from the work of his hands.

She'd brought a bottle of water, and when they locked eyes, she took his hands and poured the water on them, washing them and drying them with a cloth. He was like putty as she pulled him away, into the seclusion and privacy of the vineyard.

Rose thought of the words in Proverbs—*"There are three things that are too amazing for me, four that I do not understand: the way of an eagle in the sky, the way of a snake on a rock, the way of a ship on the high seas, and the way of a man with a young woman."* She lost herself in love and Jed did the same, their bodies expressing what words never could.

When they were spent on each other, Rose looked at the chapel through the vines. "It will look nice when it's done."

"Yeah. I wanted to finish it a long time ago. I'm sorry about that. Life got in the way."

"You'll finish it. I don't doubt that."

"We have so much to do, Rose. So much to build together."

"You've got a good start on the walls. And the roof looks—"

"I'm not talking about the chapel now."

She turned to him.

"Come with me, Rose. Please."

"On the next tour? I'm hoping we can come visit you on the road soon."

"No, not visit. Come with me to Europe."

She thought a moment and the fear crept in again. But it wasn't only fear if you were thinking about the truth. Her father was getting more and more dependent on others. His body was slowing, failing. She needed to be here for him.

"I can't, Jed. You've seen him lately. I can't leave him. Not now."

The birds sang and the sun warmed them in the vineyard rows. She could tell by the look on Jed's face that he was disappointed. And after the way they had just connected, it was hard for him to hear.

"Okay. I understand."

It wasn't the little boy pouting or kicking at the dirt because he didn't get what he wanted. It was the man in him telling her he really did understand. He didn't like the answer and wanted things to be different, but if this was what was important to her, it was important to him. Her father was sick. Jed was going back out on the road. To Europe, no less. She understood the need to travel. He would have to understand her need to care for her father. This was their life, a season, and they both had to work harder at holding on to each other.

Rose nestled under his arm, putting her head on his shoulder, and they both looked at the clouds rolling by as she wondered if the day would ever come when she'd feel they weren't being pulled apart by something.

CHAPTER 30

Shelby pushed for the *Rock & Roots* magazine shoot and article. She brought it up with Stan, who took it to the editors, who agreed it would be a great special edition for the spring. It had also been Shelby who suggested they exploit the "King" theme and take pictures with Jed sitting on a throne. Shelby had picked out the crown and scepter, too, and the dark colors with the gold accents. That color scheme went better with her tattoos, she thought.

She loved the picture they chose for the cover. It was headlined "The Son Also Rises." She sat on the floor with her head laid back against Jed's knee, a somewhat-sultry look on her face while he looked blankly into the camera. She wished she could get him to smile more, but there was something to be said for that somber look. It made him appear more brooding, more vulnerable.

Most of all she loved the equal billing she got with Jed. Her name in big letters beside his. Everything she'd planned, everything she'd hoped for, was coming true. All but one thing. And she was pretty sure that would happen too, if she could be patient. If she didn't force it. If she let it be *his* idea. She could see he wasn't happy. He wasn't all he could be. It would just take a little time to show him what he was missing, and she had time.

The lady writing the article had spent a day with Jed at his father-in-law's vineyard in Kentucky. There were shots with his son, his wife, the chapel Jed had built—or at least tried to build—for their wedding. It was all so cute, so Americana. But the better photos were at the concerts. The screaming fans in subdued light. The sweaty performances of the band. One shot showed Jed and Shelby cheek-to-cheek, eyes closed, singing their hearts out, sweat dripping from their faces. She loved that one. She'd asked for a copy of the photo so she could keep it and the photographer sent it.

"I thought you weren't big on photos," Vivian said when she saw it in Shelby's purse. Shelby had laminated it so it wouldn't bend and wrinkle. "Isn't that what your tattoos are for?"

Shelby rolled her eyes and took a draw on her cigarette, letting the smoke and nicotine reach deep into her lungs. "I guess some are worth keeping."

Vivian opened the magazine and read the story aloud.

"'Jedidiah King, the son of the late David King, makes his home on the outskirts of Louisville, only a half hour from the idyllic vineyard where his wife was born.' You sure you want to mess with that fairy tale?"

"I'm not messing with anything, girl. I'm just being who I am and letting the chips fall."

"Right," Vivian said with an edge to her voice. "I don't know, Shel. This has all the marks of a train wreck."

"What are you talking about? We're on the cover of *Rock & Roots*, for crying out loud."

"You're at the corner of home wrecker and alimony. Look at that face. Look at that sweet little kid. You want to take his daddy away from him?"

Shelby gave her a stare. "Since when did you get all religious on me? Since when did you get all judgmental?"

"I'm neither. I'm just telling you this isn't going to end well. For anybody."

"I'm following my heart, Viv. I'm doing what we've talked about all along. You put positive energy into the universe, you get back positive. And all I'm doing here is moving toward love."

"How is stealing somebody's husband moving toward love?"

"What's with you?" Shelby said, scowling. "You gonna start telling me to stop taking pills? You don't seem to have a problem with that."

"The pills are different. You're not hurting anybody but yourself."

"And you're making money on the side."

"If you'd pay me more, I wouldn't have to work on the side."

Shelby rolled her eyes. "Nice try. Look, you take care of your side business and I'll take care of mine. Okay?"

Vivian was still reading the article. "Did you read this part?" She held her finger to a place in the copy.

Shelby nodded but took the magazine from Vivian. She couldn't help reading it again.

> King and Bale make an unusual pairing. Musically, the duo has bands that play many of the same instruments. But thematically, you can't get much further apart. King's most famous ballad, "The Song," a message-driven melody about the pursuit of a lifelong love, was written on his honeymoon after waking from a dream. He worked out the words and the tune early one morning in a riverfront cabin, then played the song for his new bride when she awakened.
>
> Bale's most famous song is "Confetti," a screaming fiddle tune she wrote on the back of wet cocktail napkins after a night of inebriation and chasing a one-night stand. It's a breathless, cat-on-a-hot-tin-roof song she says is an "existential melody about the longing of the human heart."
>
> "It just kind of came out of me," Bale said from her hotel room on the current tour. "Songs are like

that for me. They come and they go through my brain like wind through the trees. Some of them I catch and some fly by. I'm a big believer that if I'm supposed to sing a song, it'll come around again someday."

How the two teamed up is not quite clear, but manager Stan Russel says they perfectly complement each other. "Shelby is the wild-eyed, free-swinging young thing who throws caution to the wind. Jed is the conservative, laid-back, solid family guy, and audiences love them both as individual artists, but love them together even more. It's kind of hard to explain. It's magic."

In a performance last fall, Bale surprised King by playing along with one of his songs, and the two have been performing together ever since. When asked about a romantic attraction between the two, which some fans say is easy to spot, King smirks and shakes his head, while Bale seems more philosophical.

"Jed would never do anything to jeopardize his image, his beliefs, or his family," she said. "He's not that kind of guy. And everybody respects him for that."

Shelby looked up at Vivian and smiled. "It's there in black-and-white. I respect Jed for his moral . . . What's the word? Dedication?"

Stan walked toward them and pulled his sunglasses up. His eyes were just as red as theirs and he looked like he needed some coffee.

"You ready for some good news?" he said.

"You're lowering your manager's rate?" Shelby said.

"I should be raising my rate. You know that single we released of the live version of 'The Song'? It's going gold. Presentation's next week between the shows in Orlando and Atlanta."

Vivian let out a whoop and Shelby gave her a high five.

"Never had a song go gold before," Shelby said, smiling.

"Technically it's his song, but you gave the momentum, little lady."

"That's Shelby," Vivian said, giving her a look. "The girl with the momentum."

"Momentum that's taking us to Europe," Shelby said.

"And what's left after that?" Vivian said to Stan.

He shrugged. "Who knows? We had a call from a network yesterday asking if Jed might be interested in hosting his own show."

"I hope you included me in the deal."

"Sweetheart, wherever Jed goes, you go."

Shelby couldn't contain her excitement. Maybe that would be how it happened. They'd get together while in Europe, Jed would see how dead-end his marriage was, and when they returned to the States, they'd start the TV show. His fans would have a hard time with him leaving his wife, at first, but he'd pick up others. They would understand a man choosing to follow his heart.

But she couldn't get ahead of herself. She needed to pull back and take things slowly. Get Jed to Europe, away from the familiarity of the States, away from the quick overnight trip home, away from Rose and his son. That would be her best opportunity to help him move forward, move toward her.

CHAPTER 31

THE FLIGHT TO GLASGOW, for the first leg of the European tour, was exhausting for Jed. They left in the afternoon and were to arrive early in the morning. He had bought a sleeping mask to block out the light because in the past few weeks he'd been unable to sleep on the plane like usual. But the mask and the neck pillow and the glass of wine he had with dinner didn't help. His mind was busy with the tour, Rose and Ray, and how much he was missing.

Way back Pastor Bingham had encouraged him to find a friend, someone to help him walk the straight and narrow. He hadn't, of course. He told himself it was just the way a man of the cloth looked at life. The pastor had no idea how hard it was when you were on the road to find someone who could fill that role. It was next to impossible and a whole lot easier to talk about than to actually accomplish. So, too, was reading the Bible. The daily rigors of life on the road and practicing and playing had made reading a chore, and Jed thought he'd get back to it as soon as life settled. He'd get back on solid ground. That would be the first thing he would do after the success of the tour.

He put all of that out of his mind and turned his thoughts to Rose. She was right about her dad. The man was slowing down. And it made sense for her to be there. If Jed could go back and have the chance to spend more time with his own dad, he would take it in a minute. But even slower, Shep was still as strong as an ox and would probably outlive them both. At least that's what he hoped.

If Rose had said yes to coming on the trip, they could be together, emotionally and physically. They could connect, but he questioned how much "connection" she needed. Would they always be at odds about this? Would he always be made to feel dirty simply because he wanted to be with his wife? Making love wasn't something perverted, it was holy, as they'd experienced in the vineyard. So why did he feel like he was asking too much when God had wired him this way?

When he got into these twisted arguments with himself, he tried to use the energy for something good, like writing a song. He pulled out the latest electronic gadget he had bought for that purpose and let the ideas flow. Phrases, ideas, concepts. The best songs, like the best stories, had some element of pain to them that connected with the hearer. They also had an element of hope because everybody wants to be able to hope that something in life is going to get better.

He was hearing a melody, but it was a little bold, a little brash, like one of those angry songs by younger artists wanting to be noticed. *Look at me, I'm angry at something.* That wasn't the feel he wanted. Not the tone he wanted to project with his music.

"Whatcha working on?" Shelby said, brushing against him and leaning over his shoulder.

From anyone else he would have felt it an intrusion, but working as closely as they had the past few months, it was okay. It was how Shelby was—in your face. She wore everything on the surface, like the tattoos on her arms and back.

"Just an idea for a song," he said, turning off the device.

"No, let me see. Maybe I can help. Some of the best songs are cowritten, you know. One person has an idea, you put two heads together, and you come up with something better. I'll work on the chorus while you work on the verses."

"It usually doesn't work that way with me."

"Have you ever tried?"

"Not really."

"Have you ever sung 'Turn Around Fast'?"

"Yeah, sure. The Transom, right?"

"Story goes that Sully, the lead singer, had a verse he was working on and Glenn Sincher asked him if he could help. Sully said no, put him off, put him off. Finally he gave it to him and Glenn finished it and the rest is history."

"You think that'll happen with you?"

"I think we'll never know unless you let me see it. Come on, what's it going to hurt?"

Shelby inched around and asked Johnny Paugh, Jed's drummer, if they could switch seats. "We're writing a song," she said.

Johnny raised his eyebrows and scooted toward the back.

"I really don't feel right about sharing this one, Shelby. Not yet."

She puckered her face in a cute, pouty way, like a kid whose lollipop just fell in the sand. "Must have something to do with the marital act, then. Right?"

How did she know that? Jed thought.

"You're blushing," Shelby said, laughing too loud for the subdued flight and the time of night. She lowered her voice and leaned toward him. "Okay, far be it from me to intrude on your bedroom. Or wherever it is you two . . ."

He almost told her about the vineyard but held back from sharing such personal information. You had to draw a line somewhere.

"Where? The laundry room? The kitchen? Your secret's safe with me, Jed."

He turned toward the window and saw his reflection. His eyes looked hollow in this light, even to himself.

"The vineyard," he said, turning back to her.

"Outside? I knew Christians could be back-to-nature kind of people, but I didn't know you'd go that far."

"That's never happened before," he said, feeling bad about revealing something so intimate. "But it was nice."

"I'm glad," she said. "I've heard that's one of the first things to go after children. You know, the desire and everything. 'All I want to be is with you' becomes 'All I've got tonight is a headache.' So good for you."

He didn't say anything and she seemed to pick up on his silence. Finally she said, "I've been working on something too. It's about this girl looking for love in all the wrong places. She gets hurt a few times. Gets angry. Tries to get even. She pours herself into her work, her art . . ."

"How does it end?"

Shelby leaned over the armrest. "She meets somebody really special. Somebody really different from her. And he gives her hope, even though he doesn't know it. But . . ."

"But what?"

"He's off-limits. So the whole thing is . . . What's the word?"

"*Unrequited*?"

"Yeah. Or maybe *forbidden*." She smiled sheepishly.

"Hey, don't feel bad you couldn't remember it. You used *existential* in the *Rock & Roots* interview. That was impressive."

"You read that?"

"Of course."

"And what did you think?"

"There were a couple of factual errors about my dad, but it was pretty good. Can't complain about the publicity."

"Stan says even bad publicity is good."

"I don't know about that," he said. "Show me your song."

"I'll show you mine if you show me yours." She winked.

He grinned and shook his head. "Maybe some other time. But keep writing. You have real talent."

Shelby grabbed her purse and pulled out some lip gloss. Jed saw a prescription bottle and pointed at it. "You don't have some serious illness you're fighting, do you?"

She jammed the bottle deep into her purse. "No, just the normal stuff. Sometimes I can't sleep. Sometimes I'm too wired. These just help."

"You should be careful with that kind of help."

"Don't worry about me, Jed. Things are under control."

He looked out the window at the darkness and the blinking plane lights. In the reflection he saw Shelby get up and leave. Part of him felt relieved. Part of him wanted her to stay.

In Glasgow the next night they sounded amazing together. The whole group did, both bands, but particularly Jed and Shelby. The houses were packed with a younger audience that clapped and screamed and sang along with every song. The sound, the lighting, the nearness of the fans—it all worked and Jed fed off the electricity in the room, fed off the chemistry between Shelby and him. He couldn't imagine them sounding better.

But the next concert in Dublin was just that, better. And their concert in London took things to another level. At the end, as they performed their finale, "The Song," Jed and Shelby sang, "Love is the power that heals."

The response rose to a crescendo and someone screamed

to Jed's left. He saw the fan break through security just before she tackled him.

"I love you," she shrieked as two guards grabbed her and pulled her away. "I want you, Jed! I love you! Your songs mean so much to me! Don't let them take me away!"

While she kept screaming over the applause, Jed looked at Shelby. She convulsed with laughter.

Jed shook the event off and waved at the audience before going backstage. Stan was elated. The band was stoked. Shelby was on some cloud enjoying the response. But Jed felt an emptiness and a hunger he couldn't explain and that no amount of adoring fans could fill.

He decided that what he needed was a good night's sleep and then he would get back to performing. He tried to convince himself that would take away the questions and the ache inside.

CHAPTER 32

ROSE AND RAY ARRIVED at the vineyard before noon to eat lunch with her dad. They brought a picnic basket filled with Ray's favorites. Peanut butter and banana sandwiches, carrot and celery sticks with peanut butter, honey and peanut butter and crackers. Ray was definitely partial to peanut butter and she would have loved to give him as much as he wanted, but for some reason the smell of the crunchy stuff turned her stomach these days. That hadn't happened since . . . well, for a long time.

As she drove, Ray nodded off and she turned the radio on low. One of Jed's songs came on and she smiled. He'd come a long way from being the only act at their festival. And it seemed like there was no stopping him or slowing him down.

He understood about her dad; she really believed he did.

But he still had the hurt look on his face when he drove away, like she should be coming with him to Europe. She decided she could either live feeling guilty or she could live fully, and she chose the latter.

She knocked on the screen door when she got to the house and called for her dad. There was no sound inside. Ray ran to the tire swing in the front yard, the same one her mother had watched her on until the day she died.

"Daddy?" The screen door creaked when she opened it and she set the basket of food down, then peeked into his office, half-expecting him to be slumped over his desk in that big chair, but he wasn't there. She looked closely at the floor, where all the animals prowled.

"Daddy?"

She walked through the kitchen and looked out the back window, thinking he might be in the barn, but she saw no movement except wind in the trees.

She found him in the living room, in his favorite chair with an afghan tossed haphazardly over his legs. He was still and lifeless and she didn't want to touch him because she knew his skin would feel cold. Just before she lost it and burst out crying, his eyes opened and he looked at her as if he was expecting someone else.

"Rose?"

She smiled, wiping away a tear. "Didn't you hear me calling you?"

"I heard something but figured it was the wind." He struggled to get up. "Where's Ray?"

"He's outside on the swing. Stay where you are. You look tired."

"Just came in for a little nap after my chores." He sat up and put three fingers to his chest and winced, then burped. His breathing seemed labored like he was trying to pull air out of a deflated tire.

"How do you feel, Daddy?"

"With my fingers. How do you feel?"

She gave him a glare.

"I've seen better days. But better days are ahead, too." He scooted to the edge of the chair and sighed. "I had a dream. Just as clear as a bell."

"What was it?"

"Your mama was sitting there at the window. Looking out at Ray. Telling me what I ought to do like she always did."

"She cared more about you than you did."

"That's a fact."

Ray came bursting through the door and found them in the living room. Her dad enveloped the ball of energy and brought him onto his lap.

"We're going to have a picnic!" Ray said.

"A picnic? That sounds like a great idea."

"You hungry, Paw Paw?"

"I was born hungry," he said, laughing. Then he coughed and wheezed a little and Rose sent Ray to wash his hands.

"You sure you're all right?" Rose said.

"You worry too much. Relax, okay?"

They took the basket to the picnic table outside and Ray

served his grandfather all the food he enjoyed. Her dad told Ray a story about saving Rose's life from a snake she found near the pumpkin patch one year.

"Was it big enough to eat her?" Ray said.

"Big enough to bite her little toe, but that's about it. It was a garter snake. Just out minding his own business and here came Rose."

"I thought I was going to die," she said.

"But the fearless father came to the rescue!" He held up his celery stick like it was a sword.

"Did you kill it, Paw Paw?"

"No, you don't want to kill something so good for your garden. I pulled Rose out of the way and let Mr. Garter Snake slither off."

"I would have killed it for you, Mama," Ray said.

Rose laughed and they talked more about old times. Ray ran back to the swing with a sandwich in his hand and honey on his cheeks. There was a time when she couldn't stand having his face dirty, but now she let it go. He'd get clean eventually.

"Is Jed playing tonight?"

Rose nodded. "London."

"Any part of you wish you were over there? Sightseeing? Spending time together?"

"That day will come," she said.

"I hope you didn't stay around here because of me."

"I stayed around here because this is where we live, Dad. The road is no place to try and raise a rambunctious child like that."

"It does help to have a big backyard, don't it?" he said, grinning. Then he turned serious. "I just don't want you two to grow apart. To stay apart for too long."

"Now who's the worrywart?" she said, packing things away. "Things are good, Dad. Not perfect, but good."

"I'm glad to hear it," he said. "Because I'd like to tell you about something I've decided."

"What's that?"

"I redid my will the other day."

"Dad."

"No, let me tell you. I'd let it go for a long time. Your mother was still in it." He smiled and looked at the house.

"What are you thinking?" Rose said.

"The joke your mother used to tell about the little boy in Sunday school. Teacher at the country church asked the kids who wanted to go to heaven and everybody raised their hands except little Johnny. 'Johnny, don't you want to go to heaven?' Little Johnny nodded and said, 'I do. I just thought you were gettin' up a load to go now.'"

Rose laughed, remembering the stories and jokes around the kitchen table when she was young. Family and friends just stopping by without calling.

"Anyway, I updated the will to reflect things as they are now. And I made you the executor."

She let the news sink in.

"It means you decide what happens to the house and the land and the vineyard."

"I know what it means."

"Your brothers are going to want to sell the place as fast as they can. I want you to do what's right with it."

"Daddy, that's not going to be easy, especially with how headstrong—"

"I know they're stubborn. They take after your mother." His eyes twinkled. "But you care about this place. If you and Jed want to move here and keep the place up, you can sell some of the bottomland and let the boys split that. If you don't want to live here, you'll sell it to the right person who will take care of it. This is not gonna happen anytime soon, mind you. I'm just making preparations."

She felt sad at first, and angry in a way, that her dad would bring up such a morbid thing at a picnic. But at least he was finally talking and not waiting until it was too late. Her mom had been sick and they'd known the end was coming, but still they had no idea what she wanted to be buried in or what songs she wanted at the funeral. It was because her dad had hung on to the stubborn belief that she would miraculously get better. She would beat cancer and everything would keep going like it always did. Her father had always seemed strong to her, like he could handle anything, but looking back, she could see how scared he was and what that fear did to him.

After lunch her dad took another nap. He said he just wasn't feeling right. Rose took Ray to show him off to some old friends in town and it was in Wilkerson's Grocery (which had become Kroger, but she'd known it as Wilkerson's since she was little) that she ran into Eddie in frozen foods. The irony was not lost on her. She hadn't seen him since the harvest festival episode with Jed, more than six years ago. He was wearing a gray uniform and unpacking frozen dinners, and when he saw her, his face both lit up and fell.

"Hey, Rosie," Eddie said. "This your little guy?" He leaned down and touched Ray's cheek with his gloved hand.

"This is Ray."

"Ray," Eddie said as if he would try to remember it. "How old are you, buddy?"

"Four," Ray said, then buried his face in Rose's skirt.

Eddie stood and looked Rose up and down. "You know, a lot of women get married, have a kid or two, and just let themselves go. You must work out."

"I spend most of my time chasing him," she said. "That's good exercise."

"How's Jed?"

"He's doing well. The tour is in Europe right now."

"I've heard. Him and Shelby Bale are tearin' it up."

"How about you, Eddie?" she said, turning the tide toward him.

"I'm okay. Just working at this job until I can find something in my sweet spot. Temporary, you know."

"Sure. And did things work out with Kristen?"

His face contorted in thought. "Kristen? Oh no, that didn't work. I'm just waitin' for the right one to come along. Again."

She blushed and Ray tugged on her skirt. "Mama, can we go?"

"We'd better get going," she said. "My dad will be expecting us."

"Listen, before you go. What happened between us. I kick myself for treatin' you how I did."

"I appreciate you saying that, Eddie."

"And if there's ever a way to make it up to you . . ."

"Mama, let's go."

"We'll let you get back to your job. It was nice seeing you, Eddie."

"Nice seeing you, too, Rosie."

She didn't look back at him as they checked out, but she could feel him looking at her, wondering, *What if?*

Rose made an early dinner for the three of them before her dad gave Ray a refresher on checkers. Ray seemed to like "jump your own man" the best, and her dad took it easy on him. After they had eaten, they skipped rocks on the pond, then cut back through the vineyard. Her dad took the gloves out of his pocket when he saw a patch of weeds he didn't like. He found a hoe and went to work while Ray pulled a fruit cocktail bowl from his back pocket.

"We just had dinner," Rose said.

"I know, but I'm hungry."

She opened it for him and he took a drink, then pointed at the chapel.

"Daddy's going to finish that when he gets back, right?"

"That's what he says," Rose said.

"Can we move there?"

"No, that's a chapel. It's like a church. It's where your dad and I were married."

"Cool." Ray took another slurp and then laughed.

"What's so funny?" Rose said.

"Paw Paw. Look at him. He's pretending."

Rose looked back and saw her father pitch forward into the vines, grasping for something to hold on to. Then he fell backward to the ground, his face ashen.

Rose rushed to him and fell to her knees beside him. "Daddy!"

She felt for a pulse and thought of doing chest compressions, but her father's eyes were open and fixed and there was no breath in him. She glanced back at Ray where he stood, openmouthed, watching as she screamed and wept.

Her cell phone. Where did she put her cell phone? It was back at the house. She ran, then turned back to grab Ray and he spilled his fruit cocktail and began to cry. Rose ran, crying too and trying to carry him, but he was getting bigger.

If only Jed were here, she thought. She'd been right about her father. He wasn't well. And she hated that her husband was a million miles away.

She made it to the house and dialed 911. The operator said an ambulance was on its way. Rose took Ray by the hand, got her cell phone, and went back up the hill, hoping her father might be sitting up, might have rallied, but he was still lying there when they reached him.

"Is he dead, Mama?" Ray said.

"I don't know. I don't know."

She dialed Jed. There was a five-hour time difference, but she didn't care where he was or what he was doing. She needed to hear his voice.

CHAPTER 33

SHELBY CHOSE AN OLD PUB across the street from their hotel for after the concert and the band basically took it over. There were a few other patrons there, but things thinned out soon after they arrived. Shelby could tell Jed tagged along out of a sense of duty and camaraderie. The band was a living, breathing organism, a team, and the more you did to foster that, the better they grew together and fed off each other. But Jed seemed to dislike the late-night meals, probably because they kept him up even later and it was clear that drinking wasn't his thing. He'd have a glass of wine, but that was it, although Shelby was on a mission to change that.

She couldn't understand why he didn't like to have fun. Was there something in the Bible about it? Maybe the fact that Jed's father had been a hard drinker at one point clouded his choices, or there could be something more. But from what Shelby had read about the story, if his dad hadn't had the affair, Jed would never have come along. So in some weird, cosmic way, God could use even that to bring about something good. Of course, Shelby preferred to think of it in terms of karma or just the luck of the draw. But if Jed wanted to believe there was some divine force that cared about him, she was content to let him.

Shelby felt Jed's eyes on her from the back of the room as she lined up a row of shots on the bar. Vivian went first and the crowd cheered when she drank the last one. Jed's drummer, Johnny, followed, but only got five down before he stopped.

Shelby patted him on the back. "That's not a bad first try."

Then it was her turn and she showed them how it was done. A roar rose when she downed the last one and she pumped her fist in the air, laughing and feeling totally alive, totally on fire. Feeling the momentum of the performance and the team together and all the shows they had done in order to get to this place, this success, this celebration.

She looked at Jed across the room and saw his melancholy face. Something inside her ached for him. And her instinct told her this was her chance to break through. This night.

She picked up a cigarette and took a pull, feeling the nicotine mix reach deep into her lungs.

"All right! Okay! Shut up, people!" she said, quieting the crowd. "Uh, Mr. King? It's your turn."

Jed waved her away. "I'm good."

The band cheered as she approached him, a shot in her hand. She looked at Vivian, tongue firmly planted in her cheek. "So I think he's adding drinking to the list of things he's only done with his wife."

Their friends laughed and egged her on.

"You guys, he has got a vineyard back home. A vineyard! Because he knows when he gets home and walks through his big front door, he can have all the wine he wants."

She was next to Jed now and only he could hear her. "Am I right?"

Jed stared at her, his face, his eyes, saying everything. "No."

Shelby studied him and took another puff of her cigarette, trying to understand all that he was saying. Quietly she said, "Are you serious?"

Jed didn't respond, just looked down.

"Okay," she whispered, hearing the concern in her voice. "I'm sorry. I didn't know. I just . . . I hate seeing you like this and I wanted you to have a really good time. Enjoy it."

With resolve and the rest of the room behind her, she coaxed Jed one more time. "Are there not shots on the bar? I think there are shots on the bar."

Jed's team responded with cheers and applause. Jed looked at Shelby, then broke into a sheepish smile.

"All I'm saying is, you've earned it," Shelby said, trying to get him the rest of the way to his feet.

Jed slapped his hand down on the table with resolve and stood, and the room went wild. Stan was already wasted and

Vivian looked at Shelby with wide, bloodshot eyes. Viv was the one who began the chant of "Jed! Jed! Jed!" Shelby and the others joined in and the bartender beamed, knowing this was going to be a very good night.

Jed reached the bar and raised the first shot glass. "Ladies and gentlemen, I think we owe it to Miss Shelby Bale this evening. Give it up!"

Hoots, hollers, cheers, and the unintelligible sounds of inebriated voices in unison followed.

"This one's for my boys, ladies and gentlemen!" Jed yelled.

Shelby stood back and let it happen as if she weren't trying to pull the strings, as if she weren't loving every second. She noticed a light in her peripheral vision. On Jed's table a phone vibrated. Rose's image flashed on the screen, Jed's son next to her, sunlight behind them. It was such a pretty picture, a pretty little family. So idyllic. Shelby hit the side of the phone to decline the call.

Jed slammed the next drink back and the noise in the room grew louder. He threw back the fourth and fifth and shook his head at the sting. The room was electric now and out of control.

Shelby slipped the phone into her pocket and took another puff from her cigarette as Jed continued down the row, slamming more shots, rising to the sound of the people around him as if he were onstage somewhere.

The phone vibrated. Rose again. Shelby hit the Decline button and shoved the phone in her purse.

Jed downed the last shot and steadied himself against the

bar, then threw his arms into the air and shouted in victory. Everyone joined him in celebration. He actually looked happy. Joyous. And he was on his way to becoming quite drunk.

Vivian came to her. "Congratulations. I think you've officially loosened him up."

"Should be an interesting night," Shelby said.

Vivian smiled. "You have to tell me all about it tomorrow." She looked at the clock. "Well, later today."

A song line came to Shelby. *"Deep dark sky, so black so bright, all curtains back tonight. I'm obsessed, I must confess, I don't care if it's wrong or right."*

There would be nothing hidden or forbidden between them. Nothing would ever be the same after tonight. Jed belonged to her.

CHAPTER 34

JED WASN'T STUMBLING down the hall like a few of the guys, but the room numbers on the fifth floor were floating in his vision. It was an interesting sensation that he'd felt only a couple of times. Once when he was a teenager with some friends at a party and another time at a bar where he was playing before he got married. His set kept getting pushed back and by the time he took the stage, he could barely walk. Both times he swore he would never use alcohol that way again.

And here he was, walking down the hallway with Shelby close to him and the others retreating to their rooms. She was laughing and there was no tension in the air, just freedom. And it felt good to feel free.

When they reached room 539, Shelby turned and leaned on the door. "So did you have a good time?"

"I really did. Thank you."

"Thank *you*. Now I get to scratch 'visit England' off my to-do list."

"Was that right after 'get a whole lot of tattoos'? That's something I've been noticing—you have one or two."

"It was after 'meet Jed King.'"

He took her hand and turned it over, looking at the tattoos on her arm, and something inside ignited. Maybe it was the liquor. Maybe it was the forbidden nature of being alone in a hotel together in a situation he should never have been in. The truth was, the excitement, the tingles she gave him, felt good.

"Seriously, what's the story with these?"

"Just my way of preserving memories, I guess."

"You should try scrapbooking."

"Scrapbooking?"

"It seems more . . . prudent." When he said the word *prudent*, he stumbled a little.

"Yeah, prudent. But it kills memories."

"It kills memories?"

"It's a fact. A photo replaces the memory in your mind." Shelby looked at her arm. "I see these, and memories just come flooding back, you know?"

"So you don't regret any of them."

The word *regret* seemed to do something to her, like lighting a flame in her mind. Her lips were wet and inviting as he stared at her. Those big eyes boring into his soul. "Feeling regret and guilt is like punching yourself in the face. Sure, it hurts. But it's self-inflicted. So don't do it."

"That's how I feel about tattoos."

She lowered her voice even more. "All I'm saying is, do what you want. And don't feel guilty about it."

She held his gaze, then glanced at his lips and let the words hang there. Jed thought about them. That could be a song. *Do what you want and don't feel guilty. Live life the way you want and taste the world.* Something like that. *Bite into some fruit and don't worry about where all the juice will go.* It felt like freedom. That's what Shelby was pulling him toward. And the pull was strong. Stronger than anything he had ever felt before.

Shelby put her key in the door, opened it, and walked inside. She turned and said, "Night, Jed," and let go of the door.

Just before it closed, he put out a hand and stopped it. He pushed it open to see her standing there, waiting for him as if she expected this, as if she had planned it. When he walked inside, the door closed tightly and they were alone. She smiled and embraced him. And when their lips met, it was like a forest fire ignited in his soul.

There was an old preacher Jed had heard on the radio who talked about the difference between love and lust. Love gives while lust takes. Sin feels thrilling for a time, and then it starts its killing work.

This ran through his mind as he kissed Shelby deeper and

deeper. Something way back in a corner of his heart screamed, *Run, get out, open the door and don't stop moving until you're in your own room, the door locked behind you.* But he couldn't move anywhere except toward this woman. She was offering herself with no strings. Willing. Open. Rose had been closed to him for so long and here was Shelby, ready and waiting.

Then all the chemistry onstage spilled into that hotel room. All the teasing and innuendo and side glances, all the brushes Shelby had given him on the plane and as they were in elevators—this was the culmination of all those innocent touches and words and it felt good to Jed to finally be doing something about it. And they were alone.

What Shelby said in the hallway about guilt made sense. Why not just do what you wanted? Why not act on the ache inside? But there was also a voice off in the distance telling him it wasn't too late. He could salvage what was left of his integrity . . .

Who was he kidding? It was too late. With the first kiss he was gone. It was as if he were on the edge of a waterfall and the current was pulling him over and into the depths of the flood.

Through the night, he had to keep telling himself not to feel guilty. That this was just him searching for life in the middle of all the toil of chasing after a living and a career. And when that didn't work, he blamed Rose. If she had come with him, this wouldn't have happened. If she hadn't said no to him all those times when he ached for her, he wouldn't have fallen.

He knew deep down that wasn't true. It wasn't her fault. But as the weight of what he had done came down on him, Shelby was there to pull him underwater again.

Jed awoke with a pounding headache and light in his eyes. He heard the snapping of a medicine bottle in the bathroom and the buzz of a cell phone. Then Shelby appeared in the doorway, wearing a robe with some kind of weird design on the back, like a kimono. Soft and silky. Her face looked different without makeup.

"Hey," she said in that little-girl voice. Like she was proud of what they had done. "Good morning."

"What time is it?" he said.

"It is 1:15."

Jed threw back the covers and grabbed his pants.

She sat on the bed and pulled her legs to herself. "You okay?" she said, tossing a cell phone on the bed.

"Yeah. You?" he said. "You can take that call if you want."

She smiled, an emotion on her face he couldn't decipher. Guilt? But Shelby didn't live with guilt.

"Actually, it's yours. I'm sorry. I grabbed it for you because you left it at the bar and obviously forgot to give it back to you. . . ."

Jed took the phone and saw multiple calls from Rose. "Whoa," he said, his heart shrinking. She'd been trying to reach him for hours. She'd been trying all night while he . . .

"Jed, I'm sorry," Shelby said. "I feel terrible."

"It's okay; it's not your fault," Jed said, forcing a smile. "I should call her back, though."

"Yeah." Shelby nodded her understanding, but the look on her face said she didn't want him to leave. The look asked him to stay for more of what they'd experienced in the heat of the night.

Jed grabbed his clothes and opened the door. "See you later, okay?" He looked back at her on the bed, knees drawn to her chest.

In his room, sitting on a bed he hadn't slept in, he dialed home and heard Rose's voice. Fear and pain came through the line.

"Jed?" she sobbed.

"Hey," he said weakly. What did you say to a wife you had betrayed?

"Where were you?"

The question stabbed him. He closed his eyes and tried to forget what he had done. Maybe it hadn't happened. Maybe it was all a dream. Maybe he could blame it on the alcohol.

"I've been trying to get ahold of you all night."

He wanted to tell her something. That he was asleep. He'd fallen into a deep sleep and hadn't heard the phone. Or that someone had picked up his phone by accident. Maybe that could work. But he had to be careful because covering your tracks with your words was a tricky thing and he didn't have much experience.

He sat there listening to her cry, the panic in her voice. At first he wondered if she knew, if she'd awoken from a dream and sensed a shift in the tectonic plates of their marriage.

"Where have you been, Jed?"

"Rose, what's wrong? What happened?"

"I called your room like fifty times." And then the sobbing and wailing overcame her and he thought it was about him. He thought their problems had boiled to the surface with her catching him in . . . He couldn't even bring himself to think of the word.

"He's gone, Jed," Rose said.

That jolted him back to life. "Who's gone? What are you talking about?"

Weeping. Gasping for air.

"Did something happen to Ray?" He ran a hand through his hair and cursed that he was so far away.

"No, it's not Ray. It's my dad. He's gone."

"How? What happened?"

And Rose began the story about being at the house with Ray and coming through the vineyard, her dad clutching his chest and falling. Jed closed his eyes and listened. She had been right. His health was failing all this time. But the news suddenly took the pressure off of his "indiscretion" and he interrupted her.

"Rose, I'll get there as fast as I can, okay?"

Her crying stopped. "You're coming home?"

"Of course I'm coming home. Let me call Stan and have them get the pilot and the plane ready. I'll call you from the airport."

"Jed, it was terrible. Watching him slip away. And having Ray there."

"I'm so sorry. I'll get there as fast as I can, okay? Just hold on."

Jed tried to sleep on the plane, but when he couldn't and when the pounding in his head increased, he asked for a drink. Something hard. Something that would take the edge off the pain.

Stan was great about the emergency. They'd have to cancel their next few shows, but it was clear Jed needed to get home and be with his family. He wanted to be there, wanted to comfort Rose and be with Ray, but already he was wondering if she'd be able to tell. Did women have some kind of innate ability to decipher unfaithfulness? He wouldn't fall that way again. He would be resolved never to put himself in that position. It was a one-time thing and nobody had to know.

The rest of the week was a blur with Rose's family gathering to say good-bye. They had her father's viewing at the vineyard instead of the funeral home, and Ray clung to Jed throughout the evening. Staying at the house was what Shep had put in his will, the same way his parents had been viewed. But the whole thing felt awkward, with family members and friends in the community bringing food that would never be eaten and standing around saying things to Rose like "He's in a better place now" and "God must have needed him more than we did."

The paramedics who worked on her dad came and Jed

thought that was nice of them. But some others came wanting to see Jed. Fans who wanted to get a look at him close-up. A middle-aged woman made her way through the line and when she got to him, she held out a Sharpie and the memorial page for Shep and whispered, "My daughter is the biggest fan. Could you just sign this for her?"

Jed's first reaction was to sign the thing and not make a scene, but the look of horror on Rose's face made him reach out and put an arm around the woman and lead her to the door. "I don't think that would be appropriate right now, ma'am. You tell your daughter I'm grateful, though."

The woman was apologetic as she walked to the car, then turned and took a picture of Jed standing in the doorway.

Eddie Edwards also came through the line, paying his respects. He shook Jed's hand and hugged Rose. "I'm real sorry about your loss. Your dad was a good man."

The whole thing surprised Jed but also gave him a little hope that Eddie might have matured in the past few years. Or maybe he thought Rose would be alone and he could comfort her while Jed was on tour. Jed pushed the thought away and focused on Ray. He could tell the boy was getting tired, so he took him upstairs to a spare bedroom to rest.

"It's weird seeing Paw Paw like that," Ray said.

"Mom said you were there in the vineyard when it happened."

Ray nodded. "I thought it was funny. I thought Paw Paw was playing a trick."

Jed hugged his son. "It's okay."

"Mama couldn't stop crying."

"I know. We just need to give her some time. Let her grieve."

There was a commotion in the hallway outside the room, voices whispering in angry tones. Jed told Ray to just rest, that he'd be right back, and the boy nodded.

In the hallway he found Rose's brothers holding a document.

"Did you know about this?" Zack said to Jed.

He took the paper and saw it was Shep's will.

"He made Rose the executor," Will said. "She makes the call on the property."

Jed handed it back. "Guys, you should hash this out after the funeral, okay?"

The two were clearly upset with him, but Jed slipped back into the bedroom and found Ray asleep. He sat on the floor and put his head in his hands. He needed something to drink.

The grave was dug beside Shep's wife on the hillside overlooking the pond. It was a cool day, and Pastor Bingham stood before them, a comforting figure in their time of grief.

"Shep would have loved this day," Pastor Bingham said. "He loved the outdoors. He loved the vineyard. The way it changed through the seasons. He loved the spring and summer and fall—the harvest. He loved being with nature and cherishing the gifts God has given us."

Jed found the spot where they had buried the old dog, Duke, a few years back. It had been a turning point, of sorts, in their relationship, Jed thought. Shep had always seemed a little suspicious of him. But when Duke had been put down and Jed walked through that with him, and then when Ray had come along, all of those fears had gone from the man. Perhaps he shouldn't have been so trusting after all, Jed thought.

Pastor Bingham looked at Jed as if he knew something was wrong. He took a breath and said, "A wise man once wrote, 'There is a time for everything, and a season for every activity under the heavens: a time to be born and a time to die, a time to plant and a time to uproot.' And that time has come not just for Shepherd, but for us as well. It is time to say good-bye to our friend and enjoy the harvest of a life well lived. It is time to give back to our Maker one of his finest creations. One of his most beautiful creations. A hard-working, life-loving, faithful husband and father."

The words cut Jed to the core. *"Faithful husband and father."* He shook them off and helped Rose make it through the rest of the service.

When everyone had left that evening and the house was silent, Rose crumbled on the couch and Jed held her head in his lap and watched her sleep. As she slept, his head hit the back of the couch. And he dreamed he was awake. He dreamed he heard a noise outside, like the firing of a rifle, and he rose and walked into the darkness toward a light near the vineyard. The air was filled with the night sounds of crickets and frogs. He came to the chapel but it only had the framing up, and at the far end hung the carcass of some freshly killed animal. It was hanging upside down from the rafters, blood spilling into a silver bucket on the floor and spattering the boards around a man's feet.

The man stepped back and saw Jed. It was Shep. His face was beet-red and filled with fiery anger. He pulled the knife from the animal, blood on his arms and clothes, and moved toward Jed with a look of determination. Three steps and he was on him and there was nothing Jed could do. He was paralyzed with fear.

"Don't! Shep, no!" Jed yelled, but Shep overtook him and plunged the bloody knife into Jed's stomach.

CHAPTER 35

SHELBY SAT SMOKING in the bar, staring at Vivian's open mouth.

"And you don't feel any remorse?" Vivian said. "I mean, her father died and you were—"

"I was taking care of her husband the way she should have taken care of him. It's obvious he's not getting what he needs at home."

"Really? And how can you tell that? Did you look in his eyes? Do a blood test?"

"I don't have to test. I can tell."

"Shelby, you know me. I'm not a prude. I like to have fun. But come on, the guy is happily married. His whole career is based on his family, his religion. You and I may disagree with him about God and all that Jesus stuff, but you're not just stealing his fidelity. You'll wreck his life."

Shelby glanced at her from the corner of her eye. "I'm not wrecking anything. I'm trying to free him from the prison he's in."

"Prison? You call his life a prison?"

"His art. He's trapped. He has to fit into the little box they've made for him. That he's made for himself. He could be so much more. With me."

Vivian took another sip, then downed the rest of the drink in one gulp. "And who says he's going to ditch his wife and his career for you? You think that's actually going to happen?"

Shelby smiled. "Judging from the other night, I can guarantee it. Once a man has seen that the grass is greener on the other lawn, he'll be back. And eventually he stays."

But as the days wore on and shows were canceled, Shelby wondered if Jed had changed his mind. She thought about calling or texting him, but she knew it was better to wait, to let Jed be the one to make the next move. *Be patient,* she thought. *It will make his return that much better.*

After she knew the funeral was over, Shelby met with Stan in the hotel lobby.

"I think we need to cancel Amsterdam," he said.

"You cancel another show and we're toast," Shelby said. "The momentum was so high after London."

"And his father-in-law died, if you hadn't noticed."

"I know his wife's dad passed away, Stan. But life is passing us by out here. You haven't even called him, have you?"

"I want to give him space. Pushing him right now is not the thing to do."

"Somebody needs to present him with reality. And reality is this: The tour is hemorrhaging money. Canceling shows ticks people off. They want to see us play. I don't care how good the reason is. There's a time to mourn and a time to sing and this is the time to get on with life."

Stan looked at his watch. "What time is it over there now? It's gotta be late morning, right?"

Shelby shrugged.

Stan dialed the number and apologized for waking Jed. He asked the time and mouthed, *"It's 6 a.m."*

Shelby leaned closer to the phone but couldn't hear Jed's response.

"We are certainly anxious and excited to have you back out here. Friday is Amsterdam. Everything is a go . . ."

Jed said something and Stan pursed his lips.

"Brother, we have lost six shows. Now I know that was an emergency, but we have an emergency here." He looked at Shelby. "Okay, here's the truth: we are hemorrhaging money. Hemorrhaging money, man. People are getting upset."

"Stan," Jed said, and Shelby could hear him now. "This is my life." There was passion to his voice and a bite to it.

Shelby raised her eyebrows and urged Stan on.

"And this is how you pay for your life," Stan said. "Now, if you were a nobody, if you were still just David King's kid,

I wouldn't care what you did. No one would. But I don't think that's who you want to be. Or is it? Because you can always just walk away."

Stan looked right at Shelby and she nodded. This was the pep talk Jed needed. This was the push she'd hoped Stan would give to bring him back to the tour. To bring him back to her.

CHAPTER 36

ROSE AWOKE under the same cover her father had loved. Jed was close, looking at her. She had cried herself to sleep on his lap and didn't remember him getting up. The funeral, the fight with her brothers, dealing with Ray and the questions about the farm—it was all a blur and she felt like her life had spun out of control. She prided herself on staying on an even keel, but the events since her father had died had put her in a whirlwind.

Jed was looking at her with a pain of his own as if there was something he couldn't tell her. She pushed the thought aside and coaxed him to talk.

"I have to go back," he whispered.

Rose melted into tears again. She didn't want the emotion, didn't want to seem needy, but she couldn't help it. "Please," she begged.

"I don't have a choice," he said.

"Yes, you do. Please, just stay."

"If I stay, we're going to owe a lot of money."

Her eyes bolted open and the tears stopped. She knew what she had to do. "Take me with you, then." She was resolved not to let anything come between them.

The look on Jed's face told her something was wrong. Something more than just her presence on the tour.

"I can't do that, Rose," he said so softly she could barely hear it.

"Why?"

"All the reasons you said. I can't do that to Ray."

The tears came again and the regret. "I should have gone with you then. I'm so sorry, Jed." She was crying like a wounded child now. "I'm so sorry. I should go with you."

"You have a lot to do here," Jed said. "Just help me get through these next eight weeks. I have a show in Cincy. Then I have a break."

"How long?"

She saw a hint of a smile on his face. "We'll start with a year."

The plane left the next day and Rose and Ray drove Jed to the airport, just to spend a little extra time with him. Ray held on to his father's neck and did that thing he used to do with his grandfather, holding on as long as he could and Jed leaning down so Ray would touch the ground as soon as he let go.

"After Cincy," Jed said to Rose, then kissed her on the cheek.

Jed had been especially kind while he was home. He hadn't even brought up the issue of intimacy and she guessed it was because of the trauma of her losing her father, that he wanted to be sensitive to her.

They watched him disappear into the airport, a few people recognizing him and pointing. Jed sauntered past them and waved.

Rose drove toward Nashville and met Denise at a park that was halfway between. It was always great to process life with her friend, and they talked about her dad's death and the big changes she was going through with decisions about the farm and her brothers.

"There's no question you'll keep the farm, right?" Denise said. "I mean, the family burial plots are enough to settle that."

"Dad left that open for us. He said we could move their graves if I wanted, but I don't want to do that. And I'll never get rid of the vineyard."

"What about your brothers?"

"I don't even want to get into it. They were so upset with me. They think I put him up to this."

"You never asked to be executor."

"Exactly. I'm going to split the land into three parcels and deed their share to them. They can do what they want."

"And how is it with Jed?"

"I wanted to go back on the tour with him but he said no."

"What? I thought he was begging you to go."

"He was, but he said it wouldn't be fair to Ray."

"Odd," Denise said.

"Why do you say that?"

"He was putting all this pressure on you and suddenly . . ."

Her voice trailed and Rose pressed her. "What are you saying?"

"I'm not saying anything, okay? I'm just hearing something I don't like."

"You think something's going on with Jed?"

"I think saying no to his wife who wants to go with him on tour is odd, especially when he was gung ho about it. And especially after you've been through this huge loss." Denise looked out at the playground, where Ray was climbing the monkey bars. "Have you seen any of the live videos of the European tour?"

"I've seen some of them."

"And what did you think?"

"I don't know much about music—"

"Not the music, Rose. Jed and Shelby."

"Nothing's going on between them. She's this wild-child, tattoo-wearing, smoking—you know. They have nothing in common."

"They have music in common. And the way she looks at him when she sings—"

"I don't need to hear this right now, Denise."

"I'm not trying to make you paranoid. But I have to tell you, those videos concerned me."

"You think Jed would go for somebody like that over me? I'm the mother of his children."

"Children? As in plural?"

"Yeah. I'm having another baby."

"That's fantastic! What does Jed think?"

"I haven't told him yet."

"Oh, boy."

"Stop it, Denise."

"Look, I'm excited for you. You're a great mom. And I'm sure Jed is pure as the driven snow. I just think any red-blooded guy who's away from his wife—"

"That's disgusting." Rose stood and called Ray. "I can't believe you'd say that."

"Rose, don't leave."

"I'm not going to sit here and listen to you drag my husband's name through the mud. I get that enough with the tabloids."

"Please, sit down."

"No." She looked at Ray. "Get your stuff, honey, we need to go."

Denise stood. "Rose, calm down."

"Don't tell me to calm down."

Denise held up her hands. "All right. You're right. I'm sticking my nose in where it doesn't belong. From now on I'll keep my observations to myself."

"We haven't had a picnic yet," Ray said behind her.

"Get in the car. You can eat on the way home."

Rose walked to the car, loaded the stuff, strapped Ray in, and got behind the wheel, not even looking at Denise when she drove away. She pulled over at the entrance to the park and looked for some napkins in the picnic basket.

"Why are you crying, Mom?"

She looked at Ray in the rearview mirror and smiled through her tears. "No reason," she said. "Sometimes moms just have to cry."

It was the first time she had lied to her son. Denise's words had struck something deep inside she didn't want to consider. Rose was sure she was right about Jed, that there really was nothing going on between him and Shelby. But what if . . . ?

She looked back at Denise finally, still sitting on the bench near the playground. Then she drove away.

CHAPTER 37

AFTER THE NIGHTMARE about Shep, it was hard for Jed to sleep. On the plane to Amsterdam he kept waiting to nod off and see the grim reaper with Shep's face under the hood, walking down the aisle. He had a couple of drinks to take the edge off, then listened to some music and fell into uneventful sleep. He awakened as they were touching down. Maybe the worst was over.

He had to admit that getting back to the tour felt exciting, like he could breathe again. He'd get back with the band and things would be normal. He'd make music and money. And he would see Shelby. His resolve to call the whole thing off had wavered. He had discouraged Rose from accompanying him because of Shelby. Though he felt guilt about what had happened, he also felt excitement every time he thought of her. Shelby wanted him, she wanted to be with him, and she was good at keeping secrets. She hadn't called, hadn't texted. She had freed him by saying, "Do what you want and don't feel guilty." It was obviously working for her, so why couldn't it work for him?

So that was it. He would decide not to feel guilt and move forward with life and things would work out.

Somewhere in the back of his mind, however, something deep inside bugged him. If he kept up the relationship with Shelby, at least the physical part, it would affect his relationship with Rose. It already had. They hadn't been intimate while he was back for Shep's funeral, partly because Rose was so undone by her dad's death and he wanted to be sensitive. But also because of what had happened in London.

How would his relationship with Shelby affect their music? Would she cling to him? No, Shelby just wanted to have fun. She enjoyed life, got tattoos, drank to the bottom of the bottle, and laughed till it hurt. She was a fresh wind blowing through his life and he envied her. He wanted what she had.

Another part of him shouted that what he was doing was wrong, that it wouldn't end well, that someone like Shelby could be a trap. That was the old, paranoid part of him, of course. The one with God trying to kill his pleasure. He deserved to be happy and he would take what he wanted and he wouldn't feel guilty. Period. End of song.

Stan greeted him at the front of the auditorium and led him backstage. "I was getting a little worried about you making it. It's good to see you, man."

"Good to be back."

Stan asked about Rose and Ray, but it sounded obligatory. He went over the itinerary for the rest of the European dates. Johnny Paugh saw Jed and shook his hand as Stan took a phone call.

"I'll take him to the stage," Johnny said. "Sorry to hear about Rose's dad. That's a big blow."

"She took it really hard."

"She was with him when it happened?"

"She was. Ray too."

"Death stinks, doesn't it?"

"Yeah."

Johnny stopped in the hallway. The two were alone. "Jed, I gotta ask you something. Straight up. We've been friends a long time and you know I respect you."

"Go ahead, Johnny."

"The night before you left, I couldn't help noticing you got a little wasted. That's not normal for you."

Jed nodded. "It wasn't the high point of my life."

"Everybody was having such a good time. It probably wasn't the high point for any of us." Johnny looked down. "Jed, I know you're serious about what you believe. And you've always lived it."

"But?"

"This is not easy."

"Say it."

"I heard Vivian say something the other day, while we were all sitting around waiting, wondering when you'd come back. It was about you and Shelby."

Jed swallowed hard.

"Is there something going on with you two?"

Jed smiled. "There's something going on with everybody and Shelby. You know that. She draws people in, you know?"

"She's never drawn me in. Not to spend the night in her room."

The hallway spun and Jed took a deep breath. "Look, I appreciate you saying something. I'll talk with Shelby about spreading rumors, okay? Vivian too."

"Yeah. Okay, let me show you to the stage. This is a sweet venue."

Johnny led him down the long hallway while Jed's heart thumped in his chest. The stage was close to the audience, the way Jed liked, where he could feel the energy coming from the fans.

"This is a nice place to come back to," Jed said.

Johnny agreed. "I'll catch you later."

"All right, dude."

Jed walked toward the stage, where the band was setting up and the roadies were loading in. And Shelby was there, walking slowly toward him in an outfit that made her look like something out of a Nashville production of *Cleopatra*. Her hair was longer—it must have been a wig or extensions—with gold tassels running through. Her shirt was gold-sequined and made her tattoos even more prominent.

She moved like a cat toward him, smiling. "Hi," she whispered, then hugged him around the neck and held on tightly. "Welcome home."

It felt good to have her so close, to have her in his arms, but there was something about what she said, something that wasn't right. The road had been his home for so long. Maybe she didn't mean anything by it. Or maybe she did. He was going to mention what Johnny had said, how they needed to keep things between them. But he didn't. He just said, "Thanks."

She led him to the stage and they worked on the set list for the night. The band ate together; then Shelby opened the show with Jed prowling backstage. Performing was a bike you got back on every time, singing the same songs, trying to make each performance fresh, but there was something different going on inside him tonight. He chalked it up to nerves and the break for the funeral. Or maybe it was something he ate.

When it was his turn, he walked out to wild applause. The audience was with them, the band sounded great, and Jed was ready. But when Shelby started playing the solo to begin "The Song," the melody and the applause and screams changed the climate of his heart. Shelby turned to him and smiled, showing him what a familiar tune could do to people.

Jed walked up to the microphone as the rest of the band

joined in. The guitar, which usually felt like an extension of his soul, felt heavy, like an albatross. He looked out at the audience, at the young girls jumping and older fans swaying to the easy beat of the tune.

And then Jed saw him. In the middle of the throng stood Shepherd Jordan. For a split second he was there, scowling, staring at Jed like he was ready to pounce on him and teach him a lesson. Pull out the knife and plunge it in again.

Jed blinked, trying to catch up with the band, but they were going too fast or he was too far behind. Music had always been intuitive to him and now he had to think about where his fingers went and how to strum. He looked again and the place where he'd seen Shep was empty. Just gone in a flash. But the effects of the vision were immediate. His heart sped up, and he struggled for even a shallow breath. He felt the sweat on his brow and his arms felt like lead.

He looked at Shelby for help, trying to communicate something with his stare, but how could he tell her with his eyes what was going on, what he had just seen? Truth was, he didn't know what was happening. He turned quickly and his guitar hit the microphone stand and toppled it to the floor, sending feedback through the hall before the sound engineer could mute the mic.

The band slowed, thrown by the fact that Jed hadn't begun the first verse, and Shelby got them going again as Jed bent over and picked up the microphone and tried to let the audience know everything was okay. But everything wasn't okay. Everything was swirling in his brain and his body. He was feeling something he'd never felt before and it had all begun with the first notes of that song. *Her* song. Rose's song.

Instead of getting better, Jed's vision blurred. He staggered backward and looked at the audience. Someone in the front row mouthed, *"There's something wrong."*

Finally he took off his guitar and set it on the floor of the stage, put a hand to his chest and gasped. The stage spun now and his legs felt like jelly. He wobbled a bit and then fell like the mic stand, hitting the stage. He heard screams from fans and the music stopped and then there were people around him, his band members—he saw Johnny, concern on his face. Shelby too.

Jed held his chest and looked at Shelby. He shook his head and mouthed, *"Can't breathe."*

"Just breathe. Breathe, baby." She put a hand on his chest.

"What happened?" Stan said, on the floor at Jed's side. He seemed more concerned about the show, the crowd, but Jed couldn't focus. Couldn't get a breath.

"Breathe, baby," Shelby said again. "Slow down."

"I can't," Jed said, panting. He felt hollow like a balloon that had sprung a leak and was limp and airless.

"You can, Jed. You're okay."

"Call 911," Stan said.

"No, it's a panic attack," Shelby said, her voice strong. "Jed, listen to me. You're not going to die, okay? Breathe."

"He needs help," Stan said.

"Help me get him backstage," Shelby said.

The feeling was crazy. Jed's whole body seized like

something inside had come loose—a fan belt in his heart. Was this what a heart attack felt like?

They got him to Shelby's dressing room and sat him in a chair. Stan said he'd take care of the crowd. "I'll have the guys play something—if you think you can help him."

Shelby put a hand on Stan's arm. "He's going to be fine. Give me ten minutes."

When they were alone, Jed dropped his face into his hands and tried to calm himself, but his heart was still racing. "This has never happened to me before."

"It's a physical reaction. Stress. It feels like the world is ending, but it's not. You just need some help."

She unscrewed a bottle of pills, poured two into her hand, and held them out to Jed. He looked at the pills and back at Shelby, and she saw his hesitation.

"To help you relax, okay? I'm just trying to help you."

Her eyes were piercing and beautiful and kind. But there was something else going on and Jed didn't know what it was. Gasping, struggling for breath, he shook his head.

"I can't sing that song, Shel."

"Yes, you can, Jedidiah."

His name. She used his real name and it felt good to hear it from her. As he struggled to get a grip, Shelby was the only one between him and the abyss.

"It's her song," he said.

She closed her eyes and with resolve said, "No, it's your song."

Shep's face flashed in his mind and he tried to get another

breath. He needed to explain something to Shelby, something she couldn't understand.

"You ever feel like you don't write your own songs? Like they were given to you?"

"By who?" she said, bewildered. Then she smirked. "God?"

"What if he takes them away?"

"Why? Because he doesn't like what you're doing? Look at the world, Jed. You like what he's doing?"

He let the thought hang there. She had a point. The world was a mess. Wars and death and poverty and starving children. Planes falling from the sky in pieces, scattered along hillsides. The world was a messed-up place, for sure, but that wasn't God's fault. Or was it?

"The first time I heard your music, I thought, *This is it. This guy really gets it. This is what I need.* But I also thought, *If only he weren't so . . .*"

"Married," Jed said, his breathing more even now.

"Narrow," she corrected, coaxing him off his ledge. "But think of the music he could write if he just let go and lived without all of these rules. And then I realized, I can help him let go. He needs me too."

He stared at her, taking in her beauty and the softness of her voice and how it brought a calm to him.

"I thought I was going to die out there," he said. "I don't ever want to feel like that again."

She smiled and drew closer. There was a twinkle in her eyes like she knew something he didn't. "You won't."

She put the pills in his hand and he took them.

CHAPTER 38

SHELBY HAD VISITED the hash bar the night before with Vivian. It was a dark place with brick walls and uncomfortable chairs, but no one came to this part of town with the flashing neon signs to find a comfortable chair. She bought a bag of the stuff that had worked the night before, and Jed, still high from the pills, was a willing subject. She wanted to loosen him up even more, and from the way he smiled when she blew smoke in his face, she knew they were in for a good, long night.

Vivian leaned in. "I thought you were dead when you fell on that stage tonight."

"So did I," Jed said.

"I guess this is Jed's resurrection," Shelby said. "And we should do something to celebrate the occasion."

"What?" Jed said. "This is not enough of a celebration?"

"It's time to give up the scrapbooking, Jed. Let's remember this night forever."

"What are you talking about?" Vivian said.

Shelby smiled. "Follow me."

They walked down the street with all the *X*s and tacky silhouettes of naked women and went into a tattoo parlor. A man who looked like a bowling ball saw Shelby and nodded. She took Jed over to the man's station in the dimly lit room, and Jed sat like a sheep ready for shearing.

"Is this the guy you were talking about?" Bowling Ball said.

"It is. I think he's ready."

Jed looked like he didn't know what was happening at first. Then, when the needle came out, he flinched. "What are you going to paint or draw or whatever you call it?"

"I've got the perfect thing." Shelby handed him something else to smoke. "All of my tattoos were done when I was high. You won't feel a thing."

The man went to work, and when he was done and had wiped the blood from the skin, Jed stared at the creation.

"What do you think?" Shelby said.

"You're the expert," Jed said, holding up his arm and showing the crown that circled his wrist. "What do *you* think?"

She leaned into him and whispered in his ear. It amused her to see that even with a thick beard, a man could blush.

Jed paid the artist and they stumbled back to their hotel. Shelby was surprised at how quickly Jed jettisoned his rules and laws and morality. She knew he'd just been waiting for something to come along and release him from the prison he'd made of his heart, but she couldn't have predicted how fast the leap into the dark would happen. And she loved leaping into the dark with him.

The tour continued; the music flowed, and so did the liquor and pills. Back in the States, in New York, they spent the night at one of the most expensive hotels Shelby had ever been in and Jed sampled more than just the wine. In Washington, DC, where the power brokers of the world came to have their way, she had hers. And the bond between them kept growing; the drugs and alcohol and sex and secrets united them, became the glue that held them together.

In Pittsburgh their performance, though fueled by their personal cocktails of booze and pills, was magical and incandescent. They were going somewhere, and not just with their music. Their hearts were beating as one, and when Shelby looked at Jed onstage, she saw the man she loved, the man who brought her pleasure and who she brought pleasure to.

There were some performances, though, that neither of them could remember. The further they went into themselves and into the substances that had now taken over, the less she remembered about the shows, and the nights all seemed to merge into each other. Cleveland was no different from Amsterdam was no different from London or Baltimore.

Shelby could feel the momentum, the push and pull toward Cincinnati. The Queen City, where she could be queen and Jed king. There was only one thing holding them back from really being together. Only one person standing between her and happiness.

CHAPTER 39

Rose drove the two hours to Cincinnati and Ray slept on the way. The car always lulled him, and she would watch him in the rearview, his eyelids getting heavier, his head nodding down and then up as he fought sleep. Finally he would surrender, and she loved the peaceful look on his face when it happened. Complete and total submission, and not a care in the world.

She hadn't told Jed about the baby. It didn't seem right to just tell something like that over the phone or in a text message. She wanted to wait and surprise him with the little bump when they were together. But the little bump had grown to a much bigger bump. Would Jed be as excited as she was? Would he understand why she had kept the news from him?

Yesterday, Denise had driven up from Nashville to spend the day. Rose met her in the driveway and told her how sorry she was for driving off and getting so upset.

"You have nothing to apologize for, but I accept," Denise said. "If you'll accept my apology, I'm sorry I came on so strong. It's not my place—I just care about you so much."

The two had hugged outside the house, in tears. They moved inside to the kitchen and Ray played with LEGOs on the floor while Rose and Denise sat at the table and had tea.

"I think one of the reasons I was so upset," Rose said, "was because I've had the feeling you're talking about. I've seen the music videos and the publicity stuff and the way she looks at him . . ."

"It's hard not to extrapolate from there, isn't it?"

"Yes. But the hardest was something I found on YouTube. Somebody uploaded a video from one of their shows—it was just a two-minute clip, but they were singing our song and Shelby was standing so close to him and looking straight at him, like he was hers."

"Have you talked about it with him?" Denise said.

"We haven't talked in so long. I get a text every now and then. A voice mail. And when we do talk, it's short. He has to go."

"Have you thought about counseling?"

"He's never home. How are we going to go to counseling?"

"Not for the two of you, for you. Maybe it would help if

you talked with your pastor or a counselor. To help you get healthy, you know?"

Rose hadn't thought about counseling for herself, but suddenly something flared up inside. "Are you saying this is my fault? That I did something to push Jed away?"

"Not at all. We don't know what's going on with him. All we know is how you feel. Distance. Dissatisfaction with the relationship. You two are not moving together, you're getting further apart."

"But isn't that the nature of his work?"

"It's part of the package, I understand. But nobody is holding a gun to his head and forcing him to be out there on the road all this time."

"Stan is. Not the gun part, but he's the one driving it."

"Really?"

"What, you don't believe me? Then you don't know Stan."

"I believe you that Stan is pushy and is in this for himself. He wants to make money and he sees Jed as his ticket. And it's working. But Jed is a willing participant. He wants this as much as Stan does—at least, that's what he's saying by being on the road as much as he is."

"But if I bring this up to Jed, he's going to say that in order to make it in the business, you have to tour, you have to pay your dues. You have to build your fan base and that's all he's doing."

"That's a choice he's willing to make right now. But every yes he says to touring is a no to something else." Denise took a sip of tea and stared at the cup. "Maybe nothing's going on with Shelby. Maybe he's having a Bible study every night. Maybe he's out there singing and touring and when he finally gets done with that, everything will get back to normal."

"That's what I'm hoping happens."

"But that's your choice, Rose. You're choosing to act on what you hope is going to happen. Not on what you feel."

"That's what you're supposed to do, right? Believe all things. Hope all things."

"True. Love forgives and keeps no record of wrongs. But it also deals with the truth. And if deep inside, you know there's something off, something not right, you have to listen to that and not shove it down."

Rose kept the radio off as she drove toward Cincinnati, thinking about Denise's words. She didn't want to think of Jed negatively. That was too easy to do. She wanted to believe he was the gentle, kind, caring man who had walked with her through her father's funeral, who had wooed her and been inspired to write a great song because of her. And all that was true. But there was the other part, the fears about him and Shelby, about his lack of communication after going back on tour . . .

"God," she prayed, "make things clear tonight. Show me what I need to do in order to love Jed and our family. Even if it's hard, Lord. Open my eyes and help me see. Make me wise."

Rose had left a message for Jed that morning, but she knew they were traveling and sometimes he didn't get his messages till later. When the Cincinnati skyline came into view, she called again but the phone went to voice mail.

"Hey, it's a big night for Ray and me," she said with a smile. "He's excited about seeing his daddy. I was thinking maybe we could do dinner beforehand, but if not . . . Well, call me, okay?"

Ray woke up and pointed at the buildings. When she hadn't heard from Jed, Rose picked a family restaurant off I-75 and Ray ordered pancakes. It didn't matter what time of day, he was always ready for pancakes or peanut butter. And peanut butter pancakes were his favorite. While it wasn't the healthiest dinner in the world, she didn't object—but she did draw the line when he wanted to order soda.

Her phone rang just as their order arrived. "Hey, sorry I didn't get back to you sooner; it's been crazy," Jed said. "We got here late and the sound check was horrible."

"I understand," Rose said. "We're at dinner now, so we'll just see you there."

"I have tickets waiting for you at the front, okay?"

"Great. Do you think we could stay overnight? With you?"

Jed hesitated. "Uhh, sure. I think the room is big enough."

"It's just that it'll take a while getting out of there tonight and then at least two hours back home—"

"Absolutely, let's do it. Just plan on staying."

"Is Daddy excited to see us?" Ray said after she hung up. He had syrup and whipped cream on his face. She hadn't realized there was going to be whipped cream on his pancakes.

"Real excited," she said. "Our tickets are waiting when we get there."

Rose picked at her salad, then paid the bill and drove the

rest of the way. Her heart felt like her stomach, empty and dissatisfied. The tickets were at the box office, like Jed had said, but he didn't come outside to see them.

When they were seated, Stan made his way to the front. He hugged her and gave a Hollywood kiss.

"I'm sorry about your dad's passing," he said. "I know it weighed heavy on Jed these last weeks, being away and all."

"He said he was going to make it to Cincinnati. We've been hanging on for tonight."

Stan's eyes shifted like he didn't know what Rose was talking about, like there were more dates booked and she hadn't heard. But maybe it was just the past and all the hurt and loneliness coming up that made her unsure.

"You're a real trouper," Stan said. "Enjoy the show."

She didn't really care for Shelby's opening act, but when Jed walked onstage and the crowd reacted, her heart fluttered. She could see why he enjoyed performing. He'd come a long way since the harvest festival.

But something was off in his performance. Something about his eyes, the way he moved, the hollow nature to his voice. Instead of seeming alive and invigorated, he almost looked high.

"There's Daddy!" Ray yelled as the people got to their feet.

"That's him," Rose said, and she felt sad in a strange way. The things Denise had said kept coming back to her, and as she watched him sing "The Song," a little part of her died. When she'd first heard it on their honeymoon, on the morning after their wedding, it had sprung from his heart and felt fresh and new. Now, the sound was fine, the harmonies good—the band played it impeccably—but his heart wasn't in it.

Or maybe it was her own heart that had stopped responding.

CHAPTER 40

JED STOPPED at Shelby's dressing room for something to take the edge off his anxiety. He hadn't passed out or anything, but he could feel himself tightening. He had some pills back in his hotel room, but he felt like he needed something right then.

Shelby was packing up her makeup and seemed preoccupied. "Congratulations," she said.

"What for?"

"You managed to eke out 'The Song' tonight." She didn't look at him. "I'm sure she was thrilled."

"Shel, we've talked about this. You said you would give me some time. That you understood how hard this would be."

"I said what you wanted me to say." She looked at him with hurt in her eyes.

"I want you to tell me the truth."

"All right. The truth is this—"

Someone passed them and Jed stepped in and closed the door. "Go ahead."

"The truth is, I can't understand why you don't want to be happy. Why you want to live with one foot in obligation and the other foot in this world. Our world."

"I do want to be happy. And I'm going to choose that. But I need some time—"

"Time to what? To keep stringing me along? Playing second fiddle? I won't do that forever, Jed."

"I'm not asking you to."

"Then do it tonight. Tell her the truth. That it's over. You want out."

"I can't do that tonight."

Shelby stood and moved toward him. He thought she was going to slap him. Instead she pressed her lips to his in a passionate kiss that left him gasping.

"Will you at least think about it?" she said, lifting her eyebrows.

He nodded and walked out the door without asking for the pills. Down the stairs and past a security guard he heard Ray's voice call out.

"Daddy!"

"Hey, buddy!" Jed said, picking him up and feeling how he'd grown. "Did you have fun?"

"Uh-huh." Ray turned and pointed. "Look at Mom's belly."

Jed looked at Rose. He searched for something to say. What was he supposed to say? He tried to think quickly, but all that came to his mind was "Wow."

He walked toward her, still holding Ray. "Wow," he said again, stooping down. "Look at Mom's belly."

He hugged Rose and she embraced him with a passion he wasn't prepared for. He pulled back and said, "Why didn't you tell me?"

She smiled with that pregnant mother glow. "I wanted to tell you in person."

He embraced her again to hide the look on his face, the feeling in his heart. This was the worst news he could imagine. This made it even harder for him to tell Rose the truth about Shelby.

The stage door opened and a group walked down the darkened hallway. Jed's heart skipped a beat when he heard Shelby's soft laughter. She stopped when she saw them together.

Rose turned. "Hi, Shelby."

Shelby broke from the group and came into the light.

Jed closed his eyes and tried to sound as natural as he possibly could. "Shelby, this is my wife, Rose."

"It's really nice to meet you," Shelby said, extending a hand.

"It was a great show tonight," Rose said, shaking with her. "You're very talented."

All Jed could think about was getting Rose and Ray out

of that hallway, away from Shelby. Before something awful happened.

"Thank you," Shelby said, staring at Rose's bump. Then she looked at Jed and gave him a smile that said too much.

"And this is my son, Ray," Jed said.

Shelby lit up with an over-the-top grin, raising her hand for a high five from his son. "Ray? You are so handsome." She stared at him, a little too close. "I've heard so much about you. I feel like I know you guys. But I did not know that you were expecting." She said it to Rose, then glanced at Jed.

"Neither did he," Rose laughed.

An awkward silence fell between them and Jed felt his heart accelerating like there was another attack coming on. Ray felt like a sack of potatoes all of a sudden. Jed wanted to run and hide. Anywhere.

Shelby said she was going to grab a drink with the guys and mercifully exited. Before she did, she looked at Jed. "Catch you tomorrow?"

Jed nodded and said he would, then turned to Rose. "Ready to go?"

They got Ray into the hotel suite; the little guy was exhausted. Jed opened the sleeper-sofa and Rose fixed his covers and tucked him in and he was gone before the lights went out. Jed wished he could sleep that way. Then he remembered he could, if he took enough pills.

Rose hugged him from behind and sighed like she had plans for the evening. "I missed you," she said.

"I missed you," Jed said to the wall, trying to mean it.

She turned him around and looked at him, but Jed had a hard time making eye contact. She took his right hand in hers, then held it up and rolled the cuff back, revealing his tattooed wrist.

"When did you get this?" she said.

"Amsterdam."

"Why?"

"I don't know. It seemed like a good idea at the time."

He could tell she was disappointed, but she wasn't about to let her discovery spoil the moment. She stroked his face and leaned into him, unbuttoning his shirt. His heart nearly exploded, not from desire but from shame and guilt and what was left unsaid between them. Air left the room and he felt trapped as if he were drowning.

Breathe, he told himself. *Just breathe.*

Suddenly he could take no more and he grabbed her hands, struggling to think through what he should do, what he should say.

"Is everything okay?" Rose said.

He pushed her back and whispered, "Yeah. Just give me a second, okay?"

Jed opened the bathroom door and went inside, his heart nearly beating out of his chest. He couldn't look Rose in the face; he had to get away. Once inside, he turned the faucet on high and opened his shaving kit, pulling out the stash of pills Shelby had so easily gotten for him. Instead of calming, his heart beat faster and he collapsed in the corner, waiting in hope that the drugs would take effect.

He stayed there until his breathing evened out, but by then his whole body felt like it was floating, and all of his guilt and shame about Shelby melted into sweet, blissful sleep.

He awoke next to the toilet, still dressed in the clothes he had worn the night before. He had dreamed that Rose was at the bathroom door, knocking and calling his name. But maybe that wasn't a dream.

And then he remembered he had passed out here with Rose waiting for him and Ray asleep in the next room. He struggled to stand and fell against the door, opening it and finding the bed empty and then the sleeper empty.

"Rose? Ray?" he called. He opened the door and looked in the hallway. No one was there.

Then he saw it. On the nightstand by the phone was a handwritten note.

Dear Jed,

I don't know what's wrong, but I know something is happening to us. I thought you would be excited to be with me tonight. I'm taking Ray and going home.

You told me you'd be taking a break after Cincinnati. I guess that wasn't true. And you'll probably blame Stan.

I can't keep going this way. I'm going to get help. And I hope you will too.

All my love, from a broken heart,

Rose

She was going to get help? What did that mean? If she knew about the drugs, why didn't she say something? If she knew about Shelby, why didn't she confront him?

The room phone rang and he thought about not picking it up. But what if it was Rose? What if it was Shelby?

"Bus is pulling out for Indy in ten minutes," Stan said. "You coming?"

Jed closed his eyes. "Yeah, I'll be there."

CHAPTER 41

Pastor Bingham requested that Melanie, one of the female counselors, meet with Rose and him in his office. He explained that it was just one of the policies of the church that there always be another pastor or counselor for meetings between opposite-sex people behind closed doors.

"Do you think Jed has some kind of addiction?" Pastor Bingham said.

"I don't know what to think," Rose said, tears falling, voice trembling.

Pastor Bingham handed her a box of tissues.

"He had a tattoo on his wrist. Jed hates tattoos. He said he'd never get one."

Pastor Bingham looked at his hands and rubbed them together as he thought. Then Melanie leaned forward. "Why did you wait until last night to tell Jed about the baby?"

"I don't know; I thought maybe he would be excited if I waited and told him. Showed him, you know?"

"And he wasn't?"

"He looked like he could hardly breathe. Kind of pale and shaky. Even when he sang, it was different. And then last night . . . We used to fight about intimacy, you know. But when I approached him . . . he didn't respond. I just want my husband back."

The two of them listened to Rose sob, seemingly comfortable with the pain that leaked out.

After a few minutes, Pastor Bingham spoke. "Rose, there may be nothing going on with Jed. But the signs you're describing trouble me. I'm guessing that Jed is in the middle of making some bad choices."

"From what I can tell, there's a lot of drinking after the shows. And who knows what else."

The pastor winced. "I think you need to prepare for the worst."

"What do you mean?"

"I think it's possible that Jed may be involved with some substances. Or with someone else. From what you describe—his erratic behavior—it sounds like that might be the cause."

"Couldn't it just be stress?"

"Sure," Melanie said. "But I tend to agree with Pastor Bingham. It sounds like something is going on inside Jed.

And you're the most likely person to help him. You're also the person who will be hurt the most by his choices, if our assumptions are correct."

"Rose, we're going to pray for you. For wisdom. Discernment. And that when the truth comes out, you'll have the courage to move forward and, if you need to, confront him in a loving way, but in a way that draws a line."

"What kind of line?"

"If he's addicted, if he's having an affair, you have every right to ask him to choose. You don't have to live with someone who is unfaithful. Love doesn't have to roll over and take that."

"Divorce?" she said.

"I'm not talking about divorce. At least not yet. You want to give Jed a chance to repent and then see if that repentance is genuine. And you can't go this alone. You have to surround yourself with people who . . ."

Rose didn't hear the rest. She was too captured by the sins of Jed's father and how they might have come back to haunt her.

But Jed wouldn't cheat on her. He loved her too much. He wouldn't get involved with another woman. She couldn't even imagine him with . . .

And then she remembered the way Shelby had looked at him backstage, when Shelby saw Rose was pregnant. Her words were fine. She said everything she was supposed to say, but the look on her face when she glanced at Jed said, *"How could you?"*

They joined hands and Pastor Bingham and Melanie prayed for Rose and Jed and Ray and the unborn child Rose was carrying. When she got in the car to drive home, she felt the door of her heart closing. And she wondered if there was any hope for them as a family.

CHAPTER 42

SHELBY WAS GLAD to get to Indianapolis. She wanted to get Jed alone to talk about what had happened in Cincinnati, but he was aloof. It was clear he wanted to be alone, so she stayed with Vivian and stewed. Maybe he'd told Rose the truth. Maybe he was just hurting now that things with Rose were coming to an end. Maybe he would come running back to Shelby's arms after the show. She decided to let him make the first move.

Through her opening set she couldn't wait until he walked onstage. She played "I Like It This Way," a sweet and melancholy song that veiled her feelings for Jed. She got to the lyric that said, "I'll show you love you can't believe" and nearly choked on the words. Sometimes Jed came out and sang with her, but he didn't show up.

When he finally walked in at stage left, he stood by Stan, looking pale and gaunt. She didn't mean for the drugs to take hold like they had, but if he could just break free from Rose, she was sure she could help him conquer them.

The audience applauded for Shelby and she took a bow. Jed walked onstage and she looked at Stan, who signaled her to start "The Song." She mouthed, *"No,"* but Stan wouldn't relent.

Shelby hesitated a moment. What if Jed did a halfhearted version? But she began her fiddle solo and the band followed and the crowd cheered. Shelby played it with everything in her, willing Jed toward her again, but his face was tight. Slowly he removed the guitar strap and walked offstage. The guys in the band looked at her as if she could do something.

Shelby ran to Jed, the band still keeping time and some in the crowd beginning to boo. Tears had begun to fall by the time she caught up with him backstage.

"Jed, please don't do this to me." She was crying hard now, sobbing, beating on his chest. Then she calmed a little and begged him, "Let's just go back out there—"

"No," Jed said. He pushed her backward and she could tell he meant more than just the song. He was under Rose's spell and was pushing her out of his life.

She narrowed her eyes and looked him in the eye and with all the resolve she could muster said, "I'll just sing it myself."

Shelby walked toward the stage, hoping Jed would follow

and put a good face on it and let the show go on. There was no reason everything had to fall apart like this, no reason they couldn't spend the rest of their lives together.

Just as she made it to the edge of the stage, she heard Jed say something; then he grabbed her arm and jerked her back into the shadows.

"You will never sing that song," he said, his jaw clenched. He said it again and shook her so hard her teeth rattled.

She pulled free and gave him a stare. No one ever spoke to her that way. No one ever shook her like that. She'd promised herself as a child that if any man grabbed her and shook her like her father had, she would get her revenge. So she ignored Jed's little power play and walked back onstage, signaling to the band to keep playing.

"I've been waitin' on you—"

That was all she got out before Jed grabbed the microphone. She stepped back and Jed grabbed her violin and with one swing smashed it on the stage. The crowd gasped, wondering if this was part of the show and then realizing it wasn't. Jed's anger and emotion were real and she'd never seen this side of him.

Jed tossed the pieces of the fiddle across the stage and the band came to Shelby's aid, taking off their instruments and going after Jed.

The crowd, once cheering, now sounded more like WWE spectators, booing and yelling at the turn of events.

Backstage, things were no better. Jed threw a chair in her dressing room and gave a primal scream.

"You think you're better than me?" Shelby screamed, following him. "You think *she's* better than me?" She hit Jed and pushed him back.

"What was that?" Stan shouted, entering the dressing room.

Shelby couldn't take it any longer. "You broke it! You broke it!" She was all over Jed now and Stan tried to intervene.

"Get off him," Stan yelled, grabbing Shelby's arm and pulling her away.

"Get off me!" Shelby yelled, gritting her teeth and hitting Stan with a fist to the face that connected with a sickening crunch. Stan went down in a heap, a hand over his nose.

"Stop!" Jed yelled, grabbing Shelby and trying to subdue her.

"No!" she wailed when Jed had hold of her. "I'm going to tell her! Let me go! I'm going to tell her!"

Jed let her back away, his eyes on fire now. He pushed Shelby against one of the posts in the dressing room, her head banging against it, the emotion and drugs and fatigue boiling. He shouted into her face with anger Shelby didn't know was there. "Are you threatening me? You don't threaten me."

Then Shelby's bandmates were on him and Shelby slumped to the floor, crying, totally undone. They let Jed go and he bent over, hands on his knees, panting.

When things had calmed, she looked at him—mascara running, tears coursing, but she didn't care. "I love you," she moaned.

He dropped to the floor across from her and stared at her. She imagined this was not what he expected to hear, but there it was.

"I love you," she said again. And as she crawled to him, the people in the room seemed in utter shock.

Stan's cell rang and he spoke with someone quickly. When he hung up, he said, "Look, I don't care what you do. I don't care who you do it with. But when you bring your problems onstage, they become my problems. My very expensive problems! Now if you can't keep your baggage off the stage, I will. Shelby, you are done! Done!"

His phone rang again and he stepped into the hall.

Jed put his hands over his face.

Shelby tried to get closer. "Jed, please. We can work this out."

He got up and looked at one of the guys. "I need to get home."

"Jed, *please*."

He stopped and looked down at her. "I'm sorry about your fiddle. I'll get you a new one."

"I don't want another violin. I want you."

But just like that, he was gone.

CHAPTER 43

ROSE AWOKE in her childhood home to the sound of a car in the driveway and the front door closing. An intruder was her first thought. She picked up the phone to dial 911, then thought better of it. She turned on the light and saw the marriage book she'd been reading. She was actually going through it a second time, looking at places she'd underlined about lovingly setting limits in a marriage.

She expected to see Jed at the top of the stairs, disheveled and falling into bed, but he never showed up. After a few moments she went downstairs and found him slumped on the couch, already asleep. She took her dad's old afghan and put it over him. Jed didn't move, so she went back up to bed.

When Jed had left for the European tour, she found herself drawn back to the vineyard. After her father passed, it gave her comfort to be here, and she and Ray had moved in. The longer Jed was away, the more consolation she felt at waking up in the old house with all the memories.

Ray found Jed the next morning and jumped on him. Jed laughed and tickled him, then sat up. His eyes were red like he'd been up all night.

"I thought you guys were headed to Nashville for the show," Rose said.

"We are. I just needed to get back here, you know?"

He went upstairs while she made him breakfast, but she found him asleep on the bed and he stayed there until the afternoon.

"Is Daddy going to eat dinner or breakfast?" Ray said to her.

"We'll eat together," she said. "He can have his dinner and call it whatever he wants."

They sat in the sunroom, one of her mother's favorite places in the house, and ate around a small table. Rose had fixed a healthy meal but Jed seemed preoccupied. His face was sunken and his color was sallow.

"Looks like it's going to rain," Rose said. "We need it."

Jed's phone chimed and he checked it.

"Can I play with your phone?" Ray said.

"We don't play with gadgets or phones at the table, Ray," she said. "You know that."

Jed put the phone in his pocket and immediately it chimed again. Then again.

"I was hoping to take Ray to your Nashville show; would that be all right?" she said. When he didn't answer, she dipped her head and tried to get his attention. "Jed?"

He looked at her like she was interrupting major surgery. "Yes. That would be fine."

His tone was off. He was touchy but she decided not to tiptoe, not to play nice. She had every right to ask questions. "Why is Shelby off the tour?"

He sat back and stared at her. He hadn't touched his food and it seemed he didn't want to touch the question either.

"I read that she was off the tour," Rose said.

"She punched Stan in the face."

"Good for her," she said, studying his reaction. He wasn't liking this line of questioning, but she thought she deserved an answer. "Why?"

"I don't know," he said quickly. "Look, I don't want to talk about work right now."

And with that, every suspicion she had, everything that Denise had said, everything Pastor Bingham and Melanie brought up, sent the red flags flapping in her mind and it was more than she could take. His hollow cheeks, red and sunken eyes, and the way he reacted when she brought up Shelby told her there was more here than just Shelby flying off the handle after a concert.

Rose gathered her plate and soup bowl and hurried into the kitchen. Jed followed.

"Rose, what?" he said.

She ran the disposal and ignored him, the bile rising, the

questions coming in a flurry, all leading to a place she didn't want to go but couldn't help going. She shut off the disposal.

"Do you not want me here?" he said.

She turned to face him. "You're not here. We have to say your name five times before you even answer. Something is wrong."

"All right, I'm just tired," he said, all puppy-dog eyes and defensive. Like he could just apologize and make everything better.

She studied his face. "Why aren't you singing my song?"

Jed looked away, then at the floor. Anywhere but at her.

Something broke inside Rose and that deep, crushing feeling came in a wave. She fought the emotion to get the words out, to get him to respond to one more question running around her mind. "Do you not love me anymore?"

"Rose," he said, dismissing her words. "Of course I do. Why would you ask me that?"

Like she was the bad person for bringing up the question. Like this whole thing was her fault. No. There was something wrong. And there had been for a long time. She wasn't crazy. This wasn't because she was pregnant or had too much on her hands with Ray and the vineyard and . . .

"Sing it," she said. "I want you to sing it right now."

He kept his distance, standing partially blocked by the overhead cabinet. "Rose, that song's special to me. All right? It holds a special place. And I'm just tired of being demanded to sing it like some sort of performance monkey—"

"What is that?" she said, interrupting. Ray's voice came

from the sunroom, sounding as if he was talking with someone.

She hurried back and found Ray at the table, a tattooed woman sitting next to him in Jed's chair.

"Shelby?" Rose said. She had a knot in her stomach as soon as she saw her, and her motherly instinct kicked in. *Get Ray away from her,* it said. *Now.*

"Hey, Jed," Shelby said, smiling, looking past Rose.

Rose reached for Ray's hand and took him from the table.

"What are you doing here?" Jed said.

Shelby was chewing gum, her face plastered with makeup. She smelled like cigarettes and looked like a scorned woman to Rose.

"Why didn't you answer your phone?" Shelby said to Jed.

Everything made sense now. Rose was looking at the mushroom cloud of his actions and seeing the fallout. The look Shelby gave Jed. His defensive posture. The two of them together backstage in Cincinnati. How he didn't want Rose in Amsterdam. The tattoo. Everything fit. And everything was falling apart right there in this place where they should have been eating and talking and connecting.

"I'm having dinner with my family," Jed said. "What do you want?"

"Okay," Shelby said, standing. She wobbled a little. "Can you just tell Stan to bring me back?"

"Shelby, don't come to my house—"

"What?" she interrupted. "Are you done with me? Is that

it?" She looked at Jed with not an ounce of shame. It was a threat, a calling out. She took a drink from Jed's wineglass.

Rose asked Ray to go back in the house and wait. Dutifully he obeyed and bounded away.

"Because of me?" Shelby said to Rose. And then she laughed and leaned on the table. It was the laugh of someone who'd had too much to drink or smoke or too many pills. "Honey, he's the druggie. He's the one that takes all my—"

"Get out," Rose said, calm and even, looking her in the eyes.

Shelby laughed again and flicked her lighter. "Seriously, dinner on the porch. How cute." She let the screen door slam and stumbled down the stairs.

Rose stared at the table, her resolve firm. Now that she knew, now that her worst fears were confirmed, there was no going back. There was no way not to know. She had to draw a line.

"You too," she said firmly, her heart breaking into a million pieces as she said it. "Get out."

"Rose?" Jed said, his voice high and pleading.

"Get out!" she screamed.

He paused and looked at her, then walked out the door and followed Shelby to her car.

Rose went back in the house to make sure Ray was okay.

"Where's Daddy going?"

"I don't know, buddy."

"Why did you yell at him?"

She looked him in the eyes. "Sometimes mommies have

to stand up and do some hard things. Sometimes they have to say things loud enough so others can hear them."

The look on his little face was more than she could bear. She hugged him and glanced out the window in time to see Jed in the front seat of Shelby's car, downing a handful of pills. She knew she needed help and that there was only one place she could go.

"Can you stay here for a little bit?" she said to Ray.

Ray nodded and she ran for the back door.

CHAPTER 44

JED COULDN'T BELIEVE Shelby had shown up at the house and he certainly couldn't believe Rose had kicked him out. He pulled Shelby out of the driver's seat, where she clearly didn't belong, and hopped into her Mini Cooper. The seat was way too close but he didn't care. He needed some relief from the pain, the racing heart, the shallow breath—it was all back again. He found a bottle of pills, popped the cap and swallowed some dry, then put the car in reverse and backed in a U but hit something on the driveway. He got out and looked at Ray's Big Wheel his grandfather had given him, busted beyond repair. He closed the door and ran inside the house.

Ray was sitting, playing one of his games. "Ray, where's your mom?"

Ray pointed to the back door.

Jed walked toward it and heard the voice of his son behind him.

"Are you leaving, Daddy?"

He turned and looked at his son and for a split second thought of his own father and the family he had left behind. He couldn't think of anything to say, so he just smiled and walked out the door.

He climbed the knoll above the pond toward the monument to his inability to finish—the chapel. One side was drywalled, the windows in. The roof was on. But the other side was exposed studs.

He stepped into the chapel, the place where they had vowed to love and honor and cherish and protect and whatever else he promised. His failure flooded like water through a broken dam. Good thing the pills were starting to kick in.

Rose was facedown on the floor at the front, her head on her arm. She wasn't moving, but she was talking to herself. Or maybe she was praying.

"Rose," he said, walking toward her. "Rose?"

She pushed herself up, holding her stomach, and a wave of guilt washed over him. He hadn't meant to put her through this. It was just something that happened. It wasn't anyone's fault. That's what he wanted to say, what he wanted to believe.

He reached out to touch her and as quick as a cat, she turned and slapped him hard on the face.

"You were with her!" she screamed, the pain leaking through every pore of her body, her voice a volcano of emotion. "While I was here carrying our child."

"You think this is what I wanted?" he yelled, matching her intensity.

"Yes! Yes, because it's what you did."

"I wanted you! But you made me beg. Girls out there are begging me and I have to beg my wife."

"Don't blame this on me, Jed. You did this! Don't blame this on me!"

"I did this," he said, his voice calming as he looked at her, wanting to hurt her. "And I'm glad I did this. I'm glad I didn't have to jump through fifteen thousand hoops or build a chapel, Rose, to do it." He was feeling more sure of himself now. The words were coming more freely and her face was showing the pain of them and that somehow made him feel good. "She wants me," he said cockily. "Me!"

"Because she doesn't know you, Jed," Rose said, breaking down.

"She does!"

"No, she doesn't!"

"She does," he screamed, stamping his foot.

"No, you think she does. *She* thinks she does. She thinks she matters to you. I used to think that."

"Yeah, Rose. You thought you mattered so much you could treat me however you wanted and not pay. Do you remember that?"

"How dare I. How dare I ask to be treated like an actual human being before I give it up. How cruel, right?"

"You told me over and over again that you didn't want me."

"I never said that."

"You did!" Jed made a fist and swung it through the air near her. "And now that somebody actually wants me, now you want to act like a wife. It's a little late."

"You didn't want a wife. You wanted a whore. Someone to just lay there, no questions asked. It's true, Jed. It clearly is because that's what showed up at our house today."

"You don't even know her!"

The look on Rose's face was incredulous. "Right. She's the wife you always wanted. She's going to raise your children?" Her eyes searched his soul. "She's going to grow old with you?" She took a breath and the pain turned to anger. "Then, even then, with her sleazy, saggy tattoos, that skank will always be in the mood, right? You're a fool, Jed. You are such a fool!"

"You're right," he yelled. "I am a fool. You're right."

He picked up a two-by-four and smashed a window, the shards of glass shattering on the floor. He swung again and again, smashing the glass and wood all the way to the frame with all the violence pent up in his heart.

Then he walked back to Rose, the board still in his hand, his heart beating wildly, ready for one last verbal swing. "I'm a fool because I married you. But I'm done."

He tossed the wood in the corner and walked away, down the hill and back to the car, where Shelby sat, passed out. Jed looked at the front window of the house and saw Ray there, staring at his Big Wheel. He wanted to tell him he would get him another one. He wanted to tell him he'd always be there for him. But he was done with promises.

He got in the car and drove away.

CHAPTER 45

SHELBY WOKE UP and looked at the empty bourbon bottles and the trash strewn about her Nashville home. Styrofoam and cardboard boxes on the coffee table.

It felt so good to have Jed back, and she made sure they had enough substances to keep the party going. Endless shots and lines of cocaine and uppers and downers and oxy this and that. Endless runs for Chinese food. They paused long enough for him to play Nashville, but the concert was a bust. Jed was so strung out he came off angry, and when the crowd chanted for "The Song," Jed threw his banjo into the crowd and told them to sing it themselves.

That didn't go over well with Stan, but Shelby didn't

care. She had what she wanted. They were together. And they would be together forever. All of this pain and partying would lead to some great songs. And someday the whole Rose chapter would be just a forgotten melody.

She looked outside and couldn't tell if it was morning or afternoon. Jed wasn't on the couch with her and she needed to go to the bathroom bad, so she stumbled toward it and saw Jed's legs sticking out beside the bathtub. He was propped up against it, next to the shower, clawing at the tattoo on his wrist.

She dropped to her knees beside him. "Jed, stop! Stop, stop, stop—what are you doing?"

"I want it off," he said, his voice slurred. He was digging deep into the flesh and it turned her stomach.

"Stop!" she yelled again and again, but he wouldn't listen, kept going back to the bloody wound.

As Shelby wrapped a towel around the wrist to stanch the bleeding, she saw the empty bottle of pills beside him.

"Did you flush them?" she said, hoping he'd say yes.

Jed's eyes were closed now, his lips motionless and a little blue.

"No, no, no! What did you do? Jed! Please."

She began to cry and tried to pick him up, but he was too heavy. Just deadweight. "Listen to me! Jed? You have to stay awake!" She slapped him. "Jed? Talk to me!"

She picked him up under his arms and tried to move him, but she could only lay him down in the shower. She stood over him, trying to figure out what to do. She'd read of famous singers and film stars who overdosed and a headline flashed through her mind: *"Jed King Dies in the Arms of His Forbidden Love."*

"Please talk to me. Please say something!"

For a moment his eyelids fluttered and he opened his mouth. "Rose" was the only word he said.

Shelby reached up and turned on the cold water, letting it cascade over both of them.

Then, wet and dripping, she slipped and slid through the house, found her phone, and dialed 911. She went back to him while on the phone and checked to see if he had a pulse, if he was still breathing. When the paramedics arrived, she felt better because they seemed to know what to do. She tried to help, tried to show them which bottle of pills he had taken, but they pushed her away.

And then the police arrived and the questions began and she didn't know what to say or how much to tell, but in the end it didn't matter because the cuffs came out and she was put in a squad car as she watched them wheel Jed to the ambulance.

"Is he going to be all right?" she yelled at the officer. "Is he going to be okay? Please, tell me!"

CHAPTER 46

JED WAS HAVING a hard time telling what was really happening and what he was dreaming or hallucinating. They'd watched some wild animal show on TV together while high, with lions pulling down a defenseless wildebeest, and Jed felt just like that, prey for a cunning lion. Except he had willingly walked into the lion's lair.

Then he was running from something in the vineyard, something big and hideous. Something that wouldn't let him go, wouldn't stop until he was cornered.

He came to the chapel and ran for the open door. And then it was on him, tackling him to the floor, and he thought in the next moment he would feel the teeth of the animal sinking into his neck. He rolled over in time to see not a lion but his father. He was wearing his old headband and the touring clothes Jed remembered from so long ago.

"Jed, stop running," his father said.

Jed took one look and scooted backward against the wall of the chapel. He looked on in horror at the sight of his dead father.

"I'm sorry, Dad," Jed said to him.

His father looked on him with compassion as if he knew what Jed was going through. "It's not me you're running from."

Jed opened his eyes in the hospital and tried to close them so he could see his dad again. But before he could, he glanced down and saw someone beside him. Her head was on the bed by his bandaged wrist, blonde hair. It was Rose, holding his hand. He moved, thinking it might be a dream, might be more hallucinations, but when he pulled his hand away from her, she stirred and looked at him with something close to relief and love all mixed together.

Jed couldn't hold her gaze. His chin quivered and his beard shook, his eyes clouding with emotion.

"What would have happened if you would have died, Jed?" Rose said.

"You would have been better off," he said, choking on the words. "You would have had everything."

"Jed, what did we have when we first got married? I had everything I needed. But you didn't. You still don't. I made mistakes. With us. There's things I'd . . . I wish I could do over, but I can't give you whatever it is you're looking for. No one can."

Jed heard her voice, but he also heard the heart monitor and felt his skin itching. He needed a drink. He needed a pill. He needed out of there. He wished he had died. He just wanted to go to sleep and never wake up.

"When Dad died," Rose continued, "I realized there's nothing in this world that won't go away. Eventually. My only hope is that there's something bigger than this world."

"What if it's a fool's hope?" he said.

"Then I'll take it. I'll take it. If I'm going to raise a son and a daughter on my own, then I need to believe there's a point."

Something came alive in him. Like a switch thrown backstage that turned the spotlight on. "A girl?" he said.

There were tears in her eyes. "I found out I'm having a girl."

"Do you want to raise them on your own?"

"That wasn't my plan, Jed. I want a man who believes in something bigger than all this. Someone greater than himself."

Jed stared at the ceiling, trying to think of the right thing to say. Anything.

"That's not you anymore," she said. "That man died a long time ago."

She sat back and Jed glanced at her, seeing the love in her eyes mingle with the pain of all he had dragged her through. He felt shame and sorrow. But he couldn't bring himself to speak. All those nights singing all those songs, her song, and he couldn't speak.

"Good-bye, Jed," Rose whispered.

After she left, Jed saw her rings on the hospital tray, the wedding band and engagement ring he had saved for. He held them in his hands and wept at what he had done, what he had caused.

A day later, Jed heard a knock on the door and his mother walked inside. He pushed himself up in the bed, still clutching Rose's rings. She kissed him and gave him a hug, a tear falling from her eyes onto his bedsheet.

"It's been a long time, Son. I've tried calling you."

"I'm sorry, Mom. Life kind of got in the way."

"The old demons," she said, rubbing his bandaged hand. "I went by and saw Rose and Ray."

"How is she?"

"Heartbroken. Betrayed. You've done a lot of damage to that girl."

"I know."

His mom had aged since he'd last seen her. Wrinkles and baggy eyes. Her hair had turned grayish-white toward the end of his dad's life and it was still that way.

"Do you think she could . . . ?"

She put a hand to his chest. "There's only one thing you should think about right now and that's getting sober. Nothing good can happen if you're strung out on whatever you're on."

"I know."

"Then what are you going to do about it?"

"I don't know yet."

She dug in her purse and pulled out a brochure. "I went by this place on my way over here. They said they could protect your privacy. It's not cheap. And it'll be six weeks."

He studied the redbrick building on the front of the brochure.

"Your dad went there for a while. Really helped him."

"Sins of the father being passed down, then."

"Don't say that," she said. "You have a choice. Your dad turned his life around with the help of God. You can experience the same thing."

"I'll never make up for the hurt I've caused."

She patted the brochure. "One step at a time, Jed. Don't get ahead of yourself, okay?"

❧

He brought his guitar and what he'd packed for Nashville to the Jefferson Healing Center in Louisville. Just stepped out of the limo and surrendered himself to the indignity of having all his belongings searched—even his guitar. He went with the detox program that gave him three square meals a day and all the counseling he could stand and then some. Pills delivered directly to his table and a nice gray robe and slippers that went with everything.

He had no visitors the first week and they suggested he refrain from calling anyone. At the start of the second week, when the shaking subsided and he didn't feel like running toward the shrubs to look for something to drink, he thought of calling Rose.

But what would he say? *"Hey, Rose, how is everything? You still hate me?"*

He was in the dayroom reading a music magazine when he stumbled onto Shelby's picture. The headline said, "Shelby Bale Given Probation, Agrees to Rehab."

Pastor Bingham walked in the door and Jed closed the magazine. The man smiled at Jed and shook hands and sat down across from him.

"You gonna preach to me?'" Jed said. "Tell me how big a sinner I am?"

The pastor shook his head. "No. You don't need that. You've been through enough without me beating you up."

"I messed up my life, Pastor. I messed everything up."

Pastor Bingham nodded.

"Is there hope for somebody like me?"

"Depends on how you define hope."

"Is there hope I could have my marriage back?"

"Is that what you want?"

"It's on the list."

"Sounds like a good list," Pastor Bingham said. "I'm going to hold judgment on that one. I've talked with Rose—she's been to see me and one of the counselors at the church in the past few weeks."

Jed's heart leaped. "Did she send you over here?"

"No. She told me you had checked in but she didn't ask me to visit you. This is about you, not about your marriage."

"You don't care about my marriage?"

"I care about your heart. The man you've tried to be. The

man you've become. I want to be here to walk through it with you. But I can't guarantee what's on the other side."

"Doesn't sound like a lot of hope to me."

"God offers us hope when we surrender. When we give it over to him. He can take the sin, the struggles, all the pain we have and bring healing to our hearts. To your heart."

"I don't think I'm exactly there yet, Pastor."

"I understand. I'm in this for the long haul, no matter what happens between you and Rose."

After the pastor left, Jed found a spot outside and sat strumming his guitar, thinking about Rose. In a weak moment he dialed her and heard it ring a few times. He was about to hang up when he heard Ray's voice.

"Hey, buddy, what are you up to?"

"Working. The grapes will be ready soon."

"I take it you're working with your mom. Is she there? Can I talk to her?"

"She's busy right now," Ray said.

It sounded like something he'd been told to say. "That's fine. I just wanted to call and see how you guys were doing. Okay?"

"Do you want to come home? Are you coming to the festival?"

"When is it?" Jed said.

Ray put the phone down and said something Jed couldn't make out. Then he came back and said, "October 12."

Just days after their anniversary. And the time of year when they first met. "All right. Count me in." Emotion gripped him and he ached to talk with Rose, but he knew he couldn't push it. Patience was better. A little boy stamped his feet and needed to get what he wanted, but a man could wait. A man could show those he loved he could wait.

"Hey, listen, I'm going to let you get back to work, okay? I love you."

"I love you too," Ray said.

Though Jed didn't want it, the counseling continued. After the shakes subsided, he could finally hear what they were saying. He could answer in complete sentences and didn't just stare. It was humbling being there, being vulnerable, but it was good. He was just another struggling guy with a substance problem. A guy who nearly died from an overdose.

They let him smoke a cigarette or two outside, and that helped calm him. He had given up so much, and he knew nicotine wasn't good for him. He'd kick that too eventually. He had to.

The counselors were overjoyed that Jed had his guitar and a journal. They told him to fill it up with ideas and thoughts and feelings he was going through. He poured himself out on those pages, asking more questions than finding answers, of course. Why had he made so many bad choices after making so many good ones? Was God punishing him for what he'd done? Was God even there? Would Rose take him back? And what would he do about Shelby?

He knew she had led him down a bad path. Her demons, her problems, had spilled over into his own life. What was it about Shelby that attracted Jed? Was it just her sexuality, the eyes, the hair—the physical package? Was there something else? She had led him down a wrong path, but he had followed willingly like a lamb to the slaughter.

He had blamed Rose. He had made his infidelity her fault and knew that wasn't fair. Yes, she could have been more open to him, but it was still his choice whether or not he would run toward the forbidden woman.

Late one night after an evening of drinking and carousing, Shelby had told him about her life, what had happened to her as a young girl. How men had used her and that's what made her feel special. The music was just an extension of all of that—people applauding and cheering gave her the feeling she needed. But she always wondered what it would be like to be with a man who valued her, who would protect her and really love her. It was clear she thought Jed was that man. And at some level he'd been ready to leave Rose and follow her.

Was that why he overdosed? Could his being rushed to the hospital have been God's way of rescuing him from himself and his choices?

Jed let the thoughts pour out and the more he worked through, the more he saw that he had almost lost everything. He was grasping for something he could never hold. He was chasing after wind.

He wrote down these few words.

Why have everything?
You're leaving here with nothing.
Can't take anything because you have to move on.
You were the wise one,
putting your disguise on
Lyin' to pretend, you're chasing after wind.

He was working on the chorus of the song one afternoon, smoking one of his last cigarettes, when he heard a familiar voice behind him.

"New song?" someone said.

Jed turned to see Stan Russel in an open-collared shirt and a suit coat.

"Hey, hey!" Stan said, laughing. "What's happenin', brother?" He sat on the bench next to Jed. "Very nice. Beautiful place. I'm serious."

"What do you want, Stan?"

"Maybe I want to come see you, see how you're doing."

"Do you?"

Stan gave him a look of recognition, a nod. "Okay. I do want to show you something." He pulled out a tablet and held the screen up to Jed. "Here, just look at this."

Stan had a video of their performance in Indianapolis, a grainy, shaky video of Jed grabbing Shelby's violin and breaking it on the floor of the stage.

Jed turned away from it, feelings of shame and guilt rising up. "Why would you show that to me, Stan?"

"Not the video. Don't look at the video. Look at the view counts."

"I don't care about the view counts."

Stan cleared his throat. "There's something here. There's something here we can build on." He leaned forward and looked Jed in the eyes. Brow furrowed, sincerity in his expression, but with a little bit of calculation. "It's a story of redemption."

"This isn't redemption. This is exploitation."

"Just listen," Stan said. Then, slowly, he began his pitch. "American Roots Music Awards. You and Shelby, if you can put your junk aside for just one second. Let the world see your healthy, redeemed, rehabbed faces on TV. Ready for a comeback."

As Stan spoke, Jed looked at the pristine grounds of the facility. Every piece of grass clipped. Every detail manicured and managed, just like his life. Except there was no way to manicure what he had made of his life. And he knew this was not the path he needed to go. But Stan did have a point. Maybe it could be used for good. Maybe it could be the start of something healthy.

"When?"

"October 12."

Jed smiled. "I can't do it. I have plans."

Stan sighed like he'd heard this a thousand times. "You can't do it."

"I promised Ray."

"Ray, who is Ray?" Stan said. Then realizing his faux pas, he said, "Ray is your son, of course. Come on, man. You know I love Ray. Hey, you know what? Ray wants to go to college one day. Ray wants his dad to shave and sing and be a rock star."

Stan was always able to convince Jed he was right because he usually was. He had that strength, that resolve to go out and get what he wanted, what he could envision. And it was clear that his vision extended to Jed and Shelby now.

He lowered his voice and leaned in so close Jed could see the pupils of his eyes, pinpoint wide. "You understand that this is a second chance? This is a chance to put everything behind you. Rehab. Rose. Your dad." He let the words hang there and Jed thought of how good it would feel to have the ghosts of the past off his back. All the mistakes, all the junk in the back of the U-Haul just dumped somewhere.

"Are you in?"

Jed tried to clear his mind, turn over another page in the journal. Maybe it would be a good opportunity for him to clear the air. A good chance to see Shelby and apologize. Set things right.

"I promised Ray I would come to the harvest festival that night."

Stan laughed. "The harvest festival? You'd turn down playing in front of millions of people to play at the harvest festival?"

"I'm not playing there. I'm going to spend time with my son and my wife."

"Man, you need to move on. You think she's going to take you back after what you did to her?"

"I don't know if she will. But even if she doesn't, I want to be there for my son."

"The show has to start early because of the Eastern time zone crowd. You and Shelby are on early. Do two songs and you can get on the road and be at the vineyard before the moon rises."

"I want to do a new song."

"That's cool. The one you were working on when I walked up?"

"Yeah. It's called 'Chasing after the Wind.'"

"Great. Get me a CD of it and I'll get the band together."

"What about Shelby? Is she okay?"

"She's doing good. Just like you. She looks good. Clean, you know? She'll be really excited to do this with you."

"She will be or she is? Have you talked with her?"

"Just a quick conversation. She's on board. What do you say, Jed?"

CHAPTER 47

SHELBY COULD TELL there was something different about Jed's new song. It wasn't that it was just him and the guitar and that plaintive melody he'd carved out. It wasn't that the lyrics seemed a little dark and introspective—that it was downright depressing to hear about everything being a chasing after the wind. It was more that she could hear the thing inside him coming out, the thing that had drawn her to his music in the first place. His raw, aching heart laid bare. And she knew she could make that song better with her voice and her new fiddle.

Stan had delivered it to the rehab place. He said it was from Jed and she believed him. Nothing would replace her old violin because—well, that thing had seen some good days. How could you ever replace something like that? But knowing Jed wanted her to have this one made her treasure it.

She put the CD in and listened to the melody first, picking up the violin and playing along with the intro and hearing where she would fill in the song. The second time through she didn't play; she listened to the words and they struck something inside. The longing, the regret, the hope for something more and the banging of the head against the wall. Yeah, the song had it all. She just wasn't sure where Jed was taking it.

It ended in a long instrumental she knew she could nail. Perfect for TV. Perfect for their comeback.

With rehab behind her, she called Vivian and told her she didn't want any of the pills, the joints, the powder, the alcohol. She was going cold turkey, not Wild Turkey. Vivian said she respected that and that Shelby's time in rehab had caused her to think about her own life. She'd cut back a lot and wasn't drunk half as much as before. But it sounded to Shelby like it was something that wouldn't last. The folks in rehab said it was all or nothing. You couldn't dabble, couldn't just have a taste, because it would pull you back in and suck you under and soon you'd be on the bottom looking up, wondering how you'd gotten there.

She thought that was how it might be with Jed, too. And she hoped—yes, she prayed—that he would feel the same way about her. One look from him would be all it would take to start something new, something fresh and good. Just like his dad had done with his second wife. She had it all mapped out. He would come live with her, and after the divorce, they'd get married. He would have to pay a lot to Rose, no doubt, but they would weather those hard financial times together.

They had one rehearsal, early in the afternoon of October 12. It was the first time she'd seen Jed in weeks. And he looked good. His long beard was gone, replaced by stubble. His hair that had grown like a mane was shorter too, and he looked like years had been added to his life.

Shelby walked up to him and said, "Hey."

"Hey. You sure you trust me around that thing?" He smiled and pointed at the violin.

"I trust you, Jed. With everything."

He turned to the band and said, "Let's run through the new one."

And they were off and the sound was amazing, like calling something from nothing, like pulling a rabbit out of a hat—a song that no one had heard, but the band just brought it to life and it sent shivers down Shelby's spine. She played the instrumental out and then went right into "The Song."

After a few bars, Jed waved them off. "We've done that one enough. Sounded good, guys. Really good."

The band surrounded him and welcomed him back, and before Shelby knew it, Jed was whisked away by some producer who wanted an interview backstage for the production piece to air during the show. When it was her turn, Jed was gone.

"What was it like to see Jed get so violent onstage? How did you react?"

"We were all pretty much on the edge emotionally," Shelby said. "I could have broken a fingernail and it would have brought me to tears. But that instrument, that was a close friend of mine. I lost two friends that night."

"Backstage—we've heard the stories about what happened. And Jed told us a little about it."

"What did he say?"

"He said it got physical between you two. He pushed you."

"Yeah, he did. And I hit Stan pretty good when he tried to separate us. But that's behind us."

"What's behind you?"

"That night. And what led to that night. The drugs, the booze."

"The relationship?"

Shelby smiled shyly and looked at the interviewer from the corner of her eye. "I'll always love Jed. His music. His heart. What happens from here on out, I don't know, but I'm not looking for revenge. Life's too short. I want to make peace with my demons and move on."

"Jed said that his relationship with God has gotten deeper because of this. Do you say the same?"

She looked at the floor. "No, I can't say that. I have a lot of questions about God. If there is one. But I don't fault Jed or anyone for going that direction. If that works for him, for anybody, I'm glad for them."

The interviewer looked at her tablet and scrolled down. Then looked up. "Anything else you want to say, Shelby?"

"I'm sorry if I caused people pain because of my actions. That wasn't my intent. And I really want this to be the start of something new. Something good for my life and the people I care about." She looked into the camera. "Thanks for not giving up on me. It really means a lot."

Backstage, before they went on, Shelby stood in the wings waiting by the red velvet curtains. Finally Jed walked toward the stage and listened to the performance before theirs. He was twirling something in his hand—was it a ring?

Her heart fluttered. Maybe his absence had caused him to realize how important she was. Maybe he was going to propose onstage. It was too much to ask, too much to even think about. As she watched him, her heart filled with love and she remembered the times they'd spent together. Even though most of those times were spent in a haze of substances, they were good together, and just seeing him there sparked hope.

She walked up beside him, smiling. "You ready to do this?"

He shook his head. "I guess we'll see."

It had been so long since he'd gone in front of a crowd without the help of pills, Shelby wondered if he would be able to get through it.

"You look really good," she said.

"Thank you. You too. Healthy."

"Thank you. And the song you wrote—it really spoke to me. I know you didn't write it to be a hit. It just kind of leaked out. That's how the good ones come, isn't it? They just happen to you and you find them."

"The good songs find you," Jed said. "I don't understand it, but it's true."

"Still think they're given to you?"

He nodded. "Oh yeah. I didn't do anything to deserve this one. Or any of them."

She looked at the ring in his hand and wondered how it would feel on her finger. "Jed, I knew you were eaten up, and I just thought if she knew, then it would be over and you and I could be together without all this guilt and you'd be at peace."

Jed stared at the faces in the crowd, the lights, the cameras, the female performer onstage. He didn't respond to Shelby, so she kept going, kept trying to see if her gut was telling her what she hoped. She reached down and took his hand in hers.

"We have a chance to start over. For things to be the way they should be, you know?"

He still didn't respond, didn't squeeze her hand, and only smiled sadly when the song was done.

"Here we go," he said.

Shelby led the way and the band took their places as the audience applauded. The preproduction piece rolled with the incident onstage in Indy and the interviews with Jed and Shelby. Then they were introduced and the crowd sat on the edges of their seats as Jed began the plaintive introduction to "Chasing after the Wind."

Shelby was into it, smiling at the camera, smiling at people she could see in the front row. The guitar and her violin and the mandolin and the rest of them were perfect together. Harmonies came shining through and there was a breathless quality to the performance as if people were waiting, pulling for them, willing them to move forward. After all, that's what life was about—hitting bottom and bouncing. Their stories were the stories of thousands of people who had, in some way, sunk so low there was no way but up. Washed-up sports legends who made a comeback, politicians who lost, then ran again—they were all the stories people loved to see because that's what they wanted for their own lives. And as Jed sang his ode to his own failure, Shelby was coming alive, seeing what might be.

But every good song has a turn, and this performance of "Chasing after the Wind" had it too. She realized it when they were in the middle, when Jed looked at the balcony or maybe something beyond it, with tears in his eyes. Not stage tears or something manufactured for effect, but real tears, wet and full, as if something inside was releasing. The camera went close on his face, and when Shelby looked at the screen at the side of the auditorium, something in her own heart broke because at that moment she knew the tears weren't for her.

And then the intensity of his voice came to a crescendo.

"Why should I be if nothing has made me?
All that I've done will flame out with the sun."

Now he was screaming, not singing, as if yelling to the stars. The veins in his neck strained and his face showed the pressure building inside.

"Why should I sing if nothing has meaning?"

As if on cue, the band stopped playing. She wanted to pull the bow across the strings and make some kind of sound, but all she could do was stare at Jed. The audience sat with their hands in their laps, their faces glued to the stage, and the camera focused on Jed in an embarrassingly tight close-up.

She caught Stan's face in the crowd and he motioned for her to start, to do anything. So she started "The Song," like they'd done a thousand times, and the silence was broken by that beautiful, haunting melody. She closed her eyes and let the music flow through her fingers, hoping it would fill the cavern Jed had carved with his voice.

They were seconds into it when Jed waved them off and sliced at his neck with a hand. One by one they stopped, and Jed, looking like a deer in the headlights, swayed toward the microphone. It almost looked like he was on something, like he was high. Maybe that's what people were wondering, but Shelby knew better. She'd never seen Jed more sober.

"You know, when you're always under bright lights, you can't see the stars." There was emotion in his voice. Searing, personal pain bubbling up from inside. "You forget things. You forget that somebody put the stars there. And that they love you enough to die for you. And it's that kind of love that makes songs worth singing. And life worth living. I had that love. And I threw it away. Because I am a fool. I'm sorry."

He shook his head and the silence of the audience was deafening. Shelby could only imagine what was going on in living rooms around the country as people watched. It was as if time stopped, and then Jed was there in front of her. What should have been a chance for him to propose gave way to the worst moment of her life.

"You're right," Jed said. "We have a chance to do things right."

Shelby's heart was pounding. She tried to control it and evened her voice. "You really think she'll take you back?"

"Either way, this is good-bye."

He didn't walk backstage to leave; he walked down the stairs and into the audience, all the way to the door leading outside. Shelby watched him go, that long, easy gait, and knew she'd never see him again.

CHAPTER 48

JED FELT LIKE HE'D JUST THROWN off a thousand pounds from his back. He walked on air through the audience, not caring what anybody whispered as he passed. For once he felt true freedom, not the kind that could be managed by someone, but the kind that set the heart loose to do what it wanted to do, what it needed to do.

He glanced at his watch as he neared the hallway and smiled. If he drove the speed limit, he would be there before the band finished at the harvest festival and he could pick up Ray and toss him in the air. He could look at Rose and tell her what he'd done, tell her the old Jed was dead and the new one had come alive. He was already practicing what he would say when Stan pounced on him in the empty hallway.

"Jed, stop. You can't do this."

"I can. You're watching it happen."

"Do you realize what you're walking away from?"

"Nothing that really matters."

Stan grabbed him and stopped him, shaking the program in his face. "Let me tell you something. You walk out that door, I will sue you for every show you cancel."

Jed smiled. Stan's power with words had been all-encompassing to him throughout the years. Now he seemed like a paper tiger. "I know. Go ahead." He put a hand on Stan's shoulder, suddenly feeling sorry for the man. "It's only money, Stan."

He clapped Stan's cheek twice and walked away. "I've lost much worse."

During the drive to the vineyard, he rolled the window down and hung his head out, letting the cool air wash over him. He drove faster than the speed limit, hoping he wouldn't be pulled over.

All he could think about was Rose and Ray and their unborn child. What would they call her? Leah? Stephanie? No, Lily. After Rose's mother. Lily Shepherd King. He couldn't wait to see Rose and tell her, to let the things on his heart explode. He'd tell her how sorry he was. He'd tell her how wrong he was. He'd give her the rings she had given back to him and she'd be crying, just like the night when he proposed. And things would return to normal. They'd spend their days and nights together and be a team again.

But he knew that was just a dream. In the real world where real hearts were involved, forgiveness didn't come that easy. What would he do if she took a swing at him? Or just ran away?

"Oh, God, give me wisdom," he whispered. "Again. I promise I won't squander it this time."

He passed the sign for Sharon and accelerated toward the vineyard, where the lights of the place shone into the night. His heart was beating fast when he parked, but the band onstage began a run with their instruments that made him smile. He scanned the crowd and saw the booths and it felt like coming home, like George Bailey running through Bedford Falls and waving at the Building and Loan. He wanted to kiss the crooked cotton candy display and give thanks, but just then he saw his son playing and called him.

"Dad!" Ray said, running into his father's arms. How easy it was to pick him up and hold him and look at him.

"I missed you!" Jed said.

"You're late," Ray said.

"I know. I'm sorry I'm a little late. But I'm here, right?"

"Uh-huh."

"Where's your mom?"

Ray pointed. "She's over there by the wine people."

Jed chuckled. "By the wine people. I'm going to go talk to her, all right?"

"Okay," Ray said.

"I love you, you know that?" Jed said.

Ray hugged him and Jed gave him a big kiss. It felt like he

was home again, like some stone had been rolled away from his heart and he had walked out with only the scars showing from the past. But the biggest hurdle lay ahead. Children can embrace and forgive because their hearts are bigger than their hands. Adults find it harder to let go of the past.

"See you in a little bit, okay?" He put Ray down and watched him run.

The sight of Rose made him smile. It was just like the first time he had seen her, right here amid the hay bales and candy apples and wine tasting in the crisp autumn air. She'd taken his breath away, and her beauty now, with their child growing inside, made him wish he could go back and relive the last few months, make better choices. But what man can wind back the hands of time?

Jed walked toward her to the sounds of the bluegrass band on the stage. It was a pure, clean sound, and the mandolin was kicking in as he caught her eye. She excused herself from the people she was with and walked past the pumpkins and cornstalks. Jed's face was cold from the drive and he figured his nose was red. His eyes watered when he saw her, but it had nothing to do with the weather.

"Rose." He said it like a prayer, like an invitation.

"What are you doing here?" she said, bewildered. "I thought you had a show tonight."

"I love you," he said. He held her gaze and said again, "I love you."

She looked away, her face tight. "Jed, stop. Just stop."

"I did," he said. "I quit it. Everything, tonight. I was onstage and I just walked away because it's not what I want. I want you."

He said it with all the feeling in his soul, with resolve and strength and desire. He said it from a heart free from everything that had enslaved him. But what he got in response was not what he had hoped.

"You had your chance, Jed." It sounded like an amen to a prayer. So be it. Then she walked away.

"Rose," he said. But she was gone. And there was nothing he could do except watch her go.

A man alone can fall toward despair. He had done that before. But as he watched her walk away, he breathed a prayer. "Oh, God, I asked you for wisdom. Give me that wisdom now."

It was an arrow prayer, shot to heaven in an instant. No sooner had he prayed it than he looked toward the band. And he knew what he needed to do.

CHAPTER 49

Rose couldn't believe Jed would show up that late, after promising Ray and then backing out because of a TV show. She assumed that Stan had set things up and that the allure of a sober Shelby was too much to resist. She was content to let him go his own way, to let him walk as far off the pier as he wanted. As for her, she was through with trying to bring him back to his senses. There was only so much a wife could be expected to do.

But showing up now, just days after their anniversary, was too much for her. She had commemorated the day alone, after she had gotten Ray to bed. She poured a glass of grape juice, not wanting to expose their daughter to the wine, and lit a fire and cried herself to sleep. Where had he been on that night? Why couldn't he have shown up then?

Jed looked good; she had to admit that. He'd shaved and had a haircut and looked like the old Jed she'd fallen in love with. The Jed she had met here at the harvest festival. The Jed her dad had been leery of, and now she realized it was for good reason.

He'd said he loved her. He'd said he'd quit his old life. Just turned his back on the music and travel and all that money, and he'd said it like a little boy showing his mother the beautiful mud pie he had made. What was Rose supposed to do with that? Pat him on the back and tell him what a good boy he was to go through rehab? Congratulate him for being so grown-up and welcome him back with open arms and not wonder if he'd return to the other life? Fall back into Shelby's arms?

She shook her head and returned to the table to help the women who wanted to know which wine was the best. She told them about the 1995 crop and the Syrah with those deep-red grapes. It was one of their best years; her dad had talked about that year and said there would never be another like it.

But one of the women in front of her had a funny look on her face. She interrupted Rose and pointed at the stage. "Is that who I think it is?"

Rose turned just as the band stopped the instrumental song they were playing and Jed stepped onto the stage with them, borrowing someone's guitar. She couldn't believe it.

How dare he interrupt the show? How dare he try to take over the festival?

She walked straight up to the stage, fire in her veins. "Jed, get off the stage," she said, pointing to the ground like he was a dirty dog who had climbed onto a leather couch.

"Rose, I want to play you a song," Jed said in the microphone, his voice carrying throughout the farm. "All right? I've wanted to play it so much, but I never can because it always makes me think of you."

She knew he meant "The Song," the one he had written her, the one that helped him climb the charts. The one she couldn't stand anymore. "I've heard it," she said. "Everyone has."

"Not like this," he said. "Please."

Crickets and frogs and night sounds. No crowd noise. Even the band was silent.

"No," she said, the final nail in his coffin. At least that's what she hoped he would feel.

Rose turned and walked away, feeling like she was doing something important for herself, for her family, the farm, Ray, their unborn daughter. She was doing something for her own dignity.

Then she heard his voice, soft at first, like he was whispering something familiar in her ear.

"To everything, turn, turn, turn
There is a season, turn, turn, turn.
And a time to every purpose under heaven."

Rose stopped in her tracks but couldn't turn around. The words and melody she had mentioned to him on that first night they met. She loved that song. And he had remembered.

"A time to be born, a time to die,
A time to plant, a time to reap
A time to kill, a time to heal
A time to laugh, a time to weep."

She slowly turned and faced him. Her eyes were filling and she wanted to control her emotion, to keep her face from showing the dam that was bursting inside.

Then the band picked up in the same key and played the intro to the old song she remembered, only with a little more pace and rhythm and flair. Jed followed along perfectly.

"To everything, turn, turn, turn
There is a season, turn, turn, turn.
And a time to every purpose under heaven.
A time to build up, a time to break down,
A time to dance, a time to mourn,
A time to cast away stones. A time to gather
stones together."

As he sang, Rose remembered all the things they'd done, all the dancing and mourning and casting stones. Everything in her felt like she needed to walk away, needed to run from Jed because she was scared of what he might do, how he might fall again. But the more he sang, the more she could tell this song wasn't being sung from sheet music but from the pages of his heart.

The band kicked the tempo up a notch and Jed laughed as he sang and it was like wine pouring over the assembly. The music was pure joy and every musician was playing his part.

Jed ended the song by singing, "'. . . a time for peace, Rose, no, it's not too late.'"

All those years ago he had sung a song about Eddie and used it to win her heart. And here he was again, chasing away the bad man, himself, in order to win her.

The band played the last few chords as Jed left the stage and walked toward her. Rose wept and shook her head at him.

"I'm so sorry," he said softly, tears in his own eyes. "Marrying you is the only smart thing I ever did. You're enough. You're a gift from God."

He held out his hand and in it she saw the wedding band and engagement ring she had given back to him. When she saw those unending circles, she couldn't hold back anymore and sobbed softly.

"All I want," Jed said, "is to be your husband. I want to raise our children." He paused until she looked up at him, and with great feeling said, "I will never leave you again."

Suddenly she didn't feel quite so cold.

"I'll never sing another note if you're not there to hear it. Please forgive me."

"It'll take a really long time," she said softly.

"I just cleared my schedule for . . . forever."

He smiled and Rose looked down, laughing through her tears. He gently took her chin and tilted her head up to look at him.

"If it takes forever, I'll be here. Forever."

He took her in his arms and kissed her cheek, and she grabbed him and held on like there was no tomorrow. As far as she was concerned, there *was* no tomorrow. There was just now. Here. This moment. This step of forgiving and welcoming him. And as she held him there, Rose thought, *Isn't it funny what a song can do to a broken heart.*

CHAPTER 50

SHELBY BALE WALKED into a darkened tattoo parlor in downtown Nashville, a Yankees baseball cap pulled down low. She showed the man what she wanted and where she wanted it.

"Gonna be painful," he said. "Ankles are pretty much the worst."

"From the looks of you, you ought to know. There's no space left."

"I got a little canvas left," he said, smiling.

"This will be the first time I've really felt the tattoo. Let's get to it."

He shrugged and prepped the area and did a sketch. She lay back and closed her eyes.

"What's the point of this?" the man said.

"The point of what?"

"The crown you want. It must mean something."

"It just seemed prudent. Better than a picture in a scrapbook."

"I don't follow you."

"I could have taken a picture of him and put it on my nightstand, but pictures kill memories."

The man looked up, finally recognizing her. "The King guy, right? You're the fiddle player, aren't you?"

She put a finger to her lips. "Keep it to yourself and you'll get a bigger tip."

He put a fake key to his mouth and locked it. "You still singing?"

"Here and there. Looking for a new manager to resurrect my career. You know, make lemonade when you're handed lemons."

"What about him? King. What's he doing?"

She shrugged. "He has a family. Two kids. A wife. I heard he's doing well. Still clean."

"That's good. Good for him. Think you two will ever sing together?"

"I doubt it," she said.

The prep work was done and he readied the needle. "Any regrets?"

"What was that?" she said.

"Any regrets about what happened? The stuff they wrote in the tabloids?"

"I don't like that word. Regret is like . . ." Her voice trailed off. Then she said, "Maybe I have one or two."

He nodded and put the needle to her skin. She closed her eyes again and saw Jed's face flash before her. The last song they sang together. The tears in his eyes. The way he walked away from the stage and didn't look back. And the words he sang about chasing after wind. Somehow she couldn't get that tune or those words out of her head. His songs always did that to her for some reason.

"Hey, hold up," she said.

"You want something to take the edge off the pain?"

Shelby got up from the chair and put her shoe on. "No, it's not about the edge anymore."

"What? You don't want the crown?"

She took out a twenty-dollar bill from her back pocket and handed it to him. "I don't think I need it."

She opened the door and walked into the darkness, but above her were the stars, sprinkling the night sky like confetti.

EPILOGUE

JED CLIMBED to the roof of the chapel with a bucket of paint to put the finishing touches on the cross. He looked out at the expanse of the vineyard. Two gravestones stood side by side next to the pond, and he remembered the old dog buried by the tree. So much had been buried, but so much remained. The dormant plants that had gone away for winter were readying themselves for new life.

The chapel had been a promise he made to Rose that he could actually keep. A man who commits adultery can never undo his sin. But there was forgiveness from God and, he hoped, forgiveness from Rose. That was taking time. A long time. But he could wait for her heart to heal and the warmth to return to her embrace. A man who has hurt his wife that deeply could listen and love and wait. What else could he do?

Rebuilding trust in a marriage that has fallen apart takes time. That's what Pastor Bingham said in the first counseling session with Jed. And the man was right. Old wounds festered and leaked at some of the strangest times. But little by little, Rose was opening. Maybe God was giving Jed the thing he had prayed for so long ago—wisdom.

Rose carried Lily to the chapel and Ray tagged along beside his little sister and mom. It was a sight Jed had pictured in his mind. His little girl, Lily Shepherd King, who had weighed seven pounds, seven ounces. The perfect number and the perfect child.

"Welcome to the grand opening of the Vineyard Chapel and Picnic Area," Jed said, smiling as he climbed down to meet them.

"We brought peanut butter sandwiches." Ray fist-bumped his dad.

"Awesome," Jed said.

Rose walked inside to look at the pews and the sun glinting through the stained glass. "It's really nice. You finished."

"I told you I would. Took a little longer than I thought."

"Some things are worth the wait," she said. She spread out a blanket and put Lily down on the floor. It was the same place Jed had found her weeping and praying when Shelby had shown up, and he couldn't help remembering the despair Rose had been in at that very spot.

"Oh, I almost forgot," Rose said, digging into the picnic basket. "This came in the mail. Looks important."

It was from a law firm that Stan used. Just the look of the three names in the left-hand corner sent a shiver down his spine. He opened it and pulled out the single page.

"Is he gonna sue your pants off?" she said.

Jed read the letter quickly.

"Why would anybody want Daddy's pants?" Ray said.

"It's an expression," Rose said. "They don't really want his pants."

"No, he's not," Jed said. He took a breath and sat beside them. "He's listed all his losses and is offering to split them fifty-fifty with me."

"Sounds like a pretty good deal."

"The guy turned out to have a heart after all," Jed said.

"When can we eat some more grapes?" Ray said, stuffing half of a peanut butter sandwich into his mouth.

"We need to wait a few months, buddy," Jed said. "You have to let them grow and be patient. Let them mature." He thought a minute. "Somebody once said, 'Treat 'em right. Give 'em time. And when they're ready, they'll let you know.'"

Rose gave him a look like she remembered. Like she knew Jed was talking about himself and about their relationship and everything in the world.

"Can I go throw rocks in the pond?" Ray said.

"As long as you stay by the tree. Don't get close to the water."

"Okay." Off he ran.

Rose pulled Lily close and began nursing her as Jed watched Ray go to the tree and toss rocks, trying to skip them like his father had shown him. Jed wished his own father could be here to see their family.

"What are you planning to use this chapel for?" Rose said.

"I thought we could have weddings here. Small ones, like ours. Maybe retreats."

"Not a bad idea."

"And I was thinking that in October, we might have a little ceremony."

"During the harvest festival?"

"Just before it. I was thinking that maybe we could renew our vows. Maybe we could start over again."

Rose looked up at him and a sad smile came to her lips. Jed felt like the sun was peeking through the dark clouds of their life.

"We have enough wine for a real celebration," Rose said.

Jed nodded. "And peanut butter sandwiches."

Lily finished eating and Rose burped her. Jed carried her in the crook of his arm to the front of the chapel, singing softly to her. He glanced out at the pond and saw Ray toss a rock with the perfect wrist flick, skipping it across the water's surface. His eyes misted and he kissed his daughter's head.

"Love is the power that heals," he whispered. It was the end of "The Song" and the beginning of a prayer he would pray the rest of his life.

ABOUT THE AUTHORS

Chris Fabry is a 1982 graduate of the W. Page Pitt School of Journalism at Marshall University and a native of West Virginia. He is heard on Moody Radio's *Chris Fabry Live!*, *Love Worth Finding*, and *Building Relationships with Dr. Gary Chapman*. He and his wife, Andrea, are the parents of nine children. Chris has published more than seventy books for adults and children. His novels *Dogwood*, *Almost Heaven*, and *Not in the Heart* won Christy Awards, and *Almost Heaven* won the ECPA Christian Book Award for fiction.

You can visit his website at www.chrisfabry.com.

Award-winning director **Richard Ramsey** has brought the story of Solomon to life. With a BA in theater from the University of Houston, he spent his early career impacting the independent film world in Texas. *The Song* marks his first feature as a writer-director. His short films, done in collaboration with his brother, John, have been featured in numerous film festivals and websites including the *New York Times*, *Huffington Post*, *LA Times*, CBS News, *The Atlantic*, and IFC. Richard serves as artistic director for City on a Hill Studio. He and his wife have four children all named after Beatles songs.

DISCUSSION QUESTIONS

1. In the prologue to the story, when Jed King's life has fallen apart, he thinks, *If this were a song, it wouldn't be worth singing.* What circumstances in your life are a song not worth singing? What circumstances are worth singing about?

2. After dealing with a difficult neighbor, Shep Jordan tells his daughter, Rose, "You have to give people who have been smacked around by life a little extra rope." How do you typically respond to difficult, ornery people? How would you respond if you remembered this advice?

3. Rose makes the decision to give away the dollhouse her father built for her when she was young. What might this symbolize? Do you think she should've kept it? Why or why not?

4. Songwriters like Jed process life's events by writing music. How do you process life's events?

5. Jed says that the past doesn't have to define you. Where do you see people you care about allowing their pasts to define them? How could it be true of your own life?

6. Jed decides that if he could ask God for anything, he would ask for wisdom. What would you ask God for and why?

7. Jed's desire to go out and sing for God has a cost—for both Jed and Rose. Do all of our callings require this kind of sacrifice? How do you determine whether a calling is from God? What would you do if you felt the calling God placed on your life came with too high a cost?

8. As Jed and Shelby grow closer, but before he has gone too far, Jed hears a voice telling him it isn't too late to run. Have you ever heard a similar voice or impression steering you away from something destructive? How did you respond?

9. Jed tattoos his arm with something permanent that he later wants removed. What else can we tattoo ourselves with—emotionally, spiritually—that we might want or need to remove later?

10. Does Rose have a role in the rift between her and Jed, or is that a wayward husband shifting the blame? If anything, what could she have done differently?

11. Jed grew up in the shadow of his father and comes to realize that a man who commits adultery can never undo his sin. Do you believe that's true? How would you advise Jed as he tries to manage his guilt and shame? What insight does Psalm 51 give you?

12. If you try to force grapes to grow faster, Rose says, you'll get bad grapes. How does this apply to people and relationships? How do you think it might apply to Jed and Rose's relationship going forward?

WEEK I

DEEPENING DESIRE

DAY 1

I Want to Know What Love Is

SONG OF SOLOMON 1:1-3

Where do we go if we want to know what love is? What are the trusted sources to help us understand romantic love? There is certainly no shortage of voices on the subject. The books we read, the music we listen to, and the movies we watch often revolve around the subject of love. Not long ago I was waiting for a prescription to be filled at a local drugstore and decided to kill time in the magazine aisle. The dominant headlines promised answers to all of our questions about love, sex, and relationships. I jotted down some of the headlines:

- What's Love Got to Do with It? (I'm not positive what It is, but It is probably what you think It is.)
- How to Make Her Jealous
- 15 Ways to Get Over a Breakup (#13: cry)

- Why You Must Date a Guy with a Cat (I'll withhold the comments I want to add in an effort to not alienate cat lovers.)
- How to Heat Things Up Fast
- 60 Tips for Sizzling Sex
- 5 Things You Can Tell about Her in 5 Seconds
- 10 Ways You Know He's Lying

I had too much pride to run the risk of being seen reading any of these magazines. In fact, as I stood in the aisle I pretended to be reading *Sports Illustrated* in case someone happened to walk by and see me looking at a women's magazine. (That sounds like something a guy who owns a cat would do.) My point is that tons of advice is out there when it comes to our love lives. But if you really want to know what love is and how you can experience it to the fullest, the best source is God's Word. After all, these things were his idea. He is the architect and the creator of love, sex, and marriage, and he knows how it works best.

Specifically we will be looking at a book in the Old Testament called Song of Solomon. It may be thousands of years old but its insights about love are up-to-date. It's a book of poetic literature that I pray will do more than just inform you as a husband and wife but inspire you to see the passion and purpose God wants for your marriage relationship.

Song of Solomon as a book of poetry can be romantic and even quite erotic. At times as you are reading Song of Solomon you may find yourself saying, "Wait. What? Who put this into the Bible?" The truth is that the ancient Hebrews didn't label and separate ideas as we do. They didn't have one box for "spiritual stuff" and another for "love stuff," for example. Everything was a spiritual issue, including the mysteries between men and women. We tend to compartmentalize different areas of our lives and we often keep our love lives in a completely separate door from our spiritual lives. We don't often talk about subjects like love, sex, and intimacy in church. But this approach tends to be more of a modern-day, Western-culture phenomenon. The people of Solomon's day believed and understood a basic reality: all truth is God's truth. This is where we must begin, with an understanding that God not only has helpful wisdom for our love lives but that these areas fall under his authority. There is no way to know what love is and to experience it fully apart from God.

> Let him kiss me with the kisses of his mouth—for your love is more delightful than wine. Pleasing is the fragrance of your perfumes; your name is like perfume poured out. No wonder the young women love you!
>
> SONG OF SOLOMON 1:2-3

Our definition of love can sound a lot like a Hallmark card, but the poetry in Song of Solomon takes us to a different level. The first three verses make it pretty clear that somebody's in love. Though there are some different opinions and interpretations about who says what and to whom throughout this book, these words are thought to be written by

Solomon's fiancée; in later verses, the king himself would speak. These words are passionate, but look a little closer and you'll find that she spoke of his "name." That's a reference to his character, his reputation. When she heard people speak the name of Solomon, it delighted her because of the kind of person people knew him to be.

The focus of most of those magazines in the drugstore was on physical appearance. And while that is certainly part of attraction (when I first met my wife, I didn't think to myself, *Look at the character on that girl*), if you really want to know what love is, learn to value and admire a person's name. Love should move quickly toward an interest in the true nature of the person.

The Bridge

Today, reflect on the growth of your love during the time you've been together. Where did it really begin for each of you? It may have begun with physical attraction, but when did you first feel that their name was "like perfume poured out"?

When my wife, DesiRae, and I first started dating, I took her to the nursing home to meet my great-grandmother who, at age ninety-four, could be a bit cantankerous at times. I sometimes took my dates there to see how they responded in that environment. Before leaving my great-grandmother's room, I asked her if I could pray for her, and during my prayer I opened my eyes and saw DesiRae holding the hand of my great-grandmother. She suddenly seemed even more beautiful to me (DesiRae, not my great-grandmother . . . not that she wasn't beautiful). Take a few minutes to remember some moments when you were attracted to each other's name.

Here's a cheesy but practical exercise that can help you identify how you are attracted to the "name" of your spouse: Take each letter from your spouse's first name and come up with a character quality you find attractive in them and then share a moment when they demonstrated that quality.

Here's what DesiRae came up with for my name:

Kind
Y
Loyal
Encouraging

Apparently the *Y* was more difficult. I suggested "Yummy" based on Song of Solomon 1:1-3, but she decided to "leave it blank for now." Anyway, have some fun with this. Ask God to deepen your desire for one another by helping you look at each other through this lens.

Next Verse: Proverbs 22:1

DAY 2
That's What Makes You Beautiful
Song of Solomon 1:5-6

As the story goes, a few years ago a wife answered the door, and a man asked, "Is this the home of Robert 'Rusty' Stevens, who played Larry Mondello on *Leave It to Beaver*? We're trying to locate him because we're making a reunion show for the Disney Channel."

She looked at the man as if he were crazy. "This is Robert's home, but I'm afraid he's never been a TV star." Disappointed, the man went away. She was familiar with Beaver's pudgy best buddy, who always had an apple in his back pocket. But her husband, Robert? Come on.

"Who was it?" asked Robert. She laughed and told him. "Oh, he had the right house," he said. "I played Larry in sixty-seven episodes of *Leave It to Beaver*." "What? And you never saw fit to mention something like that to me?" Her husband shrugged; no word on whether he pulled a fresh apple out of his pocket and took a bite.

It's probably unlikely that you unknowingly married Topanga or Urkel, but ask yourself how well you really know your spouse. Have you recently taken the time to genuinely ask questions and attentively listen? Some of the best marriage advice I ever received was to become a student of my wife, to intentionally spend my life studying and understanding her. It takes time and effort, but to deepen your desire for your spouse, you need to deepen your understanding.

In Song of Solomon 1:5-6, we find Solomon's fiancée not feeling very desirable. Though he may have considered her beautiful, she didn't feel that way about herself. But she felt safe enough to be vulnerable and tell him some things about her that maybe he didn't know.

> Dark am I, yet lovely, daughters of Jerusalem, dark like the tents of Kedar, like the tent curtains of Solomon. Do not stare at me because I am dark, because I am darkened by the sun. My mother's sons were angry with me and made me take care of the vineyards; my own vineyard I had to neglect.
>
> SONG OF SOLOMON 1:5-6

In these verses, Solomon's beloved offered a kind of disclaimer. Today it would be, "Please forgive my appearance! I came straight from work." In fact, she was explaining that she was a bit too tanned for the day's standards of glamour. She had been working in the field; she had been serving her family to the neglect of her own needs.

How would that strike you? I would think, *Here is a girl who has no sense of entitlement, no pampering. She gets things done and she's willing to break a nail or two doing it.* And frankly, I'd find that attractive. It's one of the things I really love about my wife. I remember the first time I held hands with her. We were at the theater watching *The Lion King*. She had placed her hand on her leg closest to mine giving me the green light to grab it. I interlocked my fingers with hers and noticed right away that her hands were much rougher than mine. I married a farmer's daughter who grew up raising pigs and driving combines. She may have been self-conscious, but I loved these things about her. The more we are genuinely interested in getting to know our spouse, the deeper our desire for them will be. Some of the vulnerability and insecurity that your spouse may be reluctant to share has the power to draw in your heart.

The Bridge

As we've discussed, romantic love may begin with a little eye candy, and that's natural. We're human, and God made us to admire and appreciate beauty. But what are some surprising things you have learned about your spouse along the way that have deepened your desire? What are some of your spouse's insecurities where a few words of encouragement from you might go a long way to make them feel desired? Instead of paying them the same compliments as usual, think through what affirming words they need to hear.

Solomon grew up as the privileged son of a king. His experiences and background were very different from the girl he loved. What are some of the ways God has made you different from your significant other? Instead of assuming that your spouse needs to be more like you, take a few minutes to affirm and value what makes you different.

Next Verse: Proverbs 31:16–18

DAY 3
I'll Be There for You
Song of Solomon 1:7

What's your favorite genre of movies to watch? I read an article that explained the reason we often choose to go to a certain kind of movie is more than just about entertainment. It may be on a subconscious level, but apparently we are drawn to movies that allow us to experience an alternative reality. So if your life is boring and mundane, chances are you love a good action-adventure movie. If your life is safe and comfortable, you may be drawn to a scary movie. If your life is predictable and certain, you may love a good mystery. And if you feel lonely or disconnected, you may love a romantic tearjerker or a romantic comedy. (Don't get defensive. I'm not saying these are exclusively the reason you would enjoy a certain kind of movie. Yet there must be some truth to it because I read it on the Internet.)

One of the primary reasons your desire for your spouse diminishes instead of deepens is that you just accept your current reality. You just accept that things are the way they are, and the passionate kisses, the long walks hand in hand, and the uncontained laughter are just for the movies. In Song of Solomon we consistently witness the husband and wife pursuing each other and making time together a priority.

Here's an example:

> Tell me, you whom I love, where you graze your flock and where you rest your sheep at midday. Why should I be like a veiled woman beside the flocks of your friends?
>
> SONG OF SOLOMON 1:7

In today's verse, the fiancée made a simple request: Give me your work address. She wanted to know where he hung out during the day, and of course the right question for that was "Where do you graze your flock?"

The point here is not too complicated—she wants to go where he goes.

When two people are very much in love, they have no trouble figuring out ways to spend time together. As a matter of fact, time becomes their canvas for creative expressions of love. They try new restaurants or maybe they consistently visit the same one where they order the same thing. They find time and a place to run or take walks. The point is that time together is a priority. The question for you and your spouse may not be "Where do you graze your flocks?" Instead the questions might sound more like this:

- Do you want to start blocking off Tuesday nights for dinner?
- Do you mind if I run to the grocery store with you?
- Are you free to join me on the porch for a few minutes?
- What if we started going for bike rides in the evening together?
- Do you want to run over and spend some time with your mother?

In struggling marriages, which crumbles first, quality time together or romantic feeling? The answer is yes! Those two things are tightly enmeshed. Time builds love and love makes time. It may come easy when you're head over heels, but in a great marriage it will take a little work. It has to be an intentional priority. You're going to pursue spending time with your spouse because your relationship is worth it. Sometimes we think romantic desire shouldn't require effort, that it should come naturally. But that's not true. Deepening any desire requires time and energy. You make pursuing time with your spouse more of a priority and your feelings of desire will start to catch up with your intentional actions.

Sometimes it's the small stuff that pays the big dividends. He's not really into *Downton Abbey*, but she likes it—so he sits down and watches with her, sparing the snarky comments. She's not really into watching basketball, but she loves his passion for it. So they watch together (and only talk during the time-outs).

We feel most attracted to people when we see them at their best. I'm impressed with this woman that Solomon loved. She was willing to meet him in the pasture. Not a super romantic place, last time I checked. Sheep do not make for an interesting evening, but she wanted to be where he was.

The Bridge

It's trite to say it, but let's be trite: Love takes time. It takes patience and the willingness to go somewhere—literally or figuratively. For today, let me suggest doing something together out of the normal routine. Find ways to "go" somewhere new, to be together under new circumstances. I'm not so sure about Red Lobster and bowling, but whatever it takes, be there for each other.

Now that our four kids are a bit older, here's how we try to spend time together:

- **Daily:** We take time to talk and pray together without interruptions.
- **Weekly:** We go on a date. We try to go out one evening a week, but sometimes it's just connecting for a short lunch.
- **Quarterly:** We leave town for a two-night romantic getaway (full disclosure: sometimes she comes with me on a work trip).
- **Annually:** Just the two of us go somewhere for a week and have as much fun as possible.

It may look different for you, but I know this doesn't happen by accident. Pull out the calendar and agree together about some times and places where you can connect.

Next Verse: Ruth 1:16-17

DAY 4
Shout It Out Loud
Song of Solomon 2:4

I read a story in the news about a billboard off I-95 in North Fort Lauderdale that simply read, "Brad Loves Melissa." Brad had noticed that a jewelry company had a prominent billboard that his wife passed by every day on her commute to work. Over the years Brad has found different ways to publicly declare his love for his wife. He has put the message

"Brad Loves Melissa" on everything from a side of a building to a giant inflatable advertising balloon. Brad contacted the jewelry company who owned the billboard and asked for their help in making his declaration of love. Sean Dunn from the jewelry company said, "It was a no-brainer for us, as we are in the business that is all about creating things that show people you love them; 99 percent of the time it is a stunning piece of designer jewelry, but this time it is a billboard."

Can I be honest with you? I don't really like Brad. I don't actually know Brad, but I know enough. He makes the rest of us guys look bad. Can't he just go by the Hallmark store on the night of February 13 like the rest of us? He's like the kid in school who studies for the test and sets the curve high. He's like the neighbor who has a perfect lawn and uses some sort of dark magic to create a checked pattern in his grass. He's making it difficult for the rest of us. The truth is that when it comes to declaring our love for our spouses, most of us aren't too proactive or creative.

Solomon and the girl he loves are not shy about their feelings for one another. Like passionate sports fans they want the world to know of their love. There is something about declaring our love that deepens our desire. It's a way of choosing sides and stepping over a line. Solomon's bride-to-be knows how Solomon feels about her, and so does everyone else.

> Let him lead me to the banquet hall, and let his banner over me be love.
>
> SONG OF SOLOMON 2:4

Solomon's fiancée spoke of him leading her to the banquet hall. So she likes eating out? Well, that's probably true, but what counts is he's showing her off in public. He takes her hand and says, "I want you to meet the guys." What message does that send? It says, *I love you and I want everyone to know it.* And she feels special. She says, "Let his banner over me be love." That's what flags are for, right? We wave them to show our allegiance.

Then there's the opposite: that sad situation when people disparage their spouses in public. Both men and women do this, dragging their banner in the mud. Wives dish the dirt about their husbands. Men belittle their wives. And it's all passed off as something light, just joking. "Take my wife—please, take her!"

I've heard Christian leaders speak little one-liners about their wives in sermons. Don't they get it? Marriage is a powerful, sacred bond never to be displayed at half-mast. Real love—well-tended, nurtured love—bears a fierce pride in the objects of our affection. We want to take the ones we love with us wherever we go. And when we're apart, the love still shows.

The Bridge

Look for opportunities to fly your banner in public today. Just be sincere about it, and nobody said you have to rent a billboard or write a love sonnet and post it on Facebook. It doesn't need to be on the scale of a Lifetime movie; just find a simple way to let others know you are excited about your marriage. If nothing else, when you're around some friends or extended family, let your spouse overhear you express your love and admiration for him or her.

Keep this in mind, too: When we say a good word to the world about our marriages, we're saying a good word about marriage itself. In case you haven't noticed, the institution has fallen on hard times in some quarters. People are afraid of becoming another divorce statistic. We could use a few voices that make it clear that marriage is no burden; it's a gift from God that keeps on giving.

Take some time to pray together as a couple and thank Jesus for letting the whole world know of his love for you. When he died for you on the cross, he forever made it clear that his banner over you is love. The more deeply you experience his love, the more deeply you are able to love others.

Next Verse: James 3:9-12

DAY 5
Killing Me Softly
SONG OF SOLOMON 2:15

I've talked a lot about the positive things we can do to deepen our desire for our spouses, but identifying what detracts from our desire is also important. When you fall in love, you need to address a number of potential challenges to your relationship. When DesiRae and I were first married, we moved into a starter home, and though we had never talked about it, it soon became clear that we had some unspoken and unexpressed expectations of one another. My wife grew up on a farm and the men in her family built their own homes, changed their own oil, and repaired their own leaks. I grew up in a home where I was taught you only needed two tools to fix anything: a telephone and a checkbook. So when things needed to get done, she expected me to fix it, not write a check. Chances are you also married someone who is much different from you.

You face hundreds of issues as a couple. Let me guess: You prefer structure and like to stay organized, but you married someone who is more unstructured and spontaneous? Or what about this? You are a night person but you married a morning person? One of you is more outgoing and loud and the other is more quiet and introverted? Instead of deepening our desire for each other, these inevitable issues have the potential to divide us.

Instead of ignoring our differences and pretending as if they don't exist, we need to identify them and deal with them so the fruit in your marriage, what Solomon called your vineyard, will grow.

> Catch for us the foxes, the little foxes that ruin the vineyards, our vineyards that are in bloom. My beloved is mine and I am his; he browses among the lilies.
>
> SONG OF SOLOMON 2:15-16

Solomon's fiancée, who was speaking again, referenced catching foxes in the vineyard. In the Mediterranean climate, grapes have always been plentiful. Growers tend the soil and the vines all year to produce a great crop. But in those days, little foxes snuck in at night and wreaked havoc. Actually, the experts think these "foxes" were more like jackals. They weren't particularly sly—they just liked digging things up and leaving a mess. Maybe they were looking for henhouses.

So she was saying, "Let's hunt down these pests." She was really talking about the little things that uproot relationships. "We're growing something delicious in this vineyard of ours," she was saying, figuratively. "Let's keep watch and lock out the intrusions."

And what are those little relationship varmints? You name it: Bad habits. Issues from the past. Personal flaws that may not seem like much but begin to grate over time. In-laws become outlaws. Intimacy is close-up work—it's going to reveal problems. This is a tough hunt, and it has to be carried out constantly. Guarding your relationship takes vigilance. Are you willing to work at it?

The Bridge

While discussing the little foxes in your relationship, take care! The discussion itself could dig up a few problems. But it's a good idea to do some hunting together; just be sure to agree first on a few rules of grace and patience.

I suggest each of you offers up one fox. She might say, "Sometimes I feel as if your mind is wandering while I'm telling you something important." (At least I think that's what she said.) He might mention some little habit of hers that is bothersome. (I'm not going to tell you; remember yesterday's devotion?) Remember, we're not going after the giants here—Solomon's dad, David, was the one who took on Goliath. Sometimes the devil is in the details.

Don't forget, Solomon's fiancée suggested this hunt in the context of powerful, loving conversation. What happens if you don't do that? You let things build up and then you broach the issue at the worst time and in the worst way.

At that point, the foxes are hunting you.

Next Verse: Ephesians 4:22-24

EVEN THE WISEST OF MEN WAS A FOOL FOR LOVE
INSPIRED BY THE SONG OF SOLOMON
THE SONG
IN THEATERS SEPT. 26TH
THESONGMOVIE.COM

THE SONG